THE CAIRC

The Fourth of the

CW01301791

Principal Characters in the book

The Algarve, Southern Portugal

Michael Turner

Me, a murder mystery & travel writer

Dr Samantha Turner

My wife, a private doctor based in Quinta do Lago

London

Superintendent Stephen Colshaw

Metropolitan Police Officer, based in Greenwich

Detective Inspector Paul Naismith

Metropolitan Police Officer, based in Greenwich

Detective Sergeant Richard Thorpe

Metropolitan Police Officer, Technical Division, based in Greenwich

Sergeant Don Priestly

Metropolitan Police Officer, Desk Sergeant at Greenwich

Craig Overton

Head of Operations at MI6 Headquarters in London

Roy Simpson

Technical Specialist at MI6 Headquarters in London

Sir Duncan Greenhall
Director of Overseas Communications at GCHQ in Cheltenham

Amsterdam, Netherlands
Senior Superintendent Helena Van Houten
Interpol Officer - Head of European Operations
Inspector George Copeland
Interpol Officer - Senior Pilot & Covert Operative
Inspector Colin O'Donnell
Interpol Officer - Co Pilot & Covert Operative
Inspector Willie Schuster
Interpol Officer - Covert Operative
Sergeant Jo Sylvester
Interpol Officer - Covert Operative
Martin Smith
Interpol Officer - Covert Operative & Specialist Burglar
Marika van Groen
Interpol Officer - Communications expert & translator

The Terrorists
Jahangir Ahmadi
Iranian Terrorist & Conspiracy Leader
Akram Lajani
Iranian Kurd Terrorist

Youssef Mahrez
Moroccan Terrorist & Communications expert
Sadiq Rouhani
Pakistani Terrorist
Khalid Khan
Afghan Terrorist
Sergei Polyakov
Russian Cyber Terrorist
Mohamed and Ali Shafer
Egyptian Brothers, both terrorists, based in Cairo
Nigel Collins
British Terrorist, based in Norfolk, UK
Faisal Al-Hasawi
Kuwaiti Cultural Attaché, based in Kuwait's Embassy in Cairo
Madam Favreau
Algerian Undercover terrorist based in the south of France

Israel
Moishe Kravitz
Mossad – Director of Operations
Rivka Meyer
Mossad - Undercover Operative & Moishe's 'right hand'.

World Leaders

Charles Fisher

Prime Minister of the United Kingdom

James Conway

Foreign Secretary of the United Kingdom

Mary Connelly

Home Secretary of the United Kingdom

George Wagner

President of the United States

Gilles Cazeneuve

President of France

Helmut Groening

Chancellor of Germany

Chapter One

Life for Sam and I had more or less returned to normal, whatever that was these days. In theory I was a reasonably successful author, originally writing what turned out to be incredibly lucrative murder mysteries, of which twelve had been published worldwide. However, lucrative as they were, I decided I both wanted and needed a change. I started writing travel guide books, but homing in on real crime locations for the traveller to visit that wants to do more than just lay on a beach slowly roasting in the sun, and for added interest I also include locations that have been used in films and TV series based around crime. They seem to be selling quite well, and I'm now working on my fifth travel guide.

My wife Sam, who is still called Samantha by her parents, was a successful doctor in the UK, and an occasional police surgeon, working mainly with the Metropolitan police in South London, but she then moved to Portugal where she now runs her own private medical practice. It's located in an area of the Algarve in southern Portugal known as Quinta do Lago, which is where we met and where we live. To be honest, there are some days when I wish that was all we did, me writing books and Sam seeing her patients. But then a few years ago everything changed for us when Malcolm Tisbury, one of my neighbours was brutally murdered in his own home. To cut a long story short, Sam and I got involved in trying to find the killer. We worked with both the local police, who are known as the GNR, the London, or the more correctly entitled Metropolitan police, and then Interpol. Somehow or other we ended up going undercover, travelling to South Africa, the Bahamas and half of Europe in the process, but if I say so myself we did a pretty good job of bringing the Mijas Murderer as he became known to justice.

A few months later, we were approached again by the Metropolitan police and Interpol, and asked if we would help them in their search for a brilliant counterfeiter known only as the Faro Forger. Again, our undercover investigations took us all over the world, and having successfully found the Faro Forger we thought life would get back to normal. It did - for all of sixteen days. The first fourteen of those days Sam and I spent on our honeymoon, and we'd only been back just over twenty four hours when Sam received a phone call from Salzburg informing her that her ex flat mate had committed suicide. Sam refused to believe her friend would have taken her own life, and so we were off again looking into what became known as the Salzburg Suicides. That case was concluded quite recently, and I'm pleased to say that I'm now spending my days writing and Sam spends her mornings doctoring. We both made the decision to take afternoons and weekends off, and we spend plenty of time relaxing, visiting friends and doing what we want. Recently Sam and I very reluctantly got talked into trying our hand at golf by a good friend and his wife who live locally to us, and despite our initial wariness we are actually quite enjoying it. Neither of us is very good yet, but we're taking lessons, we enjoy the exercise and most importantly we love the opportunity to sit and chat with folk at the nineteenth tee, the golfers' term for the bar in the clubhouse. I have to say, I'm beginning to see the attraction, and why there are thirty eight golf courses in the Algarve, and no doubt even more will soon be built.

Sam was working, seeing a couple of patients at her surgery, and I was sitting outside by the pool working on my laptop. I had just started on a new chapter about a crime scene location for my new travel guide. I'd already had guides published about Italy, France, Germany and Russia, and my publisher thought it was about time I tackled what was probably going to be the biggest of my guides - Spain. It was mid-morning when the telephone rang, and so I closed my laptop and went into the villa to answer the phone. Whoever it was had telephoned me on our landline rather than my mobile. That in itself I thought was a bit unusual as hardly anybody uses telephone landlines these days.

'Michael Turner' I answered picking up the phone.

'Ah, excellent, you're in. This is Craig Overton.'

I'd met Craig Overton several times during our last 'adventure' with the Salzburg suicides, but I still didn't know that much about him other than he was the Senior Operations Officer at MI6, and as far as I was concerned a fairly scary individual.

'Oh, hi Craig' I replied, wondering what was coming next.

'Any chance I can call in and see you and Sam this afternoon old chap. I'm in the area and I'd like to pop by and run something past you both.'

To be honest I really wanted to say no. I had nothing against him, but Craig Overton is never 'in the area' unless he wants to be 'in the area', and whatever it was he wanted, I felt sure I wasn't going to like it. But before I knew it I'd replied

'Of course Craig. Do you know where to find us?'

What a damn silly question. The guy ran all of MI6's operations. He could find anybody.

'Yes, I know where you are. See you both about 3.00 o'clock.'

Of course he knew where we were, and before I could say another word the line went dead and I found myself listening to the dialling tone. Craig Overton was just one of those people that made me very nervous. Over the last couple of years Sam and I had worked with the Portuguese police, the Metropolitan police and worldwide with Interpol, and we always felt quite relaxed about all of them, but MI6? That was very different. I rang Sam at the surgery and told her about our 3.00 pm visitor and she said she would be home in plenty of time.

She was, and exactly on the dot of 3.00 pm the front doorbell rang. Credit where it's due, Craig Overton was punctual to the point of annoyance. I opened the door.

'Ah, Michael, great to see you old chap, and thank you for taking the time to see me.' He walked past me and headed into the lounge towards Sam, leaned in and kissed her on both cheeks, the normal greeting here in the Algarve. 'You see Michael, I've been swotting up on how things are done in Portugal' he continued.

'Please, sit down Craig' invited Sam. 'Cup of tea or something a bit stronger?'

'Oh I never drink alcohol before 6.00 pm and even then only the occasional sherry. A cup

of tea and a biscuit would be wonderful.'
Craig Overton was definitely old school with his constant use of 'old chap', starting every sentence with either an 'ah', an 'oh' or an 'um', and only drinking sherry, but then for no apparent reason I realised I was being very picky and a bit judgemental, without really knowing why. I think it's just that the wretched man unnerved me.

'Not that it isn't nice to see you Craig' I began 'but what can we do for you?'

'Ah, well I'd like you both to go to Egypt for me actually.'

'I think you might have to be a bit more specific if you don't mind Craig' said Sam.

'Um, well it's a long story' he replied 'and I've got a written report for each of you, so don't worry about writing any of this down, but it's fairly long and quite complicated.'
Craig continued;

'As you know from the last time we met, we are officially called The Secret Intelligence Service, or SIS for short, but we are more commonly known the world over as MI6, and to make life easier I'll only use that name. We are basically the branch of the intelligence service responsible for the UK governments national security relating to overseas matters.

Our job is mainly to obtain human intelligence, usually covertly and always gathered overseas, and then have it analysed by our people back in the UK. If some form of action is then deemed necessary then it is handed over to the ops, sorry, operations department, and that's where I come in. My job is to head up the operations division of the organization.'

'Are you sure we don't need to take notes?' asked Sam.

'Positive' replied Craig. 'Now, er, a brief bit of history for you which I think may well help clarify a few things. MI6 was formed in 1909 as a section of the Secret Service Bureau specialising in foreign intelligence, and we experienced quite dramatic growth during World War I, and officially adopted the current name around 1920. The name MI6, which incidentally stands for Military Intelligence - Section 6, originated as a sort of flag of convenience during World War II, when SIS was known by many different names, not all polite I hasten to add. Again as you probably already know, the existence of MI6 was only officially acknowledged in 1994 with the introduction of the Intelligence Services Act of that year, and that placed the entire organisation on an official statutory footing for the first time, and it also provided us with the legal basis for all our operations.

'And MI6 only deals with foreign operations?' I asked.

'Yes. Unlike both our main sister agencies, the Security Service, commonly known as MI5 and the Government Communications Headquarters, commonly known as GCHQ, MI6 works exclusively in foreign intelligence gathering. Legally, according to the 1994 Intelligence Services Act, we, that is MI6, are only allowed to carry out operations against persons outside the British Islands, and since 1995 when MI6 went public about its existence, it has been headquartered in the now famous cream and green SIS building in London, on the South Bank of the River Thames, you know the one made famous in the James Bond films, which incidentally bear very little resemblance to the work we do.'

'So Craig, I have to ask - are you the real life M?'

'Actually Michael there is no 'M' as such. The head of MI6 is actually known as 'C'. The first director of MI6 was Captain Sir Mansfield George Smith-Cumming, who often dropped the Smith in his routine communications. He typically signed correspondence with just his last initial 'C' in green ink, and this evolved over time into his code name. All subsequent directors of MI6 still use 'C' when signing documents and they are known within the organization as 'C'.

'You didn't actually answer my question Craig' I responded.

'Um. No Michael I'm certainly not 'C', or 'M' or 'Q' or any other initial you care to suggest. I don't have a codename, just my real name - Craig Overton.'

'Is it true' I continued 'that MI6 is nicknamed The Circus?'

'Er, no, I'm afraid that's not true either. The term 'The Circus' was coined by the author John le Carré, who incidentally was a former MI6 officer named David Cornwell, but he decided to change his name for his espionage novels.'

'Please forgive my husband Craig' said Sam, 'his mind is always full of questions and he usually asks them at the most inconvenient times. Please continue.'

'It has come to our attention that four known terrorists are meeting in Cairo about once a month. We don't know why, but we'd like to. As far as we know, these four men have absolutely nothing in common, and yet for some reason they have been meeting regularly for the last six months now. I want to know why.'

'Can't you send in one of your guys to investigate?' I asked

'One thing the James Bond films does get right is that everybody in the intelligence community knows everybody else. We have a lot of operatives who could easily do the job, but every one of them is known to at least one of the four terrorists. The same is sadly true I'm afraid of both the CIA and Mossad, the two security agencies we work with the most. I'm afraid the terrorists watch all of us just as much as we watch all of them.'

'So what are you asking of us Craig?' asked Sam.

'As I said earlier Sam - I'd like you both to go to Egypt for me.'

Chapter Two

Sam and I looked at each other, and Craig could tell immediately that we were not keen.

'Please don't panic, I'm not asking you to meet these guys face to face or in any way contact them. Just watch them from a distance.'

'Are they at all suspicious that they are being watched?' asked Sam.

'That's just it' replied Craig 'I em hate to say this, but they are not being watched at all at the moment, at least not closely enough. We know where they are, but not why they're there, or what they are doing. It's all very frustrating and as I said, I'm afraid we simply don't have anyone to watch them that they wouldn't recognize the minute they got off the plane. That's why you two would be so perfect. You've done undercover work before and you both know what you're doing, and none of these guys knows anything about you. Will you go and have a look for me?'

'I'm not saying yes' I said, 'but exactly who are these terrorists?'

'As I said' replied Craig 'there are four of them. Two Iranians, one Moroccan and a Pakistani. That for a start is very strange as they don't usually mix with each other.'

'So what else do you know about them?' asked Sam.

'OK. Well er, as I said there are two Iranians. The leader as far as we can tell is a hard line fundamentalist named Jahangir Ahmadi, and the other guy he's frequently seen with is an Iranian Kurd named Akram Lajani. Again, that is strange as you wouldn't expect a fundamentalist and a Kurd to be bosom buddies.

But even stranger is the two they are meeting up with every month, a young Moroccan terrorist named Youssef Mahrez, and Sadiq Rouhani, a well-known Pakistani terrorist. Nobody in MI6, the CIA or Mossad can work out what these four have in common, or why they are meeting in a Cairo hotel room every month.'

'Why Cairo?' I asked.

'Again, we don't know' answered Craig. 'We can only assume it's regarded as neutral territory for all four of them.'

'So you want us to go to Cairo?' asked Sam.

'Actually, no I don't. I would like you to take a relaxing cruise down the Nile.'

Sam and I looked at each other, and a smile soon spread over Sam's face.

'I've always wanted to go on a Nile cruise and see the pyramids' said Sam.

'Well I can offer you the Nile Cruise, but at this stage I'm not sure about the pyramids. Last week, Jahangir Ahmadi spent an hour with a travel agent in Cairo, and after a considerable amount of money changed hands, one of my men discovered he had bought four tickets for a Nile Cruise from Aswan to Luxor. Ahmadi booked the tickets in false names, but the travel agent had to photocopy the four passports before he could issue the tickets, and after even more money changed hands he gave my man copies of the four false passports. It was without doubt our four terrorists.'

'If your man can do that, why can't he go on the cruise'' I asked.

'As I said earlier, he'd be recognised immediately. My man can tail them from long distance, and then later on hopefully see what they've been up to, but he daren't be seen by any of the four.'

'So if we say yes, what do we do?' asked Sam.

'Get your bags packed for a week in the sun and we'll fly you to Aswan in time to get on the cruise ship. Just be yourselves and keep your ears open. I don't suppose they'll talk about anything important within earshot of anybody else, but you never know. They may just let their guard slip.'

'What's their excuse for the cruise and what are their new identities?' I queried.

'Ah' mumbled Craig. 'Glad you asked that old chap. Now apparently, or so the story they told the travel agent goes, they won the cruise as a prize from their company for being the top four salesmen in their respective sales

areas over the previous year. They told the travel agent that they had to pay for the trip themselves initially, but then the company would reimburse them. Load of old twaddle of course, but the travel agent bought it.
As for their story, well they are all posing as car salesmen for Mercedes Benz, representing different sales territories. We know from our long distance surveillance that they all drive new Mercedes when they're back in their home countries, and please don't be fooled for one minute into thinking that all terrorists live in primitive mud huts, wear smelly, tatty old clothes and ride around on knackered old bicycles. Most of them are stinking rich from their various ill-gotten gains. So if push comes to shove I guess it's going to be relatively easy for them to talk about Mercedes if necessary, although to be honest, nobody in our profession has ever been close enough to hear any of them speak, so we wouldn't even recognize their voices.'

'But what I don't understand is why are they going on the cruise?' asked Sam.

'No idea' replied Craig. 'That's what we're hoping you can find out.'

Craig then filled us in on their four false

identities and gave us copies of their four false passport pictures so that we'd recognise them. As you may have gathered, by this time we'd agreed to go, as long as we didn't have to meet the four men, just watch them from afar. There are no direct flights to Aswan from Faro, and not even from London, so Craig had booked us on an EasyJet flight to London, and then onto a British Airways flight to Cairo, and finally a local Egypt Air flight from Cairo to Aswan. Our cruise ship was neatly berthed at the dock, and we were only the third people to board. We'd deliberately got there as early as possible so that we could watch the other passengers arriving. We were welcomed aboard by a very nice young man named Shafra, who later proudly informed us that he was named after Chefren, the builder of the second pyramid. Shafra was dressed in neat black trousers and a very smart white jacket with gold trim, and he informed us that he was going to be our cabin steward for the next six days. He showed us to our cabin, or state room as they preferred to call them, which was on the second deck, and I have to say the facilities were excellent. The wall opposite our stateroom door was floor to ceiling full width sliding double glazed glass doors with a Juliet style balcony running the full width of the room. We had a king size double bed, lots of wardrobe and drawer space, a large flat screen TV, tea and coffee making facilities, a mini bar including a small fridge, and a decent size en suite shower room and toilet, and thankfully some really efficient air conditioning.

We quickly unpacked, or should I more accurately say Sam quickly unpacked, after which we wandered round the ship taking in everything on board. The ship, like most other Nile cruisers we had seen was painted white, and ours had some very neat royal blue trim. The ship was three decks tall, with cabins all the way down both sides of the first and second decks. The third, or top deck contained a very nice lounge area the full width of the ship, full of very comfortable armchairs, with a bar at one end, and next to it was the ship's restaurant, also the full width of the ship. We went up the stairs one more level to emerge outside at the back of the ship and onto the top deck or to be more accurate, the roof. There was a medium size shallow swimming pool and two large six person Jacuzzis at the back, all open to the sun. In the centre of the ship, under very smart royal blue canvas shading, were about thirty circular wooden tables. Each table had four wooden chairs around them, all with thick royal blue cushions, and then at the front, and out in the sun were what seemed like myriads of sun loungers, again all with thick royal blue cushions, along with a second bar, also under canvas shading.

'You know, I could put up with this for a six days if we really, really have to.' I said smiling broadly at Sam.

'Oh you're such a selfless hero.' she replied smiling as she set off towards the bar. Sam ordered a couple of cold beers and we sat at one of the circular tables under the shade, right at the edge of the deck so that we could watch all the comings and goings of people boarding the ship. We hadn't seen our four 'salesmen' arrive, although I guessed we may have missed them during the unpacking. As it turned out, we hadn't as about twenty minutes later we watched two black and yellow taxis pull up alongside the boarding gangway, and our four salesmen emerged, along with all their luggage. A different cabin steward met them and escorted them onto the ship, followed by two porters carrying their luggage.

'So that's who we have to watch.' I said, stating the blindingly obvious.

'They don't look like terrorists' said Sam

'although I do realise you can't tell a terrorist or a burglar or a con-man by just looking at them, but you know what I mean.'

'Yes, I must admit, they look just like you would expect four car salesmen to look.' And then I realised I was doing it as well - judging people by their looks.

'Do we try and get near to them, or just wait and see what happens?' asked Sam.

'Remember what Craig said, they'll be on the lookout for anyone following them, so we need to be very careful. Let them get near to us if possible, but if we're getting nowhere after a couple of days then we'll review what we do.'

Chapter Three

Our luxury Nile cruiser, incidentally not very originally named the 'Tutankhamun', eventually set sail as they say, although it didn't actually have any sails, at five o'clock in the evening. We cruised for about an hour towards the Aswan dam and berthed for the night with the walls of the dam in full view. We had a very pleasant evening meal in the ship's restaurant and then went along to the lounge with everybody else, where a very experienced Egyptologist and our guide for the duration of the trip told us in perfect English of all the delights we would be seeing the following day. Our four salesmen all sat together in a corner of the lounge and kept themselves very much to themselves, not talking to anyone other than each other. Sam and I were both worn out having had a long days travel, so around ten thirty we decided to call it a day and get a good night's rest.

The following morning after a hearty breakfast of fried eggs, sausage, bacon and fried tomatoes, all very British, the passengers were all invited to take an hour long trip on a felucca, a small traditional Egyptian single masted sailing boat that carried about ten passengers. Sam and I hung around near the exit as everyone milled around the door as one felucca after another drew alongside our cruise ship, picked up ten passengers, then moved off to make way for another felucca. After the fourth boat had left, our salesmen found themselves at the front of the queue and they immediately boarded the fifth felucca. Sam and I managed to upset an elderly lady as we barged through carefully managing to manoeuvre ourselves on to the same felucca, where Sam and I very carefully sat together in the centre of the boat hoping we could hear anything our four 'salesmen' said.

We'd been in the felucca for about forty five minutes and learnt nothing. The 'salesmen' had been speaking very quietly to each other throughout the trip, almost whispering and with the constant chatter from the other passengers we couldn't really hear anything our four terrorists were saying, just vague mumbling. Then suddenly they all started laughing and Mahrez, the Moroccan said something we could both hear. At that moment it dawned on us - they weren't speaking English and even if we could hear them we wouldn't understand a word they were saying. Sam had managed over the years to pick up a few words of various different languages through having patients who originated from many different countries, and she gently leaned across to me and whispered in my ear what looked like sweet nothings to all the world, but in reality she said

'That sounded like their speaking Pashto to me, but I'm not a hundred percent sure as I only know half a dozen words.'

'Great' I replied smiling 'what do we do now if they don't speak English?'

'Leave it to me' Sam said, and at that moment she unexpectedly stood up in the boat. She wobbled slightly, and then fell, not very gracefully straight into the lap of Jahangir Ahmadi, who automatically reached out, caught her and brought her safely to the floor of the boat again.

'Oh I'm so, so sorry' Sam said smiling at him 'I feel such a fool.'

'Do not worry' he replied in perfectly refined English. 'As long as you are OK?'

'I'm fine' replied Sam 'and thank you very much Mr?'

'Cartwright, Joseph Cartwright.'

'Well thank you Mr Cartwright.'

'Yes, thank you' I echoed.

'Please forgive my rudeness' Sam continued smiling at Ahmadi 'but you don't look much like my idea of a Mr Cartwright.'

'No, perhaps not' he said smiling at Sam. 'My mother was Iranian, but my father was English, and I was educated at an English owned and run International School in Tehran, where I grew up learning how to drink tea with my little finger in the air, while eating cucumber sandwiches without any crusts. All very British.'

'I'm afraid nobody eats cucumber

sandwiches in England anymore Mr Cartwright' I said 'but I do sincerely thank you for stopping my wife going for an unscheduled swim with the local crocodiles.'

'That is quite alright. My turn to ask - Mr and Mrs?'

'Oh sorry' said Sam. 'I'm Susan Gregson and this is my husband Peter.'

Those were the names we'd agreed upon with Craig, although to be perfectly honest, we didn't really have much choice as he'd presented us with two false passports before we left, with those names and our photographs already in them.

'Well perhaps you'll allow us to buy you and your colleagues a drink at the bar later Mr Cartwright' I said 'just as a way of showing our appreciation?'

'That would be very kind. Thank you'.' he replied.

At that point conversation stopped as we were now back alongside the 'Tutankhamun', and our 'Mr Cartwright' and his three colleagues left the felucca and immediately disappeared inside the cruise ship.

Later that afternoon we met Ahmadi in his guise

as 'Mr Cartwright' and co at the outside bar on the top deck, and we all sat round a couple of tables in the shade, all drinking bottles of Sakara, the local Egyptian beer.

'So are you going to swim with the crocodiles today Mrs Gregson?' asked Sadiq Rouhani, the Pakistani 'or are you going to satisfy yourself with the ship's pool?'

'I think the pool will be quite sufficient for my aquatic needs on this holiday.' replied Sam giving Rouhani her best smile.

'I'm so sorry Mrs Gregson' said Ahmadi 'I've been very rude. I should have introduced you to my three colleagues. This gentleman is Mr Shahid Khan and he is from Faisalabad in Pakistan, this gentleman is Mr Ahmed Virenque from Tangiers in Morocco, and my other colleague is my good friend Mr Akram Barzani, also from Iran.'

They all leant forward in turn and shook hands with Sam and myself. Craig had told us before we left not to engage with them and just listen to their conversations whenever possible, but as neither of us spoke Pashto, that option was no longer on the table. I decided to push my luck and ask what I hoped were a couple of fairly innocuous questions.

'So Mr Cartwright' I began, 'what made you all decide to take a Nile cruise?'

'We didn't actually' said Mahrez. 'We all work for various Mercedes distributors in our own countries, and there was an exotic holiday offered as a prize to their top four salesmen around the world, and this year that happened to be the four of us.'

'To be honest' said Rouhani 'it is not a holiday I would have chosen for myself, but it would have been churlish to have said no to a paid week off work and a free trip.'

'Well I have to say' said Sam jumping in 'this is a trip Peter and I have looked forward to taking ever since we've known each other, but married life has been hectic to say the least, and this has been our first opportunity.'

'So did you all meet for the first time on the ship' I asked.

'No' replied Ahmadi 'we'd met each other at various Mercedes sales conferences and training courses. Akram and I knew each other anyway as we both work in Iran, although Akram is at our Shiraz showroom, and I am based in our head office and main showroom in Tehran.'

Cartwright was very confident in telling the

story, and it tied in exactly with what Craig had told us before we left.

'So are you all looking forward to seeing the temple at Philae tomorrow?' Sam asked, giving the impression of being really excited, and to be honest we both were quite excited at seeing the ancient temples and monuments of Egypt, as a cruise down the Nile was something we'd hoped to do at some point anyway. But this way was so much better as MI6 were paying for it.

'It sounds absolutely wonderful' Sam continued to enthuse 'Our Egyptologist tour guide said last night that the original ancient temple at Philae was flooded when the dastardly British decided to build the Aswan dam in 1902. Then in 1960 UNESCO decided to dismantle the original temple which was slowly being destroyed by the flood water and rebuild it, stone by stone on a different island that puts it safe and sound on much higher ground. But then I guess you knew all that as you were probably at his lecture as well.'

'Yes we were, but to be perfectly honest Mrs Gregson' said Mahrez 'I'm not really bothered about looking at a load of old stones, however neatly they've been put together. I'll probably stay on the boat, have a swim and a few beers.'

'Please excuse our Mr Ahmed' said Ahmadi. 'I'm afraid he's a bit of a philistine when it comes to admiring the glories of ancient Egypt. We hope to have educated him by the time we reach Luxor and the temple of Karnak, which I gather is the biggest and the best. Anyway, thank you both so much for the drink, but we have a video conference scheduled with Mercedes headquarters in Munich, so we must take our leave of you.'

With that they all left and went downstairs to one of the cabins.

'Jo Cartwright indeed' I said to Sam. 'Does the man think we've never seen Bonanza? I'm surprised his mate isn't named Matt Dillon or Rowdy Yates.'

'Bonanza was a TV Western wasn't it' asked Sam?

'Yes it was, but a very long time ago. Still' I continued 'at least we now know they're not infallible. They do make mistakes.'

'Why, what do you mean?' she asked.

'Mercedes headquarters. It's in Stuttgart, not Munich.'

Chapter Four

We'd been on board the 'Tutankhamun' just over 24 hours, and we'd met and spoken to our four suspected terrorists, but we'd not really gained any information that we hadn't known before getting on board. Sam and I sat on the bed in our cabin pondering what, if anything, we'd learnt.

'Well as you said, they're not infallible.' began Sam.

'We know they're lying about their real names' I sort of muttered more or less to myself 'but what I'd ideally like to know is why they're on this cruise ship.'

'What do you mean?' asked Sam.

'Well there are far easier ways of visiting Luxor, Karnak, Edfu and all the other stops on this journey, so why not just drive or fly to wherever it is they need to be?'

'I guess this way they don't look suspicious.'

'But what are they doing' I repeated 'or I suppose what I'm really asking Sam is why are they making so much effort to look so innocuous?'

'I guess because they are going to do something they don't want to be caught doing, and tourists mostly look anonymous?' said Sam.

'That's it.' I said with satisfaction. 'It's the only thing that makes any sense. They are going to do something, somewhere on this trip that they don't want to be suspected of, or associated with.'

'Agreed, but what, when, where and why?' asked Sam

'Four great questions, but as yet I've no idea.' I sighed 'but whatever it is they're up to, it can't be good.'

The following day Sam and I decided to split up. I stuck behind Ahmadi, Lajani and Rouhani, and joined the trip to Philae, while Sam claimed a splitting headache and stayed on the 'Tutankhamun' to keep an eye on Mahrez. She changed into a white bikini which helped show off her great figure and Algarve tan, but she put a light blue virtually see through top over it when she wasn't sun bathing or swimming. To be honest, my three did nothing in the least bit suspicious on my trip to Philae, at least, not that I could see. When we got back to the boat, I changed into a pair of swimming trunks and joined Sam on the top deck by the pool. She was on her own and Mahrez was still drinking at the bar.

'Anything interesting to report?' she asked.

'No' I replied despondently. 'They just did the usual touristy things, nothing suspicious at all. I kept well away from them and just watched from a distance. As I say, nothing of any interest. What about your man Mahrez?'

'Ah, well nothing I could really report on, but he did spend ages on his mobile phone chatting away in what I'm pretty sure was Arabic. I kept my distance as we'd agreed, but with everyone off on the trip the boat was really quiet and I could hear quite a lot of what he was saying. I did recognize a few words he said however as they were mostly place names, and I guess they are more of less the same in most languages.'

'Where were these places?' I enquired.

'He mentioned Paris twice, Munich once, London three times and San Diego once.' she replied. 'He also mentioned Israel several times, at least half a dozen times I should think, and you know how you can sometimes tell what people really think of something by how they say things?'

'Yeees' I slowly replied 'I think I know what you mean.'

'Well if I'm right, and I'm pretty sure I

am, the way he was saying the word, I'm convinced our Mr Youssef Mahrez absolutely hates and despises Israel.'

'Interesting, and I trust your instincts implicitly. Look, we can't keep chatting to them or they'll get suspicious. But we need to try and hear what they're saying and better still if we can do it without getting caught, record a conversation or two.'

Over the next three days we visited the Kom Ombo Temple, which to be honest I'd never heard of before, Edfu by horse carriage which was great fun, Hatshepsut Temple and the Colossi of Memnon, and we were now on a coach on our way to the place I really wanted to see more than anything else - the world famous Valley of the Kings.

We arrived in the coach and car park and all straggled out from the cool of the coach's air conditioning into the stifling heat of the Egyptian desert sun. Our guide asked us to keep together as much as possible as he led us from one tomb to another. The Valley of the Kings comprises of a pair of valleys where, for a period of nearly 500 years from the 16th to 11th century BC, rock cut tombs were excavated for the Pharaohs and powerful nobles of Ancient

Egypt.

The two valleys stands on the west bank of the Nile, opposite Thebes, or modern day Luxor as it is now called. The wadi consists of the East Valley, where the majority of the royal tombs are situated, and the West Valley. With the 2005 discovery of a new chamber and the 2008 discovery of two further tomb entrances, the valley is known to contain a total of 63 tombs and chambers ranging in size from a simple pit, coded KV54 (KV stands for Kings Valley) to a much more complex tomb with over 120 chambers coded as KV5. I have to say, I was completely fascinated as we wandered from tomb to tomb. We could see that in particular the royal tombs were decorated with incredibly beautiful and rich scenes from Egyptian history and mythology and they gave great clues as to the beliefs and funerary rituals of the period. Like Sam, who I could see was in her element, I was completely entranced by what I was seeing, and if I'm honest, I had totally forgotten all about Ahmadi and his three mates, until I saw Ahmadi chatting with a man outside the entrance to one of the closed off tombs. We'd not seen this guy before, and I was pretty sure he wasn't a passenger on the boat, so as discreetly as I could I took half a dozen photos on my iPhone, general views of the valley, but I made sure I included one of the man Ahmadi was talking to. I just hoped it hadn't look too suspicious, and as far as I could tell Ahmadi was oblivious to my Stephen Spielberg impression.

Sadly almost all of the tombs seem to have been opened and robbed in antiquity, but despite that, the few that were open to the public still gave us an idea of the amazing opulence and power of the Pharaohs. In modern times the valley became famous for the discovery of the tomb of Tutankhamen, which like all tombs now has a number, in this instance KV62, and with its rumours of the 'Curse of the Pharaohs', it has now become one of the most famous archaeological sites in the world. It is located in the centre of the East Valley, and was discovered by Howard Carter on November 4th 1922, although clearance and major conservation work continued for a further ten years, right through to 1932.

After four hours in the Valley of the Kings, Sam and I were totally exhausted. We'd drunk half a dozen bottles of water between us, and we now longed to get back to the promise of air conditioning on our coach. Ahmadi and co were travelling on a different coach to us, but we all arrived back at the boat around the same time. When we entered the dining room that evening, we saw that our four terrorists were sitting on the far right, so we decided to go left and keep our distance. After the meal we sat in the dining room and had coffee, and then like everybody else we slowly drifted into the lounge and grabbed a couple of armchairs. Our Egyptian guide was due to give a talk on what for a lot of people would be the highlight of the cruise, tomorrow's visit to the magnificent temple at Karnak. I noticed out of the corner of my eye that Youssef Mahrez had got up from his chair, left the other three sitting with their drinks, and was heading out of the dining room with his mobile phone clutched in his hand.

'Stay put Sam and keep an eye on the other three. If any of them follow me, ring my mobile. I'm going to see what Mahrez is up to.' He went up the stairs and outside onto the top deck. I was fairly close behind him, but I stayed back in the stairwell where I could still see him, but hopefully he couldn't see me. He wandered over towards the bar, where the barman was still serving, and ordered a beer. Once he had his beer he walked over to a table and sat down. As he picked up his mobile phone, I pressed the record button on my mobile and held it out towards him. Mahrez dialled a number and a few seconds later he started talking. Like every night in this part of the world, it was very quiet and very still, and although he wasn't speaking very loud, I could just about hear what he was saying, although as he was speaking what I assumed was Arabic I didn't understand a word of it. I just hoped Craig's whizz kids could make use of the recording. In all I ended up with just over eleven minutes on the recording, and when Sam and I played it back later in our cabin, neither of us had a clue what it was about, apart from the fact he again mentioned Paris, Munich, London and San Diego, and like before, he virtually spat the word Israel into the phone several times.

We felt we could get no further with Ahmadi and his colleagues, and so we decided to completely ignore them and just enjoy our trip round Karnak. Our guide was right, it was by far the biggest and the best of the Egyptian temples, and I really wished I could have seen it when it was originally built. We had another quiet night in the restaurant and the bar, and the following morning we left the ship, flew from Luxor to

Cairo, and then caught our flight back to London.

Chapter Five

Craig had asked us to report to him at MI6 headquarters when we got back, and with a bit of fear and trepidation we approached the now famous building we'd seen being blown up in the James Bond films. Strangely enough it looked perfectly intact, and it made us realize just how much of an impression the Bond films had made on us. As we entered 85 Albert Embankment in Vauxhall, MI6's London address, I remembered some of the information I'd read up on about the building. Although MI6 are now officially known about and acknowledged, there is still one thing they won't confirm or deny, and that is the rumour that there is a tunnel between the MI6 building and the Foreign Office in Whitehall.

The building was agreed to by Margaret Thatcher when she was Prime Minister, and the numerous layers over which the building is laid out created 60 separate roof areas, and in total 130,000 square feet of glass and aluminium were used in the construction. All the windows in the building are triple glazed for security purposes, and due to the highly sensitive nature of MI6's work, large parts of the building are below street level, with a host of underground corridors serving the building. Amenities for staff include a sports hall, a gymnasium, an aerobics studio, a squash court and a restaurant. I also remembered that like some ancient castles, the building also features two moats for added protection. The building work was completed in April 1994 and it was officially opened by Queen Elizabeth II and the Duke of Edinburgh, in July of that year.

After receiving two visitor passes at reception, Craig sent down one of his staff to collect us, and we were escorted to his office near the top floor.

'Welcome back.' he said 'and tell me, how did you get on?'

'Great' began Sam 'and we really enjoyed the temples, particularly Karna ...'

'I couldn't give a stuff about the wretched temples' interrupted Craig, cutting Sam off in mid flow. 'How did you get on with watching Jahangir Ahmadi and his cohorts?'

'You don't really do social graces do you Craig?' I asked 'that was just plain rude.'

'You're right Michael, and I'm sorry Sam.

That was extremely rude of me, and I guess I'm just keen to know if you learnt anything or was it all just a waste of time?'
Sam just smiled at him and said 'No problem, and no offence taken.'

'Actually' I replied 'we think it was quite useful. We watched them for the first 24 hours, but got nothing. They didn't mix with anybody, and they just whispered amongst themselves in quiet corners of the boat. Then everybody went out on various feluccas, they're small sailing boats by the way, and we managed to get ourselves onto the same felucca as Ahmadi.'

'Did they suspect anything?' Craig asked.

'No, they just talked quietly amongst themselves and then Mahrez, the Moroccan said something out loud and they suddenly all laughed.'

'I recognized the word he'd said as being in Pashto' said Sam 'as I have a family in my medical practice that speak Pashto and they taught me a few words and phrases.'

'We realized we'd get nowhere if we didn't understand the language' I said 'so Sam decided to throw herself to the crocodiles.'

'Good grief' said Craig aghast.

'Actually I just stood up in the boat' explained Sam 'and then deliberately sort of wobbled a bit, and then I accidentally on purpose fell straight into Ahmadi's lap.'

'He was the perfect gentleman' I said 'and when Sam thanked him in English he replied in perfect English. To cut a long story short Craig, what we discovered is they always speak in Pashto amongst themselves, they speak in English to all the passengers, including us, and Mahrez occasionally wanders off from the other three and makes mobile phone calls in Arabic.'

'I don't suppose you have any idea who he's telephoning or what he says.'

'None at all I'm afraid.'

'Oh well, at least we know they can speak English. That's something we weren't aware of before. Mahrez speaking Arabic is to be expected, after all, he is Moroccan.'

'There is one other thing which might be of interest.' I said.

'And what might that be?' enquired Craig.

'I managed to record Mahrez's last phone call. Admittedly it's only one sided, and the quality is not brilliant, but you might get something from it.'

'How the hell did you do that?' he asked. 'No, don't tell me. Just promise me they didn't see you.'

'No, they have no idea. Sam overheard another one of Mahrez's phone calls earlier in the week, and in both calls he mentioned London several times, Munich, Paris and San Diego, and we both got the distinct impression that he absolutely hates Israel.'

I handed Craig my mobile, and he pressed play. He listened for about thirty seconds then turned it off. He picked up a telephone and summoned someone to his office. Twenty seconds later a middle aged man in a white coat came in and Craig held the phone out to him.

'Ah, Simpson. Copy the recording on here, clean it up, have it translated into English, and then bring me three double spaced printed transcripts of what it says. Oh, and then let Mr Turner here have his phone back when you've finished.'

'Yes Sir' he replied.

'Oh Mr Simpson' I called, stopping him in his tracks 'there is also a photograph on there of Ahmadi talking to someone outside one of the tombs in the Valley of the Kings. Whoever it was he was talking to he certainly wasn't from the cruise ship, and we have no idea who he is, but I thought you folk might know him.'

'Thank you Mr Turner. I'll check it out.' and with that he scuttled out of the room.

'So' mused Craig 'London, Munich, Paris and where else did you say?'

'San Diego' answered Sam.

'Why those four, and what are they up to?' mused Craig.

'We asked ourselves the same questions' I said 'and the only thing we could come up with was that as they're four terrorists, and there are four cities on their list, perhaps they are going to set off four suicide bombs. One in each of those four cities.'

'No chance of suicide bombs' said Craig very confidently. 'Those four don't do the dirty work themselves or risk their own lives, they employ others, or better still save money by brainwashing others into the cause, whatever the hell that is.'

'You said when you first briefed us Craig that these four had very little in common.'

'Ah, yes, that's right. Jahangir Ahmadi is a very big wheel in the world of international terrorism. As you know he's Iranian and we know that over the years he has done paid contract work for numerous terror organizations including Al Qaida, ISIS and Hezbollah, but he's very much an organizational brain for hire, not an action man.'

'Why not dispose of him. I assume MI6

does what I believe is called 'wet work?'

'I'm afraid you've been watching too many spy films Michael. My people do not all have a licence to kill, and the intelligence community does not in general execute people, although exceptions can of course be made if they pose what our American colleagues call 'a clear and present danger.'

'Ah yes' I replied 'I've read both the Tom Clancy book and seen the film.'

'Yes, well don't believe everything you read in books or watch in films. Now Akram Lajani as I said before is also Iranian, but he is a Kurd, and Kurds and the likes of Jahangir Ahmadi usually detest each other because of Iran's view of Kurdistan in the north of the country and their claims for independence. Those two would by most people be regarded as enemies, not colleagues.

Youssef Mahrez is tenth generation Moroccan, and as far as we know his main beef is with the Spanish. He has always been angry at the way his father was treated by Spain when they took the enclave of Ceuta. His father had worked for the Moroccan government there most of his life and when Spain moved in, his father and mother were kicked out. His father protested, it led to violence and his father was killed during the conflict. Mahrez's beef is with Spain, not with any of the countries you mentioned.

'What about the other one – Rouhani?'

'As for Sadiq Rouhani, well to be honest, I haven't a clue. His argument is with India and it always has been. If you remember your history, you will know that relations between India and Pakistan have been complex and largely hostile due to a number of historical and political events. Relations between the two states have been defined by what turned out to be the violent partition of British India back in 1947. Then there was the very nasty Kashmir conflict, and numerous other military conflicts that have been fought between the two nations ever since. The extremely difficult relationship between the two countries has for years been plagued by hostility and suspicion, and what relations there are between the countries remain frigid, following repeated acts of cross-border terrorism. Rouhani has been heavily involved in a lot of those acts, but that has nothing to do with London, Paris, Munich or San Diego, or for that matter Iran and Morocco. I'm at a total loss to know what any of this is all about.'

We discussed various possibilities for about

forty minutes but came to no conclusions, when there was a knock on the door and Simpson returned.

'Your phone Mr Turner' he said handing me back my mobile.

'OK Simpson' said Craig 'I can read through the full transcript later, but for the time being just give me the basic Janet and John version.'

Sam and I smiled at each other at his use of Janet and John.

'Yes sir. The recording Mr Turner made lasted eleven minutes and fourteen seconds in total, and after we'd cleaned it up we could hear Mahrez's side of the conversation quite clearly, but not what was being said to him. We also have no idea who he was talking to. We got the entire conversation translated from the Arabic into English, and as far as we can tell, it looks like Mahrez is the group's communications man, as he seemed to be both reporting to and getting instructions from we assume someone in Iran, although as I said, we don't know who or where for sure. From what we could gather from only hearing that one side of the conversation, Ahmadi and co are being paid a lot of money by someone in we assume Iran, but it could be elsewhere, to put together a sophisticated terror campaign using the world's best terror experts. The idea seems to be to run a campaign that will strike at the heart of four of Israel's biggest supporters; the USA, the UK, France and Germany. Their objective seems to be to ensure the blame for each and every terrorist act or incident they arrange is firmly put on Israel, and in doing so force those four countries that are currently backing Israel to withdraw their support, and so isolate Israel. I'm afraid we have no idea what form these incidents will take, when any of these incidents are likely to take place or where exactly. Just those four cities. That in a nut shell sir is the basic Janet and John version.'

'Thank you Simpson. Well done.'

'Oh, and by the way sir, that man you photographed outside the tomb. One of our people did recognize him from our files.'

'And who was it?' demanded Craig.

'It was Khalid Khan sir, who we all thought was long dead.'

Chapter Six

'So who is this Khalid Khan? I asked as Simpson left the room.

'He was, or should I now say is, an

Afghan and the main brains behind a lot of the planning for most of Al Qaida's biggest terror acts during all the Afghan troubles a few years ago. The Americans dropped a bomb on his home and we all thought he was dead. If Khalid Khan is still alive and he's now talking to Ahmadi, then this is an extremely serious new development.'

'Well we wish you luck with it all Craig' I said standing up to leave.

'Where the hell do you think you're going?' he asked. 'Sit yourself down. I've got another job for you.'

'I sort of assumed we'd finished.' I replied. 'Look, they all know what we look like now, and so we're of no more use to you now than your own people are, less so in fact as your guys know what they're doing. We're just rank amateurs.'

'Amateurs you may be, but you've found out more in the last week than MI6, the CIA and Mossad have discovered about these people in the last six months. No, I still need you both - that is if you're willing to continue helping?'

'Of course we are' said Sam 'but as Michael said, how can we? They know what we look like and what we sound like.'

'Not if we change your appearance. Dyed

hair, glasses, a moustache etc.'

'I assume the moustache is for Michael and not me?' giggled Sam.

'Don't be flippant Samantha, this is serious.' frowned Craig, then he smiled. 'Of course the moustache is for Michael my dear, but we can change people's appearance quite easily, and providing you stick to just watching, they won't have a clue.'

'I don't know' I said 'It worries me that they know us now.'

'They certainly know Peter and Susan Gregson, a clean shaven man with excellent eyesight and his gorgeous blonde wife. But they don't know David and Julie Potter, a dark haired archaeologist with a beard and a moustache, who has to wear black horn rimmed glasses all the time, and his equally short sighted, attractive brunette wife who has to wear blue tinted gold wire framed glasses.'

'You'd already planned all this hadn't you?' I asked.

'Of course I had. It's my job. Now um, er, look you two. I am now assuming the Nile cruise was set up so that Ahmadi could meet up with Khalid Khan somewhere not at all suspicious, yet quite public, but also quite safe and completely neutral. Well done by the way for getting that photograph. We now have the travel agent in Cairo completely over a barrel, and once the poor sop had taken our money he became ours for life. We know from him that as well as booking the trip down the Nile, Ahmadi also booked a trip to Phuket in Thailand and then on to Bali, but that trip is just for Ahmadi and Akram Lajani. Knowing what we now know, I'm assuming Ahmadi is going to meet up and try and recruit other terrorists. He's not due in Thailand for another three weeks, and I'm assuming you can grow a beard and a moustache in that time?'

'I assume that question was also addressed to Michael?' asked Sam grinning.

'You just love winding me up don't you Samantha dearest?'

'I'm sorry Craig, but you always seem so serious. It's just the way I am, and I don't suppose I'll ever change. Sorry.'

'Um. Yes, well please don't apologise dear lady, I quite like it if I'm honest. Now Michael, I um think our young Professor Potter and his studious wife would quite enjoy visiting Asia for a week or two, don't you?'

'I think they just might.' I replied.

Sam and I flew back to the Algarve and spent a couple of weeks of relative normality. I wrote a few more chapters on my Spanish tourist guide of crime scenes, and Sam went in to the medical practice and reacquainted herself with Jan, her receptionist and several of the patients she hadn't seen for a while. At the beginning of our third week back home I received an email from Craig with our E tickets for the flights and two vouchers for our hotels. One in Phuket and one in Bali. Obviously the email didn't have Craig's name printed on MI6 headed notepaper, but it was from a travel company that Craig had told us handled the travel arrangements for all government departments.
We would be flying from London Heathrow to Dubai with Emirates airlines, then we had an overnight stay in the Arabian Courtyard Hotel & Spa, near Dubai Creek. The following morning we were due on another Emirates flight, this one to Thailand, where we were booked into the Wyndham Grand Phuket Kalim Bay five star hotel. Craig had told us we would be staying at the same hotel as Ahmadi in Phuket. I thought it was really nice of Ahmadi to choose five star hotels.
The flights were long and tedious, not Emirates fault, they were very comfortable and their

Dreamliner's are excellent aircraft, but after the private Gulfstream we'd got used to flying in with Interpol, any commercial airline was going to feel a bit inferior.
I hadn't really thought about it earlier, but it suddenly dawned on me that we were on our own. There was no back up or support from Interpol or the UK police who we'd frequently worked with. Although we were working under the auspices of MI6, we were now well and truly on our own. Oh well, we were only watching, and providing that's all we did, we should be OK. My dark beard and moustache had now grown to a reasonable length and both were neatly trimmed, although my hair was much longer than I normally wore it and it was definitely not its usual neat and tidy self. I'd got used to wearing the black horn rimmed glasses with plain lenses, and sometimes I looked at myself in the mirror and didn't recognize the guy looking back at me. As for Sam, well I now found myself married to a short sighted brunette who like me wore glasses all the time, but despite that, I still loved her dearly.

We checked into the Wyndham Grand Phuket Kalim Bay hotel, and went straight to our room where we both crashed out. Craig had ensured we arrived 24 hours before Ahmadi was scheduled to land so that we would be quite relaxed and refreshed before following him and Akram Lajani. The following day we were sitting on a very comfortable sofa in the large reception area when Ahmadi and Lajani checked in. We were sitting sharing a bottle of excellent merlot as I read a copy of the Daily Telegraph and Sam was flicking through Hello magazine. I'd thought about this earlier, and I got out my iPhone, put it in camera mode and zoomed in as tight as I could get on the rack of keys on the wall behind the reception desk. I pressed record and hoped the receptionist booking them in would reach back and take down a key. He did and handed Ahmadi the key to room 114. Although it was a very modern and luxurious hotel, they still used old fashioned keys as back up for the modern electronic key cards.

The following morning, we went down to breakfast but Ahmadi and Lajani were both no shows, however we did see them later at the excursions desk next to reception booking a trip to somewhere or other. I got up and wandered over to the excursion board hanging up near the desk to see if I could hear where they were going. Fortunately they were speaking English with the excursion clerk, and I heard Ahmadi booking a boat trip for the following day to somewhere known as 'James Bond Island'. Most appropriate I thought.

'James Bond Island' turned out to be the small little island located of the coast of Thailand that was used as the home of 'Francisco Scaramanga' in the Roger Moore Bond film 'The Man with the Golden Gun'. I booked Sam and I onto the same trip, and returned to our comfy sofa in reception.

'We're off on a trip to 'James Bond Island' tomorrow.' I informed Mrs Potter.

'Where and what is 'James Bond Island' she asked.

'If you remember the 007 film 'The Man with the Golden Gun' it's the private island where Scaramanga lives.'

'Who?' Sam asked.

'Francisco Scaramanga.' I answered

'No, sorry' said Sam. 'Don't know who you mean. You know my view. If you've seen one James Bond film you've seen them all. Villain tries to take over the world, 007 rides in and saves the day, whilst seducing every female in sight.'

'You can be a very cynical woman at times Mrs Potter.' I said. 'Anyway, getting back to the truly excellent film - Scaramanga, who is played by Christopher Lee, wears white suits all the time, has three nipples instead of the standard two, and charges exorbitant sums of money, a million pounds to be exact, to carry out various assassinations for his clients using a golden gun and solid gold bullets. In the film he has built a luxurious home on his own personal little island somewhere off the coast of south east China, although I gather the place where they filmed it is actually off the coast of Phuket. Anyway, we're going there tomorrow by boat, and so is Ahmadi.'

'Doesn't that mean we'll have to be quite close to him?'

'Not if we sit right at the back of the boat. We don't need to talk to him, just watch him from a distance and try and get a photograph of anyone he meets up with. I assume he's going to meet someone on the island, and I don't think he's going on the trip because he's a closet James Bond fan, do you?'

'No, you're probably right, and yes, I think we can assume he's meeting someone.'

Chapter Seven

The following morning we joined the boat trying

as hard as possible not to look like ourselves. It was a hot day, so we couldn't hide under loads of clothes, but with my now quite longish dark hair, a beard, a moustache, horn rimmed sunglasses and all topped off with a white panama hat, my mother would have been hard pushed to recognize me. Sam was wearing a pair of red shorts and a bright yellow tee shirt from Las Vegas, and with her brunette hair under a red headscarf and her gold rimmed glasses, she too looked nothing like the woman I'd married. We boarded the boat, which I estimated held about fifty people, and we headed straight for the seats at the back. Ahmadi arrived with Lajani, and they headed to the front. That was fine by us, we didn't want them anywhere near us.

The boat cast off and we headed down what was basically a wide river towards the area of national park where the island is located. It took well over an hour to get there, but we didn't mind in the slightest as the scenery en-route was absolutely amazing. When we eventually arrived at the island, which is actually located in somewhere called Phang Nga Bay, I was surprised at how small it was. Our tour guide told us that when they made the film they actually used two separate islands, one named Ko Khao Ping Kan and the other going by the name of Ko Tapu, in order to make Francisco Sacaramanga's lair seem much bigger than it actually was. We watched Ahmadi very carefully all the time he was on the island to see who he talked to, but as far as we could tell he didn't meet anybody. It was only when we were about half an hour into the journey back to the marina that I suddenly realised something. Ahmadi no longer had his shoulder bag with him. I simply hadn't noticed earlier. When we left this morning he had a small grey canvas bag slung over his shoulder, now he didn't. I told Sam what I was thinking.

'So you think he's left it on the island for someone else to collect?' she asked.

'Yes, I'm afraid so. We just weren't watching him closely enough. If you remember Craig told us all about drop boxes and how they work before we left, and I guess there is a crevice in the rock or something on James Bond Island where Ahmadi left the bag.'

'But even if we'd seen him leave it, there was nothing we could do about it.'

'True. There are boats coming and going from the island every five minutes, and whoever he left it for could have picked it up five minutes after it he left, or five hours after he'd left the island.'

'The important thing is, we know Ahmadi used the island as a drop box, and there's nothing more we could have done without raising suspicion. The tour guide was checking everyone both on and off the boat, and they wouldn't have left without us.'

'No, your right love. We did all we could.'

Back at the hotel we had a shower and then went down to the restaurant for our evening meal. To be honest, I'm not a great lover of spicy food, although Sam will eat almost anything put in front of her. Fortunately for me the hotel was used to western tastes and catered for everyone. I had an excellent sirloin steak and French fries while Sam had a Thai green curry. We both enjoyed the really good local beer. The following morning we were off again, this time to the Indonesian island paradise of Bali. We flew with KLM, and it was only a short flight of about ninety minutes. We caught a taxi to our hotel, which we found quite amusing as the signs on the roof are spelt 'Taksi'. Anyway, we checked in, and we were just leaving reception when Ahmadi and Lajani arrived. We ignored them and headed for our room, which I have to say was interesting to say the least.

It was quite a large room, with a large flat screen TV facing a massive super king size bed. There was plenty of cupboard space, a small safe, and a decent fridge. On the opposite wall were two sinks, but for the life of me I couldn't see a bath, a shower or a toilet anywhere. Then Sam slid back the glass patio doors at the far end of the room which had closed venetian blinds covering the glass, to reveal a corner bath with a shower above it, and the toilet, both of which were outside in a private walled garden. The walls were about eight feet high and we weren't overlooked by anyone, so it was all very private, but not quite what we were expecting. At least I thought we weren't going to need any air freshener, although I decided not to share my thoughts with Sam. Humidity was quite high, so we both tried the outside shower, which was actually quite good, and we then got changed into some fresh shorts and tee shirts, and headed for the bar to try the local beer which was called 'Bintang'. Again, very good and very refreshing.

We saw Ahmadi and Lajani wander past us, but they never even glanced in our direction, and they climbed into the back of the hotel's shuttle bus. We immediately drained our beers and jumped into the back of one of the 'Taksi's' waiting in the hotel's courtyard.

'Can you follow that shuttle bus please?' I asked our driver.

'Fantastic' he said. 'I've waited years to be asked to follow the car in front. Tell me please,' he said very politely 'Why are you following that bus?'

'We're secret agents from London' I said 'and we're following a couple of hardened terrorists who want to blow up the world.'
Sam looked at me with a look of horror on her face.

'Well' I smiled 'He's not going to believe me is he?' and to prove my point he said

'Seriously, why are you following the bus?'

'Oh simple really. We meant to catch it, but we'd just missed it.'

'Do you need me to overtake it?' he asked

'No' I replied 'just take your time, but don't get too close, and don't lose it.'

'Mm, I think you are probably secret agents after all' he said.
Our driver dropped us off outside a big shopping centre, and we followed Ahmadi and Lajani inside. We kept well back and out of sight

and just followed them around from a distance. Shopping centres in Bali, well at least this one, contained all sorts of things you wouldn't find in a UK shopping centre, such as four different men's tailoring shops where they'll make you a brand new made to measure suit and have it ready in 24 hours. We'd just decided we needed to rest when Ahmadi and Lajani disappeared inside one of these tailoring shops. We couldn't see inside, but Sam sensibly said

'Try and photograph everyone going in and coming out until Ahmadi reappears.'

'Good idea' I said, and I got my iPhone out of my pocket. I set it to camera mode and waited. During the next hour, three people went in, and only two came out. Then roughly an hour after he'd gone inside, Ahmadi came out and he and Lajani walked off back towards the entrance to the shopping Mall. Three minutes later, the third man who'd gone in about 45 minutes earlier came out, looked around and then headed off towards the back of the Mall. I'd managed to get photographs of everyone, and I just hoped Craig's people could recognize someone.

Later that evening Sam and I, seeing Ahmadi and Lajani were ensconced in the hotel bar for the evening, we decided we needed a break from following them everywhere, so we went to see a wonderful show which was a bit like an Indonesian version of 'Cirque du Soleil'. It was absolutely fantastic, and we got back to the hotel completely exhausted. The following day Ahmadi and Lajani headed for the hotel's private beach and so we decided to do the same. We got a couple of sun loungers about thirty feet away from them, and worked out a routine where one of us read or sunbathed, while the other watched them.

We'd been on the beach for about an hour when about six local women descended on us offering everyone full body massages. Now we still hadn't really come to terms with Balinese money, with the exchange rate being roughly 19,000 rupiah to the pound, or roughly 14,000 to the US dollar. When I asked one of the women how much she charged I thought I must have got the conversion wrong, but no, she was charging 100,000 rupiah for an hour long full body massage, about five pounds or seven US dollars. Sam and I both said yes, and two hours later we both felt truly amazing. What an experience. The following day our time in Bali came to an end, for the simple reason Ahmadi checked out and flew off somewhere. Sam and I checked out and after two long flights we eventually landed back in London.

Chapter Eight

The following morning we headed back to the MI6 building on the Thames for another briefing with Craig Overton. We handed my iPhone over to Simpson again and sat chatting while we waited. We didn't have long to wait. There was a knock on the door.

'Enter' instructed Craig, and Simpson came into the office with a big goofy smile on his face, and handing me back my phone.

'So?' asked Craig.

'Well we've no idea who the first two from the tailors shop in Bali are, probably real customers I should think, but we certainly know who the third man is.'

'Do you intend to tell us Simpson, or are you waiting for us to all die of suspense?'

'Sorry sir. It's Sergei Polyakov.'

'Oh God' said Craig leaning on the desk and holding his head in his hands.

'Who the hell is Sergei Polyakov?' asked Sam.

Craig waved an arm at Simpson who explained.

'Sergei Polyakov is Russian, ex KGB and

one of the top three cyber terrorists in the world, if not the best of the best. He went freelance about five years ago, and if he decides to hack into something and destroy it, there's very little anyone can do to stop him. As well as working with terror groups he still does odd jobs for the Russian government. About two years ago he hacked into Vienna's electricity supply and turned the entire grid off for fifteen minutes because an Austrian politician had compared Russia's then recent land grabs as being similar to Hitler taking over Austria at the beginning of World War Two. Polyakov was given the job of demonstrating to Austria that they should not criticize Russia, or if they do, take the punishment.'

'It looks' began Craig 'very much like Sergei Polyakov is working with Khalid Khan, Jahangir Ahmadi, Akram Lajani, Youssef Mahrez and Sadiq Rouhani, plus whoever picked up Ahmadi's bag at the drop box in Thailand. We apparently have a group of the world's top freelance terrorists, all working together under the direction of some as yet, unknown sponsor. I don't like it, and I'm not sure what the hell we can do about it.'

'Can't you just arrest them all?' asked Sam

'Oh, if only we could my dear. Tell me, Er, what would I charge them with? Talking to each other in a tailor's shop, chatting to each other whilst cruising down the Nile? No, I'm afraid unlike them, we have to play by the rule book.'

'Sorry Craig' I said, 'but if they're known terrorists who kill innocent people, can't you have them killed, taken out, assassinated or whatever you call it?'

'We may know they're terrorists Michael, but like all the top criminals in any field, they've never been caught in the act and we have zero proof of them ever doing anything wrong, and having proof is the important bit. Plus it would never be sanctioned by the government. There has been a strict no assassination policy amongst all the intelligence agencies for the last twenty five years, and I assure you, for every one of theirs we 'took out' as you so graphically put it, they would 'take out' ten of our people'.

'But there must be something you can do' said Sam.

'Come on Craig' I said 'for goodness sake. We know these creeps are soon going to start a massive terror campaign in four different European countries, including this one, and they are going to do it in such a way that Israel cops all the blame. As Sam said, surely there is something that can be done?'

'Oh there is.' replied Craig. 'But I can't do it myself unfortunately, so I'm going to ask you two to do one more favour for me.'

'Whatever it is, why can't you do it?' asked Sam.

'It involves travelling to another country again and I have to be here for a series of meetings with the government over the next four days, including two security briefings I have to give to the Prime Minister personally. Those meetings can't be moved, so I'm er, asking you two to go for me.'

'Go where?' I asked.

'Israel' Craig bluntly replied. 'They need to be warned so that they can start planning a response for when whatever is going to happen, happens. Will you go?'

'Of course' replied Sam looking at me. I nodded my agreement at her.

'You will be meeting a man very few people in the world know. He is my direct counterpart in Mossad, and for obvious reasons his identity is a closely guarded secret.
I will telephone him and arrange a meeting for later in the week if that is OK with you two. It is also I think time to bring in some reinforcements

to help you, so as this suspected campaign is a definite threat to Europe and our American allies, I think it is time to ask Interpol to get involved.'

Sam and I looked at each other and smiled a massive smile of relief.

'I will contact Senior Superintendent Helena Van Houten, head of European operations, and I gather your good friend?

'Yes' smiled Sam. 'Helena was my chief bridesmaid at our wedding.'

'Good' Craig replied. 'I only met her a couple of times during that Harry Greenly business, but she impressed me greatly. Because she is involved with crime, she is an unknown in the world of terrorism, which is very different, and so she can give you the back up and support that my people can't.'

'You don't know what a relief it will be to have some support with us.' I said.

'Well I don't know if she can get away until I telephone her, but I'll do my best. Look, why don't you two pop along to the canteen and have a coffee while I make a few telephone calls. I'll get Simpson to come and collect you when I've got everything tied up.'

In fact I had a mug of tea and a small individual packet of bourbon biscuits, which happened to be my favourites, whereas Sam had a mug of tea and a packet of custard creams, her favourites. We chatted about everything we'd experienced in the last couple of weeks and we both realised how nervous we had been in Egypt, Thailand and Bali, being out there totally on our own with no back up if needed. It was a new experience for us, and now we'd thought about it, one we didn't particularly wish to repeat. About forty minutes later Simpson walked into the canteen and beckoned for us to follow him. As we were walking back to Craig's office I asked him:

'Tell me please, I assume you have a Christian name, but Craig never uses it. That seems awfully rude to me.'

'Yes, well my Christian name is actually Roy, but nobody uses Christian names within the service, it's all surnames or initials, and I really don't mind, I've got used to it.'

Simpson knocked on Craig's door, we heard a gruff 'Enter' and so we bid Simpson farewell and walked in.

'Right you two. There's good news on the Interpol front. I've spoken to Helena, and she says she can arrange to be away for a few days and can fly into Biggin Hill tomorrow. She said she will use Interpol's own aircraft and her own flight crew who you apparently already know.'

'Fantastic. That means George, Colin and Jo.' I said.

'No Michael, that's only three. Helena told me there would be four of them coming in addition to herself, and she also said you'd worked with all of them before. She mentioned all the names you said, but also someone called Willie?'

'Great' beamed Sam. 'Willie Schuster worked with us on that nasty Harry Greenly business, and in fact it was Willie who got the ball rolling for us when he was a Police Inspector in Salzburg. He is now part of Helena's Interpol team.'

'Fine. Well you'll need to be at Biggin Hill at 10.00 am in the morning. Helena said you can use her aircraft to fly to Israel. Now, the man you're meeting has as I said, one of the most closely guarded identities in the world. If his face became known there are thousands of Arabs who would happily, to use your expression, take him out. His name is
Moishe Kravitz, and as I told you earlier, he is Mossad's Operations Director. He has a permanent bodyguard who goes everywhere with him, night and day.'

'And what's his name?' I asked.

'Rivka Meyer' Craig replied.

'But that's a girl's name isn't it?' asked Sam.

'Certainly is' replied Craig 'and what a girl. She is an absolutely stunning thirty two year old blonde, and she poses as Moishe's girlfriend when they are out in public. In fact, she is by far Mossad's best undercover operative and she is absolutely deadly if needs be.'

'But they are not boyfriend and girlfriend?' asked Sam.

'Good heavens, certainly not' answered Craig. 'For a start Moishe's wife would kill him, plus he is very much the family man when he's not 'on the job' so to speak. Rivka like all Israeli girls did her two years conscription in the army, where they discovered two things about her. She was deadly and a crack shot with a gun, any gun, and she was the coolest of customers in difficult situations and was able to make fast decisions and act on them. When she'd completed her two years she was approached by Mossad who had been tipped off by the army, and she joined them as a trainee. She graduated with honours after five years of very intensive training, and she has been Moishe's personal bodyguard for the last two and a half years.

Incidentally, Rivka is also god mother to Moishe's youngest daughter.'

'So where are we meeting them?' I asked.

'Somewhere very private where you won't be disturbed.' Craig answered.

'Any chance of telling us a bit more detail?' Sam enquired.

'Um, yes, well, I suppose so. You're not going to tell anyone else where are you?'

'Well I assume Helena will need to know as she's taking us there?' I said.

'Yes, well that's all right then. You're meeting in the remains of Herod's northern palace on the top of Masada.'

'Masada?' queried Sam 'I've heard of it, but I can't think why, where or what it is.'

'In that case' said Craig 'let me tell you about Masada. Masada itself is basically a 2,000 year old fortress built on the top of a flat topped mountain. That's a very crude description, but it gives you the general idea. The cliffs on the east edge of Masada are about 1,300 feet high, and the natural approaches to the cliff top are incredibly difficult to navigate. The top of the mountain, or I guess I should more accurately call it a plateau, is flat and sort of rhomboid or diamond like in shape. It's about 1,800 feet long by roughly 900 feet at its widest point. A stone wall was constructed right around the top of the plateau totalling about 4,300 feet in length and just over 12 feet high. The wall contained internal walkways from which you could look down on any enemy below, and many lookout towers. The fortress included barracks, storehouses, an armoury, a superb palace, and cisterns that were refilled by rainwater. The only way to get to the top of Masada was via three narrow, winding paths up to highly fortified gates.

You have to understand' continued Craig 'that Masada has a very special place in both Israeli and Jewish history. Almost all historical information we know about Masada comes from the famous first century Jewish Roman historian Josephus. He tells us that King Herod the Great captured the original mountain top in the power struggle that followed the death of his father Antipater. Then between 37 BC and 31 BC, we are told that Herod built a large fortress on the plateau as a refuge for himself in the event of a revolt, and he also erected two palaces, one of which is the famous northern palace.

In AD 66 a group of Jewish rebels led by a man

named Elazar Ben-Yair, overcame the Roman garrison in Masada with the aid of a clever ruse, and then four years later in AD 70, additional rebels, or zealots as they became known, fled Jerusalem and they all settled on the mountaintop. By AD 73, the Romans had had enough, and the then governor of Judaea, Lucius Flavius Silva, headed an entire Roman legion of 5,000 troops who then laid siege to Masada. The Roman legion surrounded Masada, but after numerous failed attempts to get to the summit, they eventually gave up and decided the only solution was to build a massive siege ramp against the western face of the plateau.'

'Why was it so difficult to get to the top?' asked Sam.

'Well you see' continued Craig 'Masada is as I said earlier, over 1,300 feet high, and the problem facing the Romans was that the only way to get to the top was up what is called the snake path. It is very narrow, and even if you are extremely fit, it still takes over an hour to climb to the top from its starting point which is at the lowest place on earth, alongside the Dead Sea. Two thousand years ago, ten zealots could easily defend Masada from the entire Roman Legion as the only way for them to get to the top was climbing virtually single file up the narrow snake path.

So, after three years of frustration Flavius Silva called in Rome's top military engineer who oversaw the construction of the siege ramp, which was eventually completed in the spring of AD 73. The Romans had employed an entire Legion and several auxiliary units, plus an amazing number of Jewish prisoners of war, totalling some 15,000 men in eventually crushing the Jewish resistance at Masada.'

'So what happened in the end?' I asked.

'A giant siege tower with a battering ram was constructed by the Romans and moved laboriously up the completed ramp. After two to three months of siege, the Romans finally breached the wall of the fortress with the battering ram on April 16th. According to Josephus, when the Roman troops eventually entered the fortress, they discovered that its defendants had set all the buildings ablaze, and every last one of them rather than become slaves of the Romans had committed mass suicide, with the last few men left standing killing each other, a total of 960 men, women, and children'

'That's horrendous' said Sam screwing up her face.

'Not if you're an Israeli' replied Craig.

'As Judaism prohibits suicide, Josephus said each man killed the women and children in his own family, and then the defenders drew lots and killed each other in turn, down to the last ten men. Nine of them then laid on the ground in a row face up with their necks bared, and the tenth man killed the other nine by slashing their throats with his sword. He then killed himself meaning he would be the only one to actually take his own life. Josephus also very clearly states in his account that Eleazar Ben-Yair ordered his men to destroy everything except the food stocks, in order to show that the defenders retained the ability to live, and so had chosen death over slavery. To most modern day Jews it's a moment from history that they are extremely proud of.'

'And people can still visit Masada today?' asked Sam.

'Oh yes' answered Craig 'but when you meet Moishe and Rivka, it will be inside the middle tier of the northern palace which will sadly not be open to the public that day due to unavoidable and necessary preservation work. One other thing you might find interesting. Many years ago, the chief of staff of the Israeli Defence Forces, Moshe Dayan, initiated the practice of holding the swearing-in ceremony of new Israeli Armoured Corps soldiers who had completed their basic training on top of Masada. The soldiers had to climb up the Snake Path at night, and they are then sworn in with torches lighting the background. The ceremony ends with the declaration: 'Masada shall not fall again.'

Chapter Nine

Later that afternoon, we headed down to Kent and stayed overnight in a hotel just down the road from Biggin Hill Airport, where we both took time getting back to our original selves. Sam washed the brunette dye out of her hair returning to her natural blonde, and I happily shaved off the beard and the moustache, and trimmed my hair back to its normal length. I have to say, it felt good to be our normal selves again. After breakfast we arrived at the small airport just in time to see Interpol's shiny Gulfstream come in to land. After the necessary passport checks etc we walked out to the plane, which had now taxied to an area just outside one of the hangers and shut down the engines. Helena emerged down the Gulfstream's steps and we were both greeted like long lost friends.

'So, here we go again' said Helena

beaming at us both. 'I got this very mysterious phone call yesterday from Craig Overton at MI6, who informed me that you two were helping him out, but that it was something Interpol really should be involved in and you desperately needed our help. I asked him for details, but he refused to tell me anything other than you would fill us in and tell me where we were going. So, what gives?'

'So you know nothing about this?' I asked her. 'You're very trusting of Craig to come all this way not knowing why?'

'Oh believe me. I don't trust Craig Overton one little bit, but I trust you two implicitly, and if you're involved I know it's going to be interesting and exciting.'

'Oh thank you Helena' gushed Sam. 'That's so nice of you.'

'Oh stop being so girly you two' I suggested 'and let's get on board. It's probably easier if we brief everyone at the same time if that's OK with you?'

'Of course O great one' Helena replied and smiled at me. 'Your wish is of course my command.' I like Helena.

We climbed up the steps into the body of the aircraft where we had a few hugs with George,

Colin, Jo and Willie who were all really pleased to see us, but also all inquisitive as to what was going on. We all sat down as Jo served everyone with fresh coffee from the aircrafts galley.

'OK' I began 'I'll try and keep it short and simple. Sam and I got a phone call from Craig Overton at MI6 saying he was in the area and wondered if he could call in.'

'This was at your home in the Algarve?' asked Jo.

'Yes' replied Sam

'Craig Overton is never just in the area' said Helena.

'That's just what we said' commented Sam.

'Anyway, he arrived at the villa later and said he had a problem he'd like our help with. Apparently MI6 had become aware of regular and very secretive monthly meetings taking place in Cairo between four known terrorists. He had no idea what they were up to, but he was convinced there was some sort of conspiracy taking place. He asked us if we'd be prepared to try and find out what they were up to.'

'No disrespect intended guys' said George 'but why you two. Surely MI6 is awash with agents who are trained to do that sort of thing?'

'We said as much ourselves' I replied 'but Craig said all his people were known by the terrorists and although they could watch them from a distance they couldn't get close to hear what was being said.'

'What about bugging where they meet?' asked Colin

'Craig said the venue changed every month' I answered 'different hotels, different rooms etc and he also said the terrorists knew all the CIA and Mossad agents as well, so they couldn't help.'

Sam chipped in with an explanation:

'Craig told us the terrorists watch MI6, the CIA and Mossad just as much as those three watch the terrorists. Apparently most terrorist groups have photographs and descriptions of every agent that belongs to any of the different intelligence communities.'

'Mm, I see the problem.' mused Helena. 'So what did he want you to do?'

'Well' I began 'one of the terrorists, an Iranian named Jahangir Ahmadi, had booked four tickets on a cruise down the Nile, and Craig wanted us to go on the same cruise and see if we could overhear anything that might help. To cut a long story short we said yes and flew to Egypt where we joined the cruise ship.'

'And did you hear anything?' asked Willie.

'No use whatsoever' replied Sam 'as they only spoke Pashto between themselves.'

'Who are 'they?' asked Helena. 'You've only mentioned the Iranian, Ahmadi.'

'Ah, sorry 'I replied. 'There was another Iranian, a Kurd named Akram Lajani, a Pakistani named Sadiq Rouhani, and a Moroccan named Youssef Mahrez. All known terrorists, but all clever enough not to have done anything provable.'

'So the trip was a waste of time?' asked Jo.

'Not at all' replied Sam looking indignant 'I got to top up my tan at MI6's expense.' Everyone laughed and then Sam continued. 'We did however discover the following day that they all spoke English when I sort of accidentally on purpose fell into Ahmadi's lap on an excursion in a small boat, and a day or so later Michael managed to get a recording of Mahrez on the phone to someone. He was speaking in Arabic, but Craig's people were later able to translate it into English.'

'Anything interesting on the recording?' asked George.

'O yes' I answered 'very much so. It turns out that these four are busy recruiting other well-known terrorists for a terror campaign that will take place in San Diego in the States, Munich in Germany, Paris in France and London here in the UK. But, and this is the important bit, they are going to do it in such a way that Israel gets the blame and the four countries I've just mentioned all withdraw their support of Israel, which will leave them very isolated in the world.'

'As well as our little cruise down the Nile' continued Sam 'Michael managed to get a photograph of Ahmadi talking to a man outside a tomb in the Valley of the Kings, he turned out to be a planner for Al Qaida named Khalid Khan who everyone thought was dead. We also followed them to Thailand where we realised Ahmadi had left a shoulder bag in a drop box, and then in Bali we saw him talking to man who Craig tells us is a well-known ex KGB Russian cyber expert, now a terrorist for hire named Sergei Polyakov.'

'This group' I interjected 'are some of the most dangerous and clever terrorists in the world, and as far as Craig is aware, they've never worked together before. This is very big business, and someone somewhere is controlling it, and is prepared to put a lot of money behind it.'

'Well off hand' proclaimed George 'I can only think of about twenty countries who would happily like to see the downfall of Israel.'

'Do you think this is state sponsored?' asked Helena.

'No idea at the moment' I replied 'but it wouldn't surprise me.'

'So where we off to, and what are we doing?' asked Helena.

'We're going to Masada in Israel' I answered 'to meet with the head of Mossad.'

Chapter Ten

We flew to Bar Yehuda Airfield, sometimes known as Masada Airfield. It's a small desert airfield located in the southern Judean desert, between Arad and Ein Gedi, west of the Dead Sea. George told us it opened in 1963, and it was ideal for us as it is just two and a half miles from the Masada fortress. These days the airfield is mainly used for charter and sightseeing flights, and being located at 1,240 feet below sea level, Bar Yehuda is the lowest airport in the world.

We were due to meet with Moishe Kravitz and Rivka Meyer in the northern palace at 7.00 pm, and five hours after taking off from Biggin Hill we touched down in the Judean desert. There were two Jeep Cherokees driven by two Israeli soldiers waiting to take us to Masada, and we all entered the cable car that took us to the top. Most visitors to Masada either visit in the very early morning to see the sun rise over the Dead Sea, or during mid-morning before it gets too hot. By the time we arrived on the summit, most of the visitors had gone for the day, and apart from about twenty people still wandering around, we more or less had the place to ourselves. A group of half a dozen soldiers were stopping people approaching the entrance to the northern palace, and Sam, Helena and I were escorted down the stairs to the upper level by two of the soldiers, a major and a sergeant. We walked out onto the balcony where we found Moishe Kravitz and Rivka Meyer waiting for us.

'Good evening' began Moishe Kravitz. 'As you know I originally suggested meeting on the middle terrace below here which is a bit more private, but I am told it is very quiet upstairs, and this balcony with its amazing views is I think by far the most awe inspiring part of the Masada fortress. Welcome to you all.' He walked forward with his arm outstretched and shook hands with all three of us, introducing himself and Rivka.

'My good friend Craig insisted I meet with you all, and he said you had something very important to tell me. I trust Craig implicitly, he is one of the few people in the world I do trust, and he tells me I can trust you all. So what do you have to tell me?'

So we told him.

'My God' Moishe exclaimed 'what is wrong with the world that there is so much hatred, and in particular hatred of Israel?'

'I'm so sorry to bring you this information' I said 'but we felt you needed to know. Craig said that once we'd brought you up to date, which we now have, we should leave it to you to see if you would like us to continue to be involved, or step back and leave it to your own people?'

'Oh, Craig is quite right, and in lots of ways we are powerless. My people are all very well-known by the terrorist community, and I fear that sadly however you try and disguise yourselves, you too will now be recognized if they see you again. These people do not take risks and they will happily remove anyone they feel is a danger to them.'

'Gee, thanks Moishe' said Sam quietly under her breath.

But not quite quietly enough and Moishe heard what she said.

'I'm sorry Sam' he replied smiling 'but it's no good warning you after they've killed you. I think it's always better to warn you first.'

'Well I can't argue with that.' she replied smiling.

'So there's nothing we can do to help?' I asked.

'Oh I didn't say that.' Moishe replied. 'Can you please give me twenty four hours, and then meet me here again tomorrow. Same time, same place, when I will have what I hope will be an interesting proposition for you all. Thank you so much for coming to see me, and I look forward to seeing you again tomorrow.'

With that, Rivka, who still hadn't said a word, smiled at us as she stepped forward and directed us towards the Major and the Sergeant, who then escorted us out of the palace, into the cable car, down the mountainside, and back to the Gulfstream.

The following day we returned to the northern palace on Masada not knowing what to expect. We had discussed various possibilities, but couldn't get past the fact that Moishe was adamant we would be recognised, so none of us could see a role that we could play.

'Hello and welcome back' said Rivka greeting us all with handshakes on the palace balcony. Moishe was busy on his mobile phone. Her voice matched her looks, very smooth and beautiful, although being a married man I guess I shouldn't notice these things, but in my defence I was simply married, not blind and deaf. Moishe finished his call and walked over to join us.

'I am so sorry, it was very rude of me to be on the telephone when you arrived, but it was the last of a very important series of phone calls, and they were also very relevant to the situation. Please, it is a hot evening and Rivka has bottles of cold water in a cool box if you would like some.'

We all helped ourselves and then sat down on some fold up 'director's style' chairs that had been set up in the shade on the palace balcony.

'As I said yesterday' said Moishe 'If you are happy to continue helping, then I have a very important job which only you can do. I don't think it is in the least bit dangerous, but it is incredibly important I believe for the future of Israel.'

Sam, Helena and I all looked at each other totally mystified as to what Moishe could want us to do that he felt nobody else could do.

'If these terrorists succeed, and manage to convince the world that the state of Israel is behind whatever atrocities they come up with, then we could very easily lose the support of four of our most important allies. If that happened then the rest of our existing allies would not be far behind them in disowning us.'

'Sorry Moishe' I asked 'but can't you just telephone your counterparts in all four countries and warn them?' I asked him.

'I could, but that wouldn't work I'm afraid. Over the years Mossad has built up a reputation as being the most, how can I say, non-conformist in our approach to everyday intelligence work. We are always being suspected of dirty tricks and having secret agendas. If I did as you suggest, then my counterparts would just say 'It's Moishe up to something or other' and they wouldn't take me seriously.'

'Really, they wouldn't believe you?' asked Sam

'No they wouldn't. Mossad has too much history of not always playing by the rules. Most of it was down to my predecessors I have to say, but never the less, mud sticks as you British say. No, I'm afraid there is only one possible way that will work and that will be believed by everyone involved, and that is for the two of you, supported by the authority of Interpol to go and explain exactly what you know and how you gained the information, and talk directly on a private face to face basis, with the President of the United States, The President of France, The Chancellor of Germany and your own Prime Minister in the United Kingdom.'

'You're joking?' I suggested.

'When it comes to the security of Israel Michael I do not joke. If you will do this for us, Israel will forever be in your debt. During the last twenty four hours I have made numerous telephone calls, stressed the importance of the matter and I have finally got the agreement of all four world leaders. They will meet with you over the next few days, and listen to what you have to tell them. All I ask of you is that you do your best to convince them of the seriousness of the situation, and most importantly of Israel's non-involvement of whatever it is that is going to happen in their countries.'

Sam, Helena and I looked at each other again and nodded, then Helena spoke for all of us.

'I promise you Moishe, both Michael and Sam, and Interpol will treat this with the most seriousness, and we will leave no stone unturned in getting the message across and believed. As head of European operations I have the authority to say that Interpol is at your disposal in this matter, and we will help Israel in any way we can.'

'Rivka is the most trusted agent I have in all Israel, and I am asking you if you would please take her with you so that she can keep me informed of your progress in this matter. She also has a copy of your schedule which starts in Washington with a meeting in the White House on Thursday morning. Today is Monday, so you have plenty of time. By the way, Rivka will also prove to be invaluable if any 'rough stuff' shall we call it should head in your direction.'

Rivka just smiled sweetly at us all.

'Thank you for your faith in us' I said shaking Moishe's hand 'and I promise you, we will do everything we can.'

Chapter Eleven

We left the northern palace and picked up George, Colin, Jo and Willie who were wandering around the main fortress and staring out from the walls at the Dead Sea.

'OK George' said Helena 'Let's all get back to the aircraft, fire up the engines and set course for Washington DC. By the way everyone, this young lady is Rivka Meyer, she works directly for Moishe Kravitz, and she will be joining us on our travels for the next week or so.'

Everyone shook hands with Rivka and then we all got in the cable car and headed back to Bar Yehuda Airfield.

'In what order are we seeing people?' I asked Rivka as we were travelling down.

'I will happily tell you' she replied 'but not until we are on the aircraft.'

She then looked at the major and the sergeant in the cable car with us, and then looked at me as if to say 'Idiot, we do not speak in front of the hired help.' I felt suitably chastised and kept quiet for the rest of the journey. As soon as we were on the aircraft, Rivka sat down next to me and said

'I am so sorry Michael if I appeared rude, but these meetings are obviously secret and cannot be discussed by anyone outside this aircraft or the people we are meeting.'

'Of course, and no offense taken. I just wasn't thinking.'

'So who are we meeting and when?' Sam asked.

'OK' said Rivka. 'Moishe has set up the

following: On Thursday you have a 10.30 am meeting with George Wagner, the President of the United States, then on Saturday afternoon you have a 3.00 pm meeting with Charles Fisher, the UK's Prime Minister. On Monday morning you are meeting with Germany's Chancellor Helmut Groening at 10.00 am, and lastly on Tuesday afternoon you are meeting the French President Gilles Cazeneuve at the Elyse Palace at 6.00 pm. They are all expecting four of us, Michael and Sam who can testify to the truth of the information, Helena who can give it the authority and backing of Interpol and myself as the representative of Israel.'

'My, my' said Colin addressing Helena 'we are mixing with the world's elite. Would you like me to get out the Rolls Royce for you milady or will you get a taxi?'

'Please excuse Colin Rivka' I said glaring at him. 'He's Irish, he has no respect for authority and he has a very unusual and usually most inappropriate sense of humour. He's quite harmless really, unless of course you're in trouble in which case you couldn't wish for better support.'

'Actually, I thought it was quite funny.' smiled Rivka. Colin gave her a little bow.

'Look, I hate to bother you Colin' said

Helena 'but is there any chance you could do what you are actually paid for, and fly the plane to Washington.'

'Yes ma'am' he said standing up, clicking his heels and saluting. Everyone smiled as he left to join George in the cockpit, and get the Gulfstream underway. George's voice came over the PA as we were taxiing to say we'd be stopping in Bristol en-route to top up the fuel tanks.

On Thursday morning, Sam and I dressed in our smartest clothes and were about to leave our hotel room in Washington DC when there was a knock on the door. I answered the door to be greeted by two men in smart suits.

'Good morning Mr and Mrs Turner' he said. 'We're here to collect you for your meeting at the White House.'

'Oh' I muttered 'Er, thank you.'

'Senior Superintendent Van Houten and Miss Meyer are already downstairs.'

'We'll be right there' said Sam handing me my briefcase.

We all descended in the lift, and waiting outside were two large black 4 wheel drive SUV's. We both climbed in the first to find Helena and Rivka already seated inside with a driver in the front. The man who had spoken to us climbed into the front passenger seat and the other man took the front seat alongside the driver in the car behind. The journey to the White House took about ten minutes and after going through a metal detector and having our bags checked we were shown into the Oval Office.

President George Wagner was seated behind a massive mahogany desk, and as we walked through the door he stood up, came round the desk and shook hands with us all. He nodded to the two 'suits' who then turned round and left the room.

'Well welcome, and please, sit down and tell me what this is all about.'

George Wagner was a Democrat, and he'd been elected two years earlier after speaking out in favour of introducing gun control after yet another mass school shooting. He told everyone that the Republicans were in reality just an extension of the NRA, and in his opinion it was time for change as the public had had enough of guns and violence. He was right, they had, and they voted him into office with a 57% to 43% majority.

There were too long sofas facing each other

which the four of us sat on, two on each side, and the president sat in a single armchair facing us all. We'd agreed that I'd start, and others would chip in as appropriate. I explained the approach we'd had from MI6, our trips to Egypt, Thailand and Bali, and then watched his face in shock as I explained what MI6 had obtained from the recordings. I laid copies of the photographs of Ahmadi's meetings with Khalid Khan and Sergei Polyakov on the coffee table, and it was pretty clear that he was distressed at the 'quality' make-up of this gang of terrorists. Sam then took over and explained that they were planning to hit four countries including the States, and that they were going to make it look like Israel was to blame. Rivka explained that she was Moishe's personal envoy and was here to assure the president that Israel valued the USA's support highly and they would do nothing to jeopardise it. Lastly, Helena assured the President that Interpol were fully behind and fully supportive of the action taken so far, and that they could guarantee that what the President had just been told was all one hundred percent true and accurate.

President Wagner sat staring at the carpet for a few moments, and then he spoke.

'Thank you all for coming this morning and for sharing this information with us. I take everything you have told me very seriously, but I need to consult with several people including David Benson, my National Security Advisor as to what course of action we should take. I will also talk to Martin Conran at the CIA and get his view on this. Please assure Moishe Kravitz that whatever happens over the coming weeks and months, the United States will not hold Israel guilty in any way, shape or form. Please, tell me, are you here in the States for long or are you off to hold similar meetings with the other countries involved in this horrendous plot?'

'We have meetings in London, Germany and France over the next few days' I told him 'before we report back to Moishe in Israel. However' I said, handing the President one of my Interpol business cards 'you can of course reach us anytime should you need to do so Mr President.'

I wasn't sure if that was the right form of address, but that was what they always said on the TV. President Wagner stood, and we took that to mean the meeting was over. He shook all our hands in turn and thanked us again for our time and the information. We'd been in the Oval Office exactly twenty seven minutes. The 'two suits' met us outside the door, and escorted us back to the two cars and then they drove us back to our hotel. None of us spoke a word during the journey.

Chapter Twelve

We all assembled in our hotel room, but it was still only Thursday lunchtime, and Helena suggested we got back to the plane and head for London. We could have a restful Friday in our London hotel before our meeting at 10 Downing Street on Saturday afternoon.

On Saturday morning, Helena and Rivka knocked on our hotel door and Sam let them in as I was still shaving in the bathroom. I was enjoying being clean shaven again after my month of scratching at my beard, which I didn't enjoy at all.

'What's your Prime Minister like?' asked Rivka.

'I don't really know' replied Sam. 'Like most people I've only seen him on the TV, plus the fact he's fairly new at the job. The previous Prime Minister lost the confidence of the MPs in the party, and there was an election in the Conservative party to elect a new PM. Charles Fisher, who was the Foreign Secretary under the previous PM won easily, and so far he seems to be doing a decent job.'

'Will he tell the leader of the opposition?' asked Helena.

'I shouldn't think so' I said, emerging from the bathroom. 'Good morning ladies. No, I don't think the PM will be telling his opposite number, they can't stand each other. The PM's an old Etonian and the Labour leader was brought up on a London council estate. Plus I've often heard MP's of all parties say that the Labour leader is not known for his tact and wisdom. To be honest I doubt if the PM will share it much beyond the Home Secretary, the Foreign Secretary and I suspect he'll call Craig in for a chat.'

'Craig?' asked Rivka

'Craig Overton' answered Sam. 'He's the guy that started all this and got the two of us involved. He runs all the operations at MI6. I assumed you'd know all about him as he's Moishe's opposite number. They must talk to each other all the time.'

'Yes they must do, but they never use real names, either false names or initials that aren't their own. Just in case the place is bugged or the telephones are tapped.'

'Good grief, what a way to have to live'

said Sam

'Oh you get used to it' smiled Rivka. 'Nobody in Mossad knows my real name, which incidentally isn't Rivka, and in Israel's intelligence community I'm just known as GB, initials Moishe gave me.'

'Why GB?' I asked.

'He says it stands for 'Gorgeous Blonde', but I think he was pulling my leg.'

'Well it fits' I commented as I received a dirty look from Sam.

'Well it does' I pleaded, and she just shook her head.

'I assume we'll just repeat what we did in the White House on Thursday' said Helena 'and then just answer any questions he might have.'

'Sounds good to me' I commented, and we all set off for the underground.

At 2 o'clock we left the hotel and caught a tube train to Westminster, the nearest underground station to Downing Street. We arrived in plenty of time, and decided we'd stop and have a coffee before walking along Whitehall. Twenty minutes later we arrived at the guarded security gate at the entrance to the street where the Prime Minister had his home and his office. We gave our names to the policeman at the gate, and we were ticked off a list, then escorted through the gate by another policeman and up to the door of number 10 where a third policeman, the one on duty outside number 10, knocked on the door. It opened a second later and we went into the hall and the door closed behind us.

From the entrance hall with its eighteenth century black and white chessboard style tiled floor, we were taken straight up the staircase adorned with pictures of all the previous Prime Ministers, and we were then shown into what we were informed is called the Terracotta Room, I guess because that's the colour the walls are painted. The ceiling and doors are all painted white with gold embossing on the doors and wonderful gold relief plasterwork on the ceiling. From the outside of the building looking at the what I think is the incredibly depressing black brickwork and the boring black door, you have simply no idea just how glorious and sumptuous 10 Downing Street actually is.

Two minutes after we arrived Charles Fisher walked in through the double doors, shook all our hands and asked us to sit down in the five blue armchairs neatly arranged around what looked to me like a white marble Adam fireplace. Again, sumptuous.

'Craig Overton tells me what you have to say is vitally important' he began 'and I know from my time as Foreign Secretary that if Craig says something is important, then it is. So I have asked both the Foreign Secretary and the Home Secretary to join us for this meeting. It saves me having to brief them both afterwards, and they can ask you questions direct that I may have overlooked. I trust that is OK with you all.'

We all muttered our approval and the Prime Minister continued.

'Miss Meyer, it has been my privilege to know and to have worked with Moishe Kravitz for more than six years, and I have the greatest respect for him doing so well what must be the most difficult job in the world. If Moishe has chosen to send you to represent him, then I can only think you must be a truly brilliant member of Mossad and you too have my greatest respect.'

You have to hand it to Fisher I thought, he certainly knows how to flatter people, and being a confirmed bachelor and a renowned ladies man, he knew that flattery usually works wonders when it comes to getting what you want.

'Thank you Prime Minister' Rivka replied 'You are most kind.'

At that point James Conway, the relatively new Foreign Secretary who had taken over from Charles Fisher, and Mary Connelly, the Home Secretary came into the room. They both introduced themselves with handshakes all round, then they pulled up two more blue armchairs from the side of the room and sat down completing a large semi-circle.

'Now please ladies and Mr Turner, can you kindly enlighten us all as to what this is all about, and what it is that has already taken you to the White House and then from here on to Germany and France.

So we did.

It took about forty minutes to go through everything in detail. Again, we showed them photographs of all six of the conspirators we knew about, but we also suggested there were probably many more behind the scenes.

'I have come across some of these people in the past who have appeared on the radar' said James Conway. 'Although I've only been Foreign Secretary a couple of months, I've been in the department for nearly five years now and Sergei Polyakov is a name I know very well as he was for years regarded as Moscow's finest Cyber expert, until he decided to go into business for himself. Likewise I know of Khalid Khan, although like MI6, I thought he was dead.

'How do we stop them?' asked Mary Connelly 'apart from the obvious, and I know we as a country don't do assassinations.'

'If you don't mind me asking you Prime Minister' asked Rivka 'Why not? Israel as you must know I am sure, has from time to time had no hesitation in removing people who are a threat to our citizens. Surely if you know there are people who are endangering the lives of the citizens you are charged with protecting, then surely from time to time it must be necessary to; how shall we say, remove them?'

'Ah Miss Meyer' mused the PM aloud 'how to answer you? Well perhaps it will help if I use the lessons we feel we have hopefully learnt from history, and how it has effected the UK's thinking on this subject. Political assassination, and that is what we are talking about here, has been around a long time and most historians agree that it was the assassination of Archduke Ferdinand that triggered World War One. Since then there have been quite a few both successful and failed attempts at political assassination. I know this was all a long time before you were even born Miss Meyer, but these things were very important events in world history, when for example Liaquat Ali Khan, the first Prime Minister of Pakistan, was assassinated in 1951, or in 1960 when Inejiro Asanuma, the Chairman of the Japanese Socialist Party, was assassinated. Most countries have been involved in assassinations, despite often repeated denials, and a prime example was when the U.S. Senate Select Committee reported in 1975 that it had found 'concrete evidence of at least eight plots involving the CIA to assassinate Fidel Castro between 1960 and 1965. Most major powers repudiated Cold War assassination tactics, though many allege that this was just a smokescreen for political benefit, and that in the real world behind closed doors so to speak, covert and illegal training of assassins continues to this day with Russia, your own country of Israel, the U.S.A, Argentina, Paraguay, Chile and numerous others who are all accused of engaging in such operations.

The problem as the UK sees it is that things can so easily go wrong. For example; in 1986 U.S. President Ronald Reagan, who incidentally had survived an assassination attempt himself, ordered 'Operation El Dorado Canyon', an air raid on Libya with the primary target being the home of the Libyan ruler Muammar Gaddafi. Gaddafi himself however escaped completely unharmed, but very sadly his adopted daughter Hanna was one of the many civilian casualties. Two assassinations you will of course be very familiar with are those of Anwar Sadat, the President of Egypt, who was assassinated in 1981, and of course that of your own Prime Minister Yitzhak Rabin who was assassinated in 1995.

'Yes, I do understand all that you've been saying Prime Minister' replied Rivka' and thank you for your very knowledgeable discourse, but you have been talking about world leaders being assassinated, ie, the good guys if you will, not the bad guys, the terrorists.'

'Yes, I do see your point, but the UK's view for many, many years, is that any form of assassination invariably leads to reprisals which usually bring death and destruction to innocent victims. A predecessor of mine as Foreign Secretary, David Owen once asked MI6 about getting rid of Idi Amin, the completely odious and tyrannical leader of Uganda, who had the habit of frequently murdering his own people just for fun. David Owen was simply told by MI6 'We don't do that sort of thing' and that has been the UK's policy ever since, unlike your own of course.

'Well' responded Rivka 'I have been authorised by Moishe Kravitz Mr Prime Minister, to tell you that with the greatest of respect, whenever Israel and its people are threatened, we have no qualms about taking action, in whatever form seems necessary, and we hope the UK government, along with the USA, Germany and France will feel the same when your freedom is threatened by terrorists.'

'I cannot speak for the government' said James Conway 'and this is my own personal view and not the official view of me in my position as Foreign Secretary, but I am in complete agreement with Israel's view of how to deal with terrorists who threaten our way of life and our freedoms. But as I say, that is just my personal view.'

'Here, here' responded Mary Connelly. 'Look, I know we may not be able to do what you're talking about officially James, but Prime Minister, couldn't we do whatever's necessary to protect our citizens as something that's kept between just the three of us in this room, and of course Craig Overton and his people.'

'You are talking about keeping secrets from the rest of the cabinet Mary.'

'Well it wouldn't be the first time would it

Charles?' said James Conway 'and as Mary and I have both said, this is to protect our citizens, which is as I'm sure you agree, is the number one priority of all governments wherever they happen to be. Plus, it's a matter of National Security, and that's always on a need to know basis.'

'And in my humble opinion Prime Minister, nobody outside this room needs to know' smiled the Home Secretary.

'I am sympathetic to what you are both saying Mary, and we'll continue to discuss this, but can I say to our visitors at this stage, a big thank you for all the information, and may I assure you the government of the UK will do everything it can to help in stopping whatever this group of conspirators comes up with, and Miss Meyer, please inform Moishe Kravitz that we completely understand the situation you find yourselves in, and we know and accept that whatever happens, none of this will be of Israel's doing.

Before you leave, just a quick word of warning to you Michael and your lovely wife. Craig here is paid extremely handsomely for risking his life and doing what he does, as are all the full time members of Interpol and Miss Rivka. Now I know you and Sam have done many undercover investigations over the last few years, Craig has passed me your very full files, and I have to say they are both most impressive, but Michael, or should I say Sir Michael and Lady Samantha, please understand, what you are getting involved in here is far more dangerous than anything you have done before, and should you both feel it is a step too far then nobody would think any less of you both.'

'Thank you Prime Minister, Foreign Secretary and Home Secretary' I said. 'On behalf of us both, we wouldn't dream of not seeing this through to the end.' I looked at Sam who nodded her head and smiled at me 'So thank you Prime Minister, thank you all for both your time and for listening.'

We all stood, shook hands all round, and as we were leaving James Conway whispered in my ear 'Don't worry Michael, Mary and I have this covered.'

I just smiled back at him.

We travelled back to our hotel in silence as we couldn't risk our taxi driver overhearing our conversation, but once we were all safely back in the room conversation flowed.

'My God Rivka, you didn't hold back did you?' exclaimed Helena.

'No, and I'm glad I didn't. I think it's important to remove this threat and asking them nicely will not work.'

'As we were leaving the room at number 10' I told them 'the Foreign Secretary whispered in my ear that he and the Home Secretary had this covered, which I took to mean they will convince the Prime Minister that theirs is the correct view re assassination, and I suspect Craig will find himself called to a meeting where he will be instructed to 'remove' any terrorists he manages to find.'

'That is extremely good news' smiled Rivka.

'I don't know' said Sam. 'I still don't like the idea of killing people.'

'Would you kill someone who was threatening to kill me if it was the only way of stopping them?' asked Helena.

'Of course' replied Sam 'but surely that's different?'

'There's no difference in my book' continued Helena 'Jahangir Ahmadi and his group are all known terrorists and they regularly kill perfectly innocent people. As Rivka said, they won't stop if you ask them nicely. I'm sorry Sam, but I completely agree with Rivka, the Foreign Secretary and the Home Secretary, sometimes it's necessary.'

Chapter Thirteen

'What are we going to do in Germany' I asked 'I don't speak German, nor does Sam, and as far as I know your German is fairly basic Helena, although I'm sorry if that's incorrect.'

'No, you are quite right Michael. Most Dutch people have a limited knowledge of German, but it is limited and I am far from fluent. I am assuming the German Chancellor will have a translator by his side. Should we perhaps ask for a translator of our own to ensure the translations are accurate?'

'I can do that if it is OK with you all?' offered Rivka.

'Oh Rivka, my apologies.' grovelled Helena. 'It simply never occurred to me that you could speak German, never mind be fluent. I'm so sorry.'

'It is OK, don't worry. After I finished my two years conscription in the army, as you know I was recruited into Mossad and underwent five years of intensive training. All Mossad trainees are expected to learn two new languages, and I chose German which I knew a little of, and Russian for no particular reason. When I graduated five years later I was fluent in both as well as my native modern Hebrew and English.'

'Rivka that is fantastic' said Sam. 'However, can I make a suggestion? How would it be if we kept that little bit of information to ourselves, and see if the German translator is being one hundred percent accurate?'

'You sound as if you suspect the Germans of skulduggery.' I suggested.

'Oh it's just me' replied Sam 'but I suppose it's a family thing. The Germans killed my great grandfather during the First World War, and they also killed my maternal grandfather towards the end of the Second World War. I'm sure they're all fine now, but as I said - it's just me.'

'Would you rather opt out of this one and leave it to the three of us?' I asked Sam. 'I'm sure neither Helena nor Rivka would mind?' I said looking at the two women.

'No, that's fine Sam' said Helena. 'Look, you stay here, get some rest and use the time to brush up on your French, which I know you do speak and Rivka doesn't.'

'Agreed' said Rivka. 'Please, leave it to the three of us, and I really do know how you feel with very good reason. I lost seven of my family members at Riga and Dachau concentration camps, plus my dear grandmother was one of the few Auschwitz survivors. As I said, I understand completely.'

'Look, I'm just being pathetic and really silly' said Sam 'and Rivka has far more reason to opt out than me.'

'Yes, that is true, but unfortunately I'm a fluent German speaker and you're not. It's decided, I go, you stay.'

'Yes Ma'am' Sam said saluting Rivka. Everyone smiled as Rivka smartly saluted back. We were just about to go down to the hotel's bar for a drink when Rivka's mobile phone rang. She walked into another room as she answered it. Two minutes later she was back.

'That was Moishe on the phone. The German Chancellor has had to move our meeting from 10.00 am to 4.00 pm on Monday, and apologises but something has cropped up that he has to deal with.'

'No problem' I said smiling 'that means we don't have to fly to Germany tomorrow, we can go on Monday morning and instead have a relaxing day here in London.'

We all spent a very relaxing day sightseeing in London, which none of us had done for years. We took a ride on the big wheel alongside the

Thames known as the London Eye which was Sam's choice, we did a tour of Buckingham Palace at Rivka's request, we wandered round the National Portrait Gallery which was Helena's request and then for my choice, the three girls and I took a London Sightseeing Tour on the top of a double decker open topped bus. We arrived back at the hotel, which like everything else was being paid for by the Israeli government at Moishe's insistence, and then we all wandered down Oxford Street and had a slap up meal with lots of wine at the Angus Steak House.

George, Colin, Willie and Jo who'd all been staying in a hotel near Biggin Hill, had like us been sightseeing, and they'd all spent an enjoyable day exploring the house and grounds at Chartwell, Winston Churchill's home in Kent located not far from Biggin Hill. The four of them were waiting for us with the Gulfstream at Biggin Hill, and we all flew to Berlin arriving just after 2.00 pm. Sam as agreed stayed with the aircraft, and Helena, Rivka and I were picked up from the airport in a government car, a shiny black Mercedes of course, and taken straight to the **Federal Chancellery building, which we were informed by the driver** is the official residence of Germany's Chancellor, or as we would say Prime Minister. He spoke perfect English and acted as a tour guide throughout the journey telling us that the building was completed in 2001, and it is part of the complex of buildings around the Reichstag built to house various branches of the government following the relocation of the German capital from Bonn to Berlin.

On our arrival we were taken straight to meet the Chancellor. He too had only been in office a short time when his predecessor had decided not to stand in the elections having already completed four terms. Helmut Groening was a big built man, and he was very similar in both appearance and demeanour to one of his predecessors and namesake Helmut Kohl. Indeed, the likeness was so similar that several journalists claimed he had only been elected because everyone assumed he was the reincarnation of modern Germany's longest serving and much loved Chancellor of the eighties and nineties. Chancellor Groening did not speak English, and sure enough he had a female translator sitting alongside him. We all shook hands and he invited us to begin. I spoke a sentence, and then the translator repeated it in

German, and then she nodded to me to continue. This went on for about twenty minutes, and then Helena, again speaking in English explained that Interpol were giving their full authority to what was being said, and finally Rivka, resisting the urge to speak in German, repeated Moishe's heartfelt request that Germany do not believe Israel was involved in whatever happened.

Chancellor Groening looked very serious and looked at each one of us in turn. He then spoke and the lady alongside him translated his words into English.

'I thank you for coming all this way, sharing this information with Germany, and for your assurances that the State of Israel is not in any way involved in whatever acts of terror may occur.'

She paused as he spoke again, then she translated again.

'I will relay all this information to our own Security Services, and I will get them to talk directly with Herr Kravitz. Please be assured, no blame will be pointed at Israel, and once again, may I thank you all for coming.'

And that was it. The meeting was over. He stood, shook all our hands and then left. I quietly shared my view with Helena and Rivka.

'Well that was bloody short and not so sweet' I moaned 'almost to the point of rudeness. Chancellor Kohl he's not, despite the rumours.'

'Never mind' said Helena, always playing the peacemaker 'let's get out of here and head for the bright lights of Paris. I never liked Berlin anyway.'

We laughed and climbed into the back of the waiting Mercedes which took us back to the airport and the waiting Gulfstream. Ten minutes later we were airborne, and an hour and forty minutes later we landed at Orly airport, less than ten miles from the centre of Paris.

Our host, President Gilles Cazeneuve had booked us all rooms at the Hôtel de Marigny, which is usually reserved for very important visiting dignitaries. We felt very honoured.

We felt even more honoured when we arrived and saw the hotel.

The Hôtel de Marigny is located on the Avenue Marigny, not far from the Elysée Palace, and it is used primarily as a residence for state visitors to France. The building has been the property of the French government since 1972, although its history dates back to 1869, when Baron Gustave de Rothschild paid the Duchesse de

Bauffremont 2,700,000 francs for the property. In 1872, the Baron decided to combine two buildings into a single property and to erect additional buildings on part of the site. We were all feeling very pampered, and we all crashed in our rooms. Sam and I had a fantastic enormous suite with a double bedroom and en-suite attached, and I have to say, the room contained the biggest bed I have ever seen in my life. Helena and Rivka, who were now getting on famously were sharing a nice suite with a twin bedroom and en-suite, George and Colin were as usual sharing a twin suite, and Willie and Jo had singles with en-suites. I have to say, the French government had done us proud and were loving every minute of it.

We had a free evening in Paris, and after much discussion we agreed we would visit the world famous Folies Bergère which had been in business since it first opened in 1869. During that time many of the world's great entertainers had graced its stage including Charlie Chaplin, Maurice Chevalier, W. C. Fields, Ella Fitzgerald, France's very own and much loved Édith Piaf, Ginger Rogers, Frank Sinatra and Elton John. Over the last few years the Folies had changed and now they mainly put on musicals, but nevertheless, we had a great night out.

The following evening Sam, Helena, Rivka and I headed for the Elyse Palace. We met the President, who spoke excellent English and Sam's A level French was not called into use, and we shared everything with him that we had said in our previous three meetings. President Cazeneuve asked a lot of questions and listened very carefully to the answers. He also kept the meeting as light as possible with a couple of jokes, both at my expense being the only man with three women to protect me as he put it. In total we were with him nearly two hours, and of all four of our meetings, we all agreed, this had been by far the most productive. We returned to the hotel, had a fabulous evening meal, turned in for an early night and the following morning we all flew back to Bar Yehuda Airfield to meet up with Moishe at Masada.

Chapter Fourteen

We met with Moishe on the balcony of the northern palace again, and this time George, Colin, Willie and Jo were with us at Moishe's request. We brought him up to date with all four meetings and I also told him what the Foreign

Secretary had whispered in my ear.
Apparently he already knew as he had spoken to James Conway since our meeting, and he'd informed Moishe that he and Mary Connelly had been successful in getting the UK Prime Minister to come round to their way of thinking.

'I have asked to see all eight of you for two very specific reasons. One, to thank you for all for everything you have done, not only for Israel, but for all civilized nations. Secondly, I have to tell you that in your absence I have spoken with the heads of all of your governments and the heads of your various intelligence and security services, and it is the wish of all of us, that the eight of you continue to work together, and form a dedicated task force to root out and find the conspirators, and once you have done so - deal with them appropriately.
Helena, I have spoken at length to Commissioner Kurt Meisner, and he is happy for you to command this task force, and in doing so take time off from your other duties until such time as this is over. I will continue to act as the link between the task force and the various governments involved. Every one of us, governments and security services alike feel there is no team better placed than the eight of

you to undertake this critically important task on behalf of all of us. I know it is an awful lot to ask, but are you willing?'

'Please excuse me asking Moishe' said Sam 'but are you asking us to assassinate these people if we find them.'

'Not you personally Sam as I know you would find that extremely difficult, but Rivka, Helena, George, Colin, Willie and Jo have all been trained in firearms as a necessary part of their job, and they have all used them in the past if it has become necessary. If it is possible to apprehend any of these people and bring them back to me for questioning then please do so, but if not .... '

'I see' Sam replied, turning things over in her mind as she spoke.

'This is probably the most important task I will ever be asked to take part in' began Helena 'and I would be proud to head up such a task force. Sam and Michael will be invaluable in all sorts of ways without having to use firearms.'

'Although I gather from Kurt you're not a total stranger to firing guns' said Moishe with a glint in his eye 'are you Sir Michael?'

'Oh, you know about Oman' I meekly responded.

'We wouldn't be asking you all to do this

if we hadn't done our research and weren't one hundred percent sure you were the right people for the job. And thank you Helena for your extremely positive response.'

'Please Moishe, I apologize if I seemed reluctant, I'm not and I will happily join the task force and do all that I can to help, I just don't think I'll be much use when it comes to firing weapons at people.'

'We know that Sam, we need your undoubted skills in other areas and thank you. In that case, can I please on behalf of the governments of all five countries involved and their respective intelligence and security services thank you and welcome you all as members of the newly appointed Special Task Force. All finances will initially be covered by Mossad and then shared between the five countries involved. We will issue each of you with a wallet full of credit cards with no limits that can be used anywhere in the world. I also have five different passports in five different names for each of you. Each photograph has been slightly doctored by air brushing in very simple ways, and Rivka can show you how to make your real selves look just like your various passport selves.

Now, regarding your targets. We have been busy while you've been hob knobbing round the globe and chatting with various world leaders, and we have a few leads for you to follow up. Oh, and by the way Helena, Kurt says you can use the Gulfstream as much as you wish, but the skinflint's making me pay the fuel costs.'

'Kurt certainly likes to get his money's worth' she laughed.

'So where do you suggest we start?' I asked Moishe.

'Simple my boy. Back to Egypt.'

We flew back to Cairo International Airport and taxied to the private area and left the Gulfstream under lock and key in a rented hanger. There was nothing on the aircraft to indicate that it was owned and run by Interpol, and if any enquiries were made, everything indicated that the plane was owned by a South African businessman who lives and works in Geneva. Kurt set all this up when Interpol first purchased the Gulfstream, and George and Colin as its pilots, and Jo as cabin staff all have contracts in the name of Kurt's bogus company, Swiss Finance International.

'So tell me again' said Colin 'why are we in Cairo?'

'Moishe said' I explained 'that while we were on our travels seeing the various government leaders, one of Mossad's undercover agents was sure he'd spotted Jahangir Ahmadi in Cairo, but he wasn't a hundred percent sure as he disappeared inside a large house in Al-Zohoor, an up market street in the city. He felt he couldn't follow him or make enquiries as he was sure he would have been recognised'

'So he reported this back to Moishe?'

'Exactly' answered Helena 'and that's why we're here - to follow up on it.'

'OK' demanded Colin. 'So what's the plan?'

'Well you, George and Jo are all unknown by Ahmadi' she continued 'or anyone else we know of in the conspiracy, so we want you two to go to the house in Al-Zohoor that Ahmadi went into, dressed in these nice blue GASCO overalls and white hard hats.'

I handed them two pairs of bright blue overalls with the GASCO logo on the pocket, and two hard hats that Moishe had given to us before we left.

'In case you're wondering' said Helena 'GASCO is the Egyptian Natural Gas Company, which just so happens to be based here in Cairo.'

'And the reason for going to the house?' asked George.

'A suspected gas leak' I replied 'It's imperative that you check it out as it could be very dangerous for everyone in the area. That should give you the opportunity to nose round the house in theory looking for pipes, leaks and anything else you can think of, but in reality you're looking for any sign of the conspirators, papers, notes, anything.'

'What if they don't have gas?' asked Colin.

'They do' Helena confirmed. 'Moishe's people hacked into GASCO's computers, put in the Al-Zohoor address, and sure enough, they get regular monthly bills for their gas supply, all paid by direct debit.'

'Can we ask them to leave the house while we search?' asked George. 'It will make life a lot easier without onlookers.'

'Good idea' said Helena. 'In fact, Willie, you and Jo go with them. Dress smartly so that you look official, and in the meantime we'll knock up a couple of GASCO badges for you to wear. We can download and print the logo from the internet and then slot a couple of official looking badges inside two lanyards. There are several inside that drawer' she said pointing at one of the Gulfstream's cabinets. 'Just take out our badges and slot the GASCO ones in.'

'Once you get there' I continued 'get everyone to stand well back from the house, that way George and Colin can conduct their search in peace.'

'OK then' said George 'How do we get to Al-Zohoor.'

'Drive that nice blue van over there' I said pointing at a shiny blue van parked in the corner of the hanger. 'Moishe had one of his guys hire a blue van from Hertz and park it in here yesterday. Moishe also had these two large GASCO logos made up on magnetic metal plates that will stick to the side panels of the van. Stick the logos on the side of the van, drive to the house, park outside and do your stuff. When you've finished, bring the van back here, remove the logo's and Moishe's man will return the van to Hertz.'

Two and a half hours later George drove the van back into the hanger, and Colin jumped out and slid the hanger door closed. Willie and Jo emerged from the back seats, pulled the logos of the sides of the van and brought them up the steps with them and into the aircraft.

'So, how did it go?' asked Helena.

'No problems getting in' said George 'Willie was great. He played the big boss, knocked on the front door and then put the fear of God into them that the house could blow up at any moment.'

'He even suggested they take their dog and parrot out into the street with them just to be on the safe side.' laughed Jo.

'Anyway' continued George 'Colin and I had the run of the house while Willie and Jo kept everyone back at least thirty feet from the front door. Colin searched upstairs and I had a nose round downstairs.'

'We found two things that might be helpful' said Colin 'or possibly not!'

'There was a detailed street map of San Diego downstairs in the drawer of a writing bureaux' said George 'interesting enough in itself knowing what we know, but it also had three red circles drawn on it in felt tip pen. I photographed it and returned it just where I found it. Upstairs Colin found a notepad beside the bed and he knicked the top sheet and went over it lightly with a pencil. There was a phone number on it that started with the international dialling code for France.'

'It might mean something or it might not.' said Colin. 'Either way, they'll have no idea what we found and copied. We left the house after an hour telling them all was now OK, and they all happily trooped back inside the house with the dog and the parrot.'

'Who lives there?' Sam asked.

'There were four of them that we saw' said Willie 'but there may of course be others. There were two men in their mid-thirties I would think, and an older man and woman. I didn't want to appear too inquisitive and ask lots of questions, but I would think it was the parents and their two sons.'

'That ties in with what Moishe's people found out from Cairo's census records.' said Helena. 'The house is owned by Mr and Mrs Shafer, and they have two sons, Mohamed aged 32 and Ali, aged 28. They also have a daughter named Shakira, but she lives with her boyfriend on the other side of Cairo.'

'We know nothing about this family' said Rivka 'other than their names and ages, but it might be sensible to watch the two sons for a couple of days and see where they go and what they get up to.'

'Agreed.' said Helena. 'Can you and Sam deal with that please? Again, the two brothers don't know either of you, so you shouldn't have any trouble following them.'

'Will do boss.' said Sam smiling.

'I also think we ought to get more details

on these three locations in San Diego' Helena said. 'Surely they have to be locations of bombs or perhaps places to be hit by cyber-attacks or chemical weapons. We need to know what is actually located at each site.'

'I can easily search all three locations on the internet' offered Willie. 'San Diego is on Google Earth and it shouldn't be that difficult, providing of course the three circles are reasonably small. If they cover a big area though it might not be quite so easy.'

'Here Willie' said George handing him his mobile phone on which he'd earlier photographed the map. 'They're fairly small and accurately drawn circles, so hopefully you can find some details.'

'See if the three locations have anything in common' I suggested.

'Will do' said Willie as he sat down and started his search on one the Gulfstream's two PC's located on a couple of desks at the rear of the plane's fuselage.

It didn't take Willie long to come back to us.

'Michael was right' he began. 'All three locations contain banks, and they appear to be the only things the three places have in common. In fact, at one of the locations there is nothing there other than a bank.'

'Are they all branches of the same bank?' Helena asked.

'No' replied Willie 'Three different banks.'

'They must have something in common.' I said. 'There must be hundreds of banks in San Diego, so why these three?'

'Can I humbly suggest' said Helena 'that finding that out is our next urgent job.'

Chapter Fourteen

I had an idea. Before we'd left Israel, Moishe had given us all a 'top security, scrambled and highly encrypted' telephone number where we could reach him, day or night, if we needed anything he might be able to help with. We needed help, so I rang it.

'Michael' he answered.

'How did you know it was me Moishe?' I asked. 'It could have been anyone of us on the phone.'

'Let's just say I have my ways. Now, what can I do for you?'

'We have found a map of San Diego during a covert search of that house in Al-Zohoor in Cairo that your man had previously seen Ahmadi entering. The map has rings round three different banks, and I wondered if your department might be able to find out if these three banks have anything in common?

'I would think that's a strong possibility. Give me the banks names and addresses please, and I'll get my people on it straight away.'

I did so, and then hung up the phone.

Moishe was back to me in less than an hour.

'That was quick' I said amazed.

'Computers Michael. They can do searches much quicker and more efficiently than us poor humans.'

'So, any joy?' I asked.

'Yes, I think so. All three banks have one thing in common, and as far as we can tell, only one.'

'And that is?' I asked

'PLO bank accounts. The PLO uses all sorts of offshore companies and shell companies to try and hide its money, but if you add together all the various factions involved that make up and support the PLO, then they are regarded as one of the richest such organisations in the world. Indeed, way back in 1993, a report by the British National Criminal Intelligence Service stated that the PLO was without doubt 'the richest of all terrorist organizations', with somewhere between $8 and $10 billion in assets, and an estimated annual income of between $1.5 and $2 billion from donations, extortion, payoffs, illegal arms dealing, drug trafficking, money laundering, fraud, etc. You have to remember that back then, the PLO was considered by both the United States and Israel to be a terrorist organization. That is until the Madrid Conference of 1991. In 1993, the PLO recognized Israel's right to exist in peace, they accepted UN Security Council resolutions 242 and 338, and rejected violence and terrorism. In response, Israel officially recognized the PLO as the representative of the Palestinian people. However, the PLO has still employed violence in the years since 1993, and relations between Israel and the PLO are not wonderful.

'Sorry to ask what must to you seem like a stupid question Moishe, but exactly what is and who are the PLO?'

'No, not stupid at all. PLO stands for the Palestine Liberation Organization. The PLO is basically an umbrella organization that includes numerous organizations or factions of the resistance movement, political parties, and popular organizations.

From its very conception, the PLO was designed

as a government in exile, with its own parliament called the Palestine National Council or PNC, which was chosen by the Palestinian people to be the highest authority in the PLO. It also has an executing government or EC, which was elected by the PNC.'

'You mentioned different factions. Sorry, but who are these factions?'

'The largest of these is Fatah, who are secular, and left-wing nationalist. Then there is the Popular Front for the Liberation of Palestine or the PFLP. They are the second largest faction, and they are pretty radical, left wing militant and definitely communist. There are numerous other groups or factions including the Democratic Front for the Liberation of Palestine or the DFLP. They are the third largest faction and also communist. There's the Palestinian People's Party or the PPP, which is a socialist group. The Palestine Liberation Front or the PLF, Abu Abbas faction, but they're a fairly minor left-wing faction, as are the Arab Liberation Front or the ALF, although they are aligned to the Iraqi-led Ba'ath Party There's also As-Sa'iqa, a Syrian-controlled Ba'athist faction, the Palestinian Democratic Union, another Minor democratic socialist, two-state solution, non-militant faction, the Palestinian Popular

Struggle Front known as the PPSF, The PAF, the Palestinian Arab Front, a minor pro-Fatah, former Iraqi Ba'athist faction. As you can see, it's not an easy task to understand the make-up of the PLO.'

'OK, I get it, I think, but if you were the terrorists, and you wanted Israel to get the blame for everything, what would you do?'

'If it was me' said Moishe, obviously thinking it through as he spoke 'I'd hack into the PLO accounts at all three banks, and transfer all the money out of their accounts and into Israeli government accounts. I'd do it in such a way that it looked as if I was trying to hide it, but leave enough clues to ensure we got the blame.'

'And in Sergei Polyakov they've got just the man to do it.'

'Exactly.' He replied.

'So how do we stop him?' I asked.

'We can't, and we shouldn't.'

'You can't mean that' I responded. 'Surely stealing all their cash is going to tip the PLO over the edge and cause major reprisals and a certain amount of violence?'

'For a start' explained Moishe 'the amount of cash held in those accounts is just a few million, and it is the equivalent of petty cash to the PLO, but it is the principal that matters. Violence is the obvious reprisal, but not if I warn them in advance and transfer their money into a new account they and only they have control of the minute we receive it. It will mean filling them in on a certain amount of what we expect, but if we want to keep the peace I don't see as we have any choice.'

'The trouble is' I mused thinking out loud 'we don't know for sure if that's what the terrorists have planned. They may not be as smart as you Moishe, and they may just decide to blow up the three banks.'

'True, but I certainly think it's worth me arranging a meeting with the head of the PLO. A chat about what's going on can't do any harm, and we are supposed to be able to talk to each other these days at least, even if certain militant groups within the PLO still use violence to get their point of view across.'

'OK, well many thanks for the info. I'll fill in everybody else.'

'Thank you Michael, and keep up the good work all of you.'

The line went dead and I sat back in the armchair and then filled in everybody else.

Chapter Fifteen

So' said Helena 'Moishe is dealing with the banks in San Diego, at least for the time being, do we know anything about the telephone number in France?'

'Yes' replied Sam. 'I traced the number to a house in Paris. It's owned by a wealthy Arab businessman who now lives in Saint Tropez most of the time, so he rents it out via a Paris letting agent. I spoke to the letting agent in my best schoolgirl French and I tried to rent the house, but she said it wouldn't be available for a month. I kept pushing and she eventually told me it wouldn't be available for another six weeks as two brothers from Egypt were renting it for a month. I'm assuming that's Mohamed and Ali Shafer.'

'Sounds reasonable' said Helena 'considering the phone number was found on a pad on Ali's bedside cabinet. Well done Sam.'

'So what's our next step?' asked George.

'I think for the time being all we can do is follow the brothers' Helena replied 'and then, when they eventually head off to France, we follow them to Paris and see what they get up to and who if anyone they meet.'

'Begosh and begorrah' said Colin 'tis sounding like a grand plan it does!'

'Oh shut up you Irish leprechaun' said Jo laughing at him.

We divided into four separate pairs, and put the house in Al-Zohoor under twenty four hour surveillance, just in case they decided to leave in the middle of the night. I did the first six hour shift with Sam, from 8.00 am to 2.00 pm then we handed over to George and Rivka who did the next six hours. Willie and Helena then took over from them and Colin and Jo completed the twenty four hours before we started all over again. This tedious, but very necessary task went on non-stop for four days, and then on day five Sam spotted Mohamed and Ali Shafer getting into their fathers BMW after putting a couple of suit cases in the car's boot. We had highly encrypted professional two way radio's or what's commonly known as 'walkie talkie's' with us from the Gulfstream's on board Interpol equipment stock, and I spoke to Helena who had access to a second hire car, a large black Citroen, besides the rented silver Peugeot Sam and I were using. She and Willie then drove following our 'walkie talkie' directions and they took over tailing the BMW as soon as possible, so that it didn't look like we were following them. Sam and I raced on ahead in our car to Cairo airport where we parked the car and waited for them to arrive.

The brothers pulled up outside the departure terminal, got the cases out of the boot and headed to the Air France desk, where they checked in for the midday Paris flight. Sam went over to the desk once the brothers had left and checked what time the flight was due to land in Paris. We then drove both cars back into the hanger, climbed on board the Gulfstream and George, who had by now already registered a flight plan, took off for Paris, roughly an hour before the Air France flight was due to leave.

We hired two cars again at Charles de Gaulle airport, and all eight of us headed for the house in Paris. Rue de Rivoli is a very upmarket street in Paris, not far from the more famous Champs-Elysees avenue, and it was to Rue de Rivoli that we headed. Fortunately for us, the particular house in question was directly opposite the Saint James Albany Paris Hotel and Spa. We booked four double rooms for two days, with open ended extensions if needed, and we then set up binoculars, telescopes and high powered rifle

microphones, all taken from the Gulfstream's stock of technical 'goodies', and trained them all on the house opposite, with everything linked to video recording devices.
Helena, unbeknown to us, had used her highly encrypted mobile and telephoned Martin Smith, one of Interpol's covert operatives, but more importantly their specialist burglar. Smith was not his real surname and none of us knew what is was, but we had worked with Martin before on several occasions and he was a real master of his trade. Martin was South African and used to burgle high-end properties in order to line his own pocket, but on one job, one of the men working under him tripped a silent alarm and they were all apprehended by Kurt Meisner of Interpol. Kurt recognized Martin's undoubted talents and offered him a deal - five years in prison or five years working for Interpol. Martin chose the latter, and that was nearly eight years ago. Needless to say, Martin loves his work and loves working for Interpol.

'Martin's on his way from Amsterdam' Helena informed us all 'and he will be here in just over two hours. Michael, could you and Sam please pick him and his equipment up from Charles de Gaulle airport. He's on a KLM flight and is due to land at 4.15 pm.'

'No problem' I replied looking at my watch. 'Plenty of time to get there. If you don't mind me asking, what's Martin going to do?' I enquired.

'We need eyes and ears inside that house. I need to know what they are doing and saying, so he's bringing all sorts of mini cameras and sound mics with him, plus a Dutch lady named Marika who speaks fluent Arabic, the same as the brothers, among several other languages. She's one of Interpol's top linguists and she's used to listening in to other people's conversations. Once Martin's here, we need George, Colin and Martin to make a covert entry into the house, and set up cameras and microphones in every room. Michael, can you and Willie play lookouts for the brothers outside the house and keep me informed of everyone's movements by radio. Sam, you and Rivka aren't known by the brothers, so when they go out, can you two please follow them, and if they look like returning to the house before we get the all clear from Martin, can you please use your undoubted feminine charms to keep them occupied in a bar or something. I leave the details to you.'

Sam and Rivka looked at each other, and then both started grinning from ear to ear.

Sam and I drove to Charles de Gaulle and collected Martin and Marika. It was great to see Martin again, and he'd taught me a lot about covert operations on one or two previous jobs we'd undertaken together. Marika I estimated was about 40 years old, a brunette with shortish hair and silver rimmed glasses. We drove back to the hotel and parked in the underground car park, from where we carried Martin's four silver brief cases up to Helena's room. After lots of hugs, handshakes and introductions we all sat in the lounge area of Helena's suite as Martin went through what he'd brought.

'Some of you I know are familiar with three of these cases as they are the same ones Michael, Colin and I used inside the apartment in the Burg Khalifa.'

'Now that was an interesting night' said George with feeling.

'So, just to remind you. There are four silver cases, each with a coloured dot next to left hand lock. The black dot is equipment for copying phones. It's full of various iPhones, Samsung Galaxy's, Nokias, Sony's, Motorola's etc and every other mobile phone you can think of, along with their connecting cables. We use the same routine as in Dubai, if you find an iPhone for example, get a matching iPhone from the case, connect them together and copy everything from their phone onto ours. Then return their phone exactly as you found it. The red dot case contains large capacity USB memory sticks for downloading information from laptops and PC's. The case with the blue dot if you remember contains scanners and other gear for copying any documents we find.

'And what's the case with the green dot?' asked Colin. 'You didn't have that one with you in Dubai.'

'No, I didn't need it for that job, but this one contains a selection of mini cameras and microphones, all built into normal household type objects. Smoke detectors we can attach to ceilings in each room, small carriage clocks we can put on a book shelf, electric sockets that aren't really electric sockets etc. Hopefully we can cover every room with just smoke detectors, but most houses have them these days anyway, so it may be a case of unscrewing theirs, and replacing them with ours.'

Just then Rivka, who was watching the house opposite spoke up urgently.

'Come on Sam, we're on. The brothers are just leaving the house.'

The two girls literally ran down the two flights

of stairs to the ground floor, and got outside just in time to see the brothers turn right into a side road. They ran after them, then slowed down as they reached the corner. The brothers were now only about sixty or seventy feet ahead of them, so they slowed to the brothers pace and simply followed them.

Meanwhile, with the house being empty, Martin, George and Colin shot across the road, and Martin used a skeleton type key from his pocket to open the back door into the house. Thankfully there was no alarm system, so the three men set to work.

Willie and I were on lookout duty outside the house, with Willie sitting reading a French newspaper on a bench up near the corner where the brothers had turned right, and I was simply wandering up and down looking for all the world like man who'd been stood up by his girlfriend. I had a tiny, but very efficient microphone attached to a radio clipped to my jacket, and a wireless Bluetooth earpiece in my left ear. Helena back in the hotel was on the other end. Helena also had a similar set up with Sam following the brothers, and George in the house, but only Helena could hear all three of us. As it happened Mohamed and Ali Shafer had simply gone to a local restaurant for a meal, and they were now heading back to the house. About the same time, roughly an hour and twenty minutes after entering the house, George informed Helena that they were finished and were leaving via the back door. Helena called Sam and Rivka back, and told Willie and I to get back to the hotel as well. Fifteen minutes later we were all back in Helena's hotel suite, which was doubling up as our office and observation room.

'OK Marika, it's now down to you' said Helena.
Marika was sitting in front of a bank of three medium size TV monitors and one much larger master screen that she had brought with her as secure hold luggage, and all cleared in advance with French customs by Kurt, along with a pair of Bose noise reduction headphones on her head. She had a notebook and a pen in front of her. Everything she was seeing and hearing was also being recorded for posterity and later review on various items of equipment I didn't understand, that we'd brought with us from the Gulfstream. As everything was quiet and nothing much was happening, we all took the opportunity to grab a nap as we didn't know if we'd have to be up all

night. Then at about 9.30 pm, two men arrived at the front door of the house and rang the bell.

'Action folks' yelled Marika 'Visitors at the house.'

We all rushed over to the TV screens and watched as Marika flicked the view from room to room following the two visitors. At this stage we couldn't see who they were, but after ensuring all the curtains were shut tight, one of the visitors turned on the main light and illuminated the room. Sam and I recognized both of the visitors immediately. They were Akram Lajani, the Iranian Kurd and Sadiq Rouhani, the Pakistani. As they spoke, Marika translated into English for us what they were saying.

'Are you both ready' asked Lajani.

'We are' said Mohamed, the elder brother.

'Everything you need is in this suitcase' said Lajani.

'You remember the time?' asked Rouhani

'Twelve noon exactly' said Ali, 'the square will be packed.'

'Very well' said Lajani. 'We won't ever meet again, but you will be remembered for what you are going to do for all time.'

With that, the two men left, leaving the suitcase behind them.

'So what do we do now?' asked Colin

'And what's in the suitcase?' I asked.

'Hopefully they'll open it and we'll find out' said Helena.

Sure enough, they did. Mohamed laid the case flat on the floor, dialled the numbers on the locks and clicked the latches open. He opened the lid and we could all very clearly see the contents. Explosives, detonators and timers.

'Oh great' I sighed 'I've just realised, tomorrow is Bastille Day, when France celebrates with a massive parade. The parade route passes down the Champs-Élysées from the Arc de Triomphe to the Place de la Concorde, where the President of the French Republic, his government and foreign ambassadors to France stand. The Place de la Concorde is the largest square in France and the parade arrives there at midday.'

'That's got to be it' said Helena 'without a doubt.'

'But why will Israel get the blame?' asked Sam.

'I think I can answer that' said Martin. 'Before I turned to crime I did my time in the South African armed forces, and I learnt quite a bit about explosives. Sadly I used the knowledge to assist me in opening safes I didn't have the combination of, but that's another story. Anyway, looking at what's in that case, I would say that the container of white crystalline powder Ali has just opened is something called triacetone triperoxide, or TATP for short. TATP was originally designed by Israel and as I'm sure Rivka will confirm, it's a well-known Mossad 'tool of choice'.

Rivka nodded her agreement.

'If that lot goes off' she said 'any later investigation will show they used TATP, and that means fingers will point at Israel and Mossad straight away.'

'Also' said Martin 'TATP is relatively easy to make, it's very hard to detect, but it is also incredibly unstable. In fact, all it takes is a firm tap to explode it with a force 80% as strong as TNT. I just hope Ali knows what he's doing or the whole street could go up with that amount of TATP.'

'We did some background checks on the brothers' said Helena 'and Ali is in his final year of a Chemistry degree, which I suspect is why he got this job.'

'But what do we do about it?' asked Sam. 'We can't just sit here and let them blow up the entire French government.'

'We can go over there and just take them

out' suggested Rivka. 'Clean kills, bury the bodies in the back garden, and hand the chemicals over to the French government.'

'I'm not sure' said Helena thinking aloud.

'Well we need to decide and decide soon' said George. 'It looks like they're getting ready to move.' We all turned and looked at the TV. Sure enough, the two brothers were getting their belongings together in preparation for leaving.

'Rivka, George, Colin, Jo.' commanded Helena 'two of you at the front, two at the back. Do whatever you need to. Go and heaven help you.'

All four of them left the room and quickly headed for the house across the road. As Interpol covert operatives, George, Colin and Jo had all been trained in firearms, and they carried them at all times, and all three of them had used them in the past on the few occasions it had been necessary. Rivka's experience with firearms we all knew about from several of Moishe's stories about her exploits. Colin and Jo went round to the back of the house, and Rivka and George went to the front door.

The rest of us were watching the TV screen, and we could see the two brothers were just about to pull their luggage into the hall when the front door bell rang. Mohamed stopped where he was, while Ali let go of his suitcase and went to answer the front door leaving Mohamed alone in the lounge. Ali opened the door to be greeted by Rivka and George.

'Good afternoon sir' said Rivka. 'Are you aware tomorrow is Bastille Day, and as the owner of this house you have won a prize draw of two tickets for the main stand in the Place de la Concorde? May I just give you the details?' and as she spoke she just walked past him. Ali just stood there not knowing what to do. Mohamed was not quite so slow in realising what was happening, and as Rivka entered the room he drew a hand gun from his pocket. Rivka already had her Beretta in her hand, but before she could do anything Mohamed's head exploded as a bullet from Jo's hand gun entered the back of his head. Jo had entered at the same time through the back door. Rivka realised what was happening and immediately spun round just in time to see Ali charging into the room with a knife in his hand. She coolly lifted her gun and shot him between the eyes. He dropped to the floor instantly and both brothers were dead. George and Colin checked over the two bodies and then checked the two women were both OK.

Both women just stood there looking at each

other, and then Rivka walked over to Jo, flung her arms round her and gave her a big hug.

'I really do owe you one' she said smiling at Jo. 'Thank you.'

'Well it wasn't what I'd hoped for' said Helena watching on the TV monitor in our hotel room, 'but we could all clearly see, the girls had no choice.'

'What do we do now?' I asked.

'I'll telephone the Elysée Palace, hopefully speak to the President, explain what's happened, and then it's up to them.' she replied and slowly sank back into her chair.

It had been a very tense few minutes, and it made me realize just how important it was to ensure the equipment issued to everyone in the field was always kept in perfect condition. You never knew when you were going to need something, be it one of Martin's super electronic gizmos, or a firearm. Mossad have equipped their agents and covert operatives, including Rivka, with the same handgun for many years, the Beretta Model 71. It's a .22 calibre semi-automatic pistol that accommodates an eight-round magazine, having a 3.5 inch threaded barrel and usually fitted with a silencer. Jo however had been using an Interpol special, a

Glock 17 with hollow point ammunition. These handguns are trusted by law enforcement officers and military personnel the world over because of their amazing reliability, its large magazine capacity of 17 rounds, and its relatively low weight. She too had a silencer fitted, and the neighbours would have heard nothing from either weapon.

Chapter Sixteen

Three minutes after Helena's phone call with the French President had ended, six officers and an Inspector from the Gendarmerie arrived at the house, and brought body bags with them for both terrorists. A plain clothes explosives expert took away the suitcase of TATP.

'Well we stopped that attempt to discredit Israel' I said 'but we're still no nearer catching Ahmadi and co.'

'Don't be so sure' said Martin. 'Marika and I have been going through all the bits of information we copied from the Shafer brother's mobile phones, and we've got several phone numbers in Egypt, Iran, Afghanistan and the UK, plus a list of addresses in the UK from the notes section of Ali's iPhone. They're all in Arabic, but Marika's translated them all and typed them up into English.

'Marika' I said to her 'you're amazing, where have you been all my life?'
She laughed.

'For the last few years of your life I've been in Amsterdam, but sadly you've never bothered to visit me!'

'Ah, well the only time I've been in Amsterdam over the last few years, I'm afraid my wife was with me, so it might have been a bit awkward.'

'I can hear every word you know' said Sam, smirking in the background.

'OK' said Helena, bringing us all back to business, 'once Rivka, Jo, George and Colin get back, can you please Marika talk us through what you've found on the phones, and it may help us decide what we do next.'

The four of them were not back for another fifteen minutes, as having gone through what happened with the French police and showing them their Interpol ID's and in Rivka's case her Israeli Intelligence pass, they still needed to retrieve their equipment. It had helped greatly that President Cazeneuve had assured the Gendarmerie Inspector that we were the good guys, and so once they had made their notes our four colleagues were all allowed to return to the hotel. Once the six Gendarmerie had all left with the bodies, leaving just the Inspector at the house to lock it up, Martin and Colin zipped round the house retrieving all the cameras and mics while George kept the Inspector chatting in the lounge. George then manoeuvred him out of the lounge and into the kitchen so that Martin could retrieve the final camera from the lounge. Once they arrived back in Helena's hotel suite, both Sam and Helena gave Rivka and Jo a big hug and then everyone collapsed in armchairs or on sofas. Just then there was a knock on the door, and room service brought in a dozen wine glasses, and three bottles of Château Le Bon Pasteur 2004 Pomerol, an incredibly pleasant Merlot.

'I think we all deserve this' said Helena 'and well done Jo and Rivka. Shooting another human being is never easy, and it leaves mental scars. But you've both been here before, and you both know you did what you had to do, and the mental scars will heal. You were both truly amazing and incredibly professional. Well done.'

'I owe Jo my life' said Rivka 'and neither I nor Israel will ever forget it.'

'Well thank you' said Jo 'but can we move on please. I'd rather try and put it to the back of

my mind if that's OK with everyone?'
We all nodded and at a nod from Helena, Marika started her briefing.

'We found some very interesting information on the brother's mobile phones. Mohamed had two telephone numbers in Egypt and one Iran, and Ali had the same three phone numbers on his phone, plus three in Afghanistan, four in the UK, and a list of addresses in both the UK and France from the notes section of his iPhone. Now obviously at this stage we don't know who any of these phone numbers belong to, or who lives at the UK addresses, but it might be worth putting them all under surveillance. Sorry Helena, I know that's your decision.'

'No Marika, you're quite right. Rivka, can you talk to Moishe please as soon as possible, bring him up to date with what's occurred here and then see if he can find out who the phone numbers belong to. In the meantime I think we've done all we can here in France, and I suggest we have a closer look at these houses in the UK. But let's take an hour to calm down, drink our wine and then pack up and head to the airport. Martin and Marika, can you two stay with us please and both come to the UK. We may need to get into the houses, and if we do find anything the chances are it will be in Arabic.'

'No problem' they replied in unison, and smiled at each other.

We arrived in the UK landing at Norwich airport. The addresses Martin and Marika had found were all in the county of Norfolk. One in Hunstanton on the coast, one in Thetford, and one in Watton, the latter two being central Norfolk market towns. Norwich was the nearest airport for all of them. We hired a couple of Range Rovers from Hertz using the wonderful 'no limit' credit cards Moishe had given us, and once we'd piled all Martin's equipment, plus several items from the Gulfstream's stock of electronic gizmos, high powered binoculars etc into the boots of the cars, we all headed for the coast.

During our flight across the channel, I logged onto the internet and read up on the places we were going to be visiting. Apparently Hunstanton is actually two towns, Old Hunstanton and New Hunstanton, and they both face west across 'The Wash', making them one of the few places on the east coast of

England where the sun can be seen setting over the sea. Hunstanton it said is a reasonably quiet and peaceful seaside town with a population of about 5,000 permanent residents, although that number trebles during the holiday season, when the peace and quiet fades with the invasion of tourists, or 'greckles' as the locals call them. The very quiet character of Old Hunstanton remains distinct from its busy sibling, New Hunstanton and complements it with clifftop walks past a privately owned redundant lighthouse and the old ruins of St Edmund's Chapel, which dates back to 1272. In 1846, Henry Styleman Le Strange, a local land owner, decided to develop the area south of Old Hunstanton as a sea-bathing resort. He persuaded a group of like-minded investors to fund the construction of a railway line from King's Lynn to bring tourists and visitors. This was a great success, and the Lynn & Hunstanton Railway became one of the most consistently profitable railway companies in the country.

We had booked five double rooms at the Golden Lion, a small hotel, but with wonderful views out to sea. It was a quiet time of year as the holiday season hadn't really got underway, so the hotel could just about accommodate us. The address we were going to take a look at was in Old Hunstanton, a place called Belgrave Avenue, and after dumping our luggage, we decided to walk along the cliff top to our destination. We came out of the hotel and turned right walking along Cliff Parade. We passed the bowling greens on our left, and eventually arrived at Clarence Road which ran inland from the cliffs. The first turning on our left was Belgrave Avenue, the location of our mystery house. We walked past it, six of us on the opposite side of the road, and the other four on the same side as the house. Willie bent down to 'do up his shoe lace' while we were opposite the house, and it gave us all an opportunity to take a casual look across the road. The house didn't look any different from the others in the street, and we moved on, not wishing to draw attention to ourselves. We took a loop around two adjoining streets and came back past the back of the house. We could see straight away that there was no access from the back, as the houses in the road that ran parallel with Belgrave Avenue had back to back gardens. Having now completed our initial survey, we headed back to the hotel to make plans.

'We need to put the house under constant

surveillance' said Helena 'with Martin, George and Colin ready to go in and install cameras and mics the minute the place is empty. How many people did you say live there Jo?'

'According to the last census, just an elderly couple, and their son, but if that is the case I can't see a couple of old age pensioners being involved in a terror campaign against Israel.'

'Oh I don't know' I replied 'I know some really scary old age pensioners.'

'Yes Michael, but they're all your relatives.' said Sam laughing.

I ignored my wife and continued.

'Be that as it may' I said laughing 'and Sam's quite right, most of my relatives are quite scary. The parents may have nothing to do with this and be totally unaware. What do we know about the son Jo?' I asked.

'Not a lot I'm afraid. His name is listed as Nigel Collins and his occupation is listed as a plumber. That's about it. As far as we know he doesn't belong to any political groups or have any record.'

'I suppose being a plumber would give him easy access to buildings' said Willie 'and plumbers always carry round a couple of bags of tools and bits of kit that nobody ever recognizes.

It could be a good cover?'

'True' said Helena, thinking aloud. 'Look, you three, get the cameras, mics, entry tools etc ready and head off in one of the Range Rovers. Park up just down the road and we'll telephone them from here and ask them to meet up for something or other. Wait till they leave and dive in there straight away. How long will you need?'

'It's only a small house, so no more than half an hour' replied Martin.

'Michael, can you and Sam go with them please and keep watch. Take a radio and keep in touch with me. I'll stay here and we'll put our heads together and come up with some pretext for getting them all out of the house.'

We parked the Range Rover about a hundred feet down the road from the target house, and Sam sat alongside me in the front passenger seat. Martin, George and Colin were all sitting behind us with their gear all stowed in the boot area behind them. The radio came to life and Helena was on the other end.

'OK, they should all hopefully be leaving in a few minutes.' said Helena 'I phoned them and said I was a solicitor in King's Lynn, and that an elderly relative of theirs had passed away in Italy leaving a considerable amount of money, and no will. I then explained that it looked like the three of them appeared to be his closest relatives, and they would be receiving the bulk of his money split equally between the three of them. They confirmed there was only the three of them, and I told them they needed to come to the office straight away and bring their passports with them for proof of identity, and then we could start the inheritance process. They said they would leave straight away.'

'Yes, they're coming out of the house now'. I said 'All three of them are climbing into an old Ford Mondeo saloon.' I continued my commentary 'They're just driving past us as we speak.'

As soon as their car turned the corner, the three men in the back collected their bags and calmly walked down the road to the house.

'What happens Helena' asked Sam into the radio 'when they get to the solicitors office and they find out nobody knows anything about a dead elderly relative?'

'I assume the solicitor will tell them someone was playing a practical joke on them, and they'll come back. But it will take them half an hour to drive to King's Lynn, and the same back again, so the boys will have plenty of time to install the various devices.'

'What if they've already got smoke

detectors and ours look different?' asked Sam.

'Martin has cameras installed in all the leading makes of smoke detectors' she replied 'and he'll just replace like for like, and if they don't have detectors he'll use wall sockets or install mini cameras and mics high up in the walls. Don't worry about it Sam, over the last few years we've learnt how to do this without raising suspicion.'

'I should know better by now' said Sam 'but I can't help it, I just seem to worry about things.'

'No need to apologize Sam, it helps keep us on our toes and stops us getting complacent.'

Forty minutes later, Martin, George and Colin walked back down the road and climbed into the back of the car.

'Home James please' said George.

'Mission well and truly accomplished' said Colin.

'We've now got cameras and mics in their lounge, kitchen, bathroom and both bedrooms' said Martin into the radio. 'They had smoke detectors in the lounge and the kitchen, and we had the same models so I just replaced them. The rest have been drilled into the walls, but they won't spot them.'

'Well done lads' responded Helena 'See you soon.'
That was my cue, so I started the car and drove the short distance back to the hotel. Back in the hotel room, Willie and Jo had set up the TV monitors and speakers, and we could now clearly see and hear what was going on in every room in the house. Not that there was anything to watch or listen to as the Collins family hadn't returned yet. They did so about twenty minutes later.

'What sort of warped person would do that to us?' asked Mrs Collins.

'Oh it's just the sort of thing your brother's kids would do' answered Mr Collins. 'I've always said there was a rogue gene in that family.'

'That's my family you're referring to' shot back Mrs Collins. 'It wouldn't surprise if it wasn't your Cousin Dorothy's idea of a joke. She's a weird one for a start. Then there's your sister's kid Gayle. It could easily have been her voice on the phone thinking about it.'

'Oh shut up the pair of you' yelled Nigel. 'It doesn't matter who it was. Someone's had a really good laugh at our expense, and it doesn't matter who it was. There are far more important things in life.' and with that Nigel slammed the lounge door and went upstairs to his bedroom, and laid on his back on the bed.

'Well you've really upset them haven't you?' I asked Helena smiling at her.

'Needs must, as you British say' she responded.

'I keep forgetting you're Dutch and not British' I replied. 'You have no accent and sound just like us normal people.'

'There's nothing normal about the British' said Rivka, joining in the conversation from the sofa. 'I ask you, keeping a stiff upper lip? What's that all about? Turning the other cheek? That's just stupid. Then you eat all those disgusting foods like pease pudding and faggots, cockles and whelks, bread and dripping, and what on earth is bubble and squeak. I'm sorry Michael, but none of that could possibly be described as normal.'

'Now, now children! Play nicely please' commanded Helena. 'Although I have to say I do know what Rivka means about bubble and squeak, but I assume what you said was meant as a compliment Michael?'

'Of course' I replied 'what possibly bigger compliment could there be for anyone to receive than someone assuming they were British'
Rivka gave a loud 'Huh' from the sofa and then

grinned at us all.

Chapter Seventeen

Marika, Jo and Willie were all busy watching the TV monitors.

'Action folks' said Jo suddenly.

'Nigel Collins has just got off his bed and locked the bedroom door.'

'He's getting a bag down from the top of his wardrobe' said Jo as she continued the commentary. We all crowded round the TV monitors and watched as Nigel Collins put the sports bag on his bed and unzipped it. He pulled out a pair of black football boots.

'Oh boring' said Colin 'He's off to play football.' At that point most of us returned to our seats. Martin, Jo, Marika and Willie however continued to watch.

'It won't do his feet any good if he tries playing football with that' said Martin quite sarcastically. 'I may be wrong, but that looks to me like several blocks of C4 explosive he's got tucked into his football boots and socks.' Needless to say, upon hearing that we all immediately ran back to watch the TV monitors.

'So what do we do about Nigel Collins then?' I asked generally.

'Kill him' said Rivka with no hesitation.

'Is that your answer to everything Rivka, kill them?' asked Sam 'Have you ever tried talking to people or simply questioning them.'

'As soon as you hesitate with these people they will try to kill you.' replied Rivka. 'Look, I know you don't understand how we feel, but you are not an Israeli who has half the world wishing you were dead. Not only that, most of them are doing their best to ensure that happens, and you've seen that for yourselves. As for the other half? Well they may well support us in public, and say the right things, but we know they secretly wish we didn't exist and therefore wouldn't be causing all this trouble.'

'Is that really how you feel?' asked Sam.

'It is reality' replied Rivka 'It is not just a feeling. It is fact. So yes, that is how we must live and that is also how most Israeli's feel about life.'

'Well none of us feel like that Rivka' chipped in Helena 'but despite what you say, I think a conversation with Mr Nigel Collins could prove very useful.'

'Do we wait until he leaves the house, and then pick him up, or do we go round there and arrest him? asked Colin.

'Neither' replied Helena. 'We watch him,

and wait till he goes out taking the C4 with him. We then follow him, see where he goes and then arrest him before he can do whatever it is he wants to do.'

'Sounds like a plan.' said George.

In fact nothing happened for four days. We took it in turns doing two hour shifts in pairs watching the TV screens, with those of us who were 'off duty' going for occasional short walks to get some air and keep fit. Most nights we either ate in two groups of five in the restaurant or we brought in local fish and chips for all ten of us. Then on Thursday morning there was some action at Nigel's house. A van pulled up outside, and a delivery man dropped of two large cardboard boxes, each box I estimated to be approximate three foot cubes. Nigel carried them up to his bedroom one at a time and then opened the first box. It contained what looked like various carved wooden clocks of various shapes and sizes. He emptied all three boxes and ended up with twenty eight wooden clocks.

'The mind boggles' said a curious Jo. 'What the hell does he want with all them?'

'I've no idea' said George 'but no doubt we'll find out.'

Nigel Collins then walked over to his wardrobe

and got down his sports bag containing the C4. He carefully took out a single block of C4 and laid it on the desk in his room. He then pulled back the edge of the rug in his room, with the point of a long screwdriver he very carefully lifted a floorboard, put his hand inside the opening and then pulled out a tin box about a foot long and six inches square. He lifted the lid, and Martin used his remote joystick to zoom in on the boxes contents. Detonators.

'Well he's definitely intending to blow something or somebody up.' said Willie.

'And I think I know who and when' I said as it suddenly dawned on me. 'He's got twenty eight wooden clocks, and it looks like he's going to stuff them all with blocks of C4. Keep them all in close proximity, then set one off and the whole lot will go up together.'

'But you say you think you know when and where?' asked Helena.

'I'm making a few assumptions here, but yes, I think I know. Those wooden clocks would be relatively easy to sell in the right environment, and this coming weekend will provide just the right place as it is the Sandringham Craft Fayre on Saturday and Sunday. The Sandringham Estate is just a twenty minute drive from here and today is setting up day for everyone who is exhibiting. I think he'll finish stuffing the clocks with C4 and detonators, then pack them all back in the original big cardboard boxes, and then take them to the Fayre and put them out on a stall he's got booked.'

'And then he'll blow up half the population of Norfolk when the place is packed on Saturday?' suggested Helena.

'No' I said 'I don't think so. I think he'll set them off tomorrow. Friday.'

'But the Craft Fayre doesn't open to the public until Saturday and Sunday' said Helena. 'There's no point in blowing the place up when there's nobody there.'

'But there will be someone there. Who owns the Sandringham Estate?' I asked.

'Well the Queen of course' answered Sam.

'And Her Majesty always gets a private tour of all the stands at the Craft Fayre the day before it opens. Just think of the horrendous impact on Israel if it gets the blame for blowing up the Queen. The UK would probably want to nuke Jerusalem in retaliation.'

'We need to stop him' said Willie.

'What if he's been radicalized by Ahmadi and co, and he would rather blow himself up than be stopped?' asked Jo. 'I hate to say it, but I think that's more than likely if he really is planning what Michael is suggesting.'

'You could well be right Jo.' said Helena 'We simply can't take the risk of him detonating his explosives anywhere.'

'I could guarantee to take him out with one shot' said Rivka 'but I would need to get back to the Gulfstream to collect my sniper rifle that was put in the hold.'

'I didn't know you'd put a sniper rifle in the hold' said Helena looking questioningly at Rivka. 'You should have told us what you were putting on board.'

'Sorry' said Rivka. 'It's automatic for Israeli covert operatives to take high powered sniper rifles on this sort of mission. It never even occurred to me that you didn't do the same. I apologise, and I wasn't trying to hide anything.'

'No, don't worry. We have similar weapons in the hold ourselves should the need arise. It's just that I'm responsible and I need to know what we are carrying. OK, so where and when would you suggest.'

'Where to do it? I don't really know this part of the world.'

'We need to separate him from all his explosives' said George. 'But surely if we can draw him away from his bedroom, I'm sure we can take him alive and then maybe find out who's running this operation.'

'He may not know' said Helena 'But it's worth a try.'

'Well we can't send him to the solicitors again. Any ideas anyone?' asked Sam.

As we discussed various ideas, Nigel Collins continued to stuff his wooden clocks with C4 explosive and detonators. In the end it was Willie that came up with the simple solution.

'Why don't we just knock on the front door, calmly walk in and arrest him?'

Thirty minutes later, I knocked on the front door of the Collin's house. I was wearing a Church of England 'dog collar' or vicar's white collar, which was actually just a piece of stiff white card I had cut to shape from an empty food carton, and a dark grey suit I had borrowed from one of the hotel staff's lockers. I should say however, the staff member who owned it was totally unaware it had gone missing, and I hoped to get it back to him long before he realized it had gone. Willie was standing alongside me as was Helena who was standing on the other side, holding a clipboard with a list on it that we'd printed off one of our laptops at the hotel, and a pen.

Mrs Collins answered the door.

'Ah, good morning' I began. 'My name is Father Anthony, and I'm working with the Rector at St Mary Magdalene Church in Sandringham. We are busy putting together the list of exhibitors at this year's Sandringham Craft Fayre, and this address is on our list as having an exhibitor, but for some reason we don't have any details. My colleague here has all the ID entry cards for the exhibitors, but we need a name and the signature of the exhibitor. Would that be yourself madam?'

'No' she laughed 'That would be my son. Hold on vicar and I'll give him a shout.'

'Nigel' she yelled up the stairs. 'Vicar of Sandringham with your exhibitor's pass.'

Ten seconds later Nigel Collins came slowly down the stairs looking pensive and just a bit suspicious. Then he looked at me in my clerical garb and glasses, and Helena grasping her clipboard and he visibly relaxed.

'How can I help you vicar?' he asked.

'Good morning Mr .... ?' I queried.

'Oh, sorry' he replied. 'Collins, Nigel Collins.'

At this point his mother turned round and walked back into the front room where the TV was blasting away in the background.

'Thank you Mr Collins. We're distributing all the exhibitor's passes for this year's Sandringham Craft Fayre, which will also act as your entry pass, but we need you to sign for it, if you don't mind?'

No, of course not' he answered.

As we had previously arranged and practised before we set off, Helena very carefully held out the clipboard in her right hand, and the pen in her left. It meant Nigel had to hold out both of his hands in order to take the two items. As he did so, Willie brought his hands from behind his back and slapped a pair of handcuffs over both Nigel's extended wrists. It was beautifully synchronized and executed if I say so myself. Nigel was about to yell and scream, as he started to struggle from the grip Willie now had on him, when just then Rivka appeared from the side of the house and held her Beretta with silencer attached, firmly against Nigel's forehead.

'Please give me an excuse' she said quietly to him.

Nigel stopped all movement immediately and all resistance went out of him.

'Do your parents know what you were planning?' I asked him.

'No, they haven't a clue' he replied, they just watch daytime TV all day.'

I believed him, and at that point Helena waved across the road. George and Colin then got out of the second Range Rover parked on the opposite side of the road, and they came and took Nigel away. Rivka went with them, but her pistol was back in her handbag.

'Helena, Willie and I entered the house, and we walked straight into the lounge. Mr and Mrs Collins sure enough were sitting in two armchairs, both totally engrossed in the chat show being broadcast on the TV. They stared at us as Willie walked over and turned the TV off. I spoke.

'I'm sorry Mr and Mrs Collins, but I'm not father Anthony, but I and my colleagues here are all officers with Interpol, and I'm afraid we've just arrested your son.'

'He will be charged later today' said Helena 'with High Treason, terrorism and plotting to kill her Majesty the Queen along with other members of the Royal Family.'

'Nigel?' exclaimed his mother laughing. 'You must be mistaken. Nigel couldn't harm a flea.'

'I'm sorry Mrs Collins' I interrupted her 'but we know for a fact that your son has at least thirty blocks of C4 explosive upstairs in his bedroom along with all the necessary detonators to set it off.'

'He was planning to blow up the Queen' said Helena 'and those with her as she toured the Sandringham Craft Fayre tomorrow. After your son has been formally charged, he will be taken to prison and held on remand until he appears in court.'

Needless to say, Mr and Mrs Collins were shocked to the core, and it was obvious they had no idea what Nigel had been planning. Jo joined us in the house, and we packed all the C4 and detonators into one of the cardboard boxes and took it all away with us in the other Range Rover. Mr and Mrs Collins get into their own car and headed for King's Lynn police station where George, Colin and Rivka had taken Nigel to be charged and held.

Chapter Eighteen

An hour later, having checked all the C4 and detonators into the evidence room at the Police Station, Helena, Willie and I were granted permission to go and interview Nigel Collins. Although Interpol has a lot of authority, a charge of High Treason is very rare in the UK, and the UK police have the ultimate authority. In fact, the last execution for treason in the United

Kingdom was held in 1946. William Joyce who was also known as Lord Haw-Haw, stood accused of levying war against King George VI by travelling to Germany in the early months of World War II and taking up employment as a broadcaster of pro-Nazi propaganda to British radio audiences. He was awarded a personal commendation by Adolf Hitler in 1944 for his contribution to the German war effort. On his capture at the end of the war, Parliament rushed through the Treason Act 1945 to facilitate a trial that would have the same procedure as a trial for murder. Before the Act, a trial for treason short of regicide involved an elaborate and lengthy medieval procedure. Although Joyce was born in the United States to an Irish father and an English mother, he had moved to Britain in his teens and applied for a British passport in 1933 which was still valid when he defected to Germany, and so under the law he owed allegiance to Britain. He appealed against his conviction to the House of Lords on the grounds he had lied about his country of birth on the passport application and did not owe allegiance to any country at the beginning of the war. The appeal was not upheld and he was executed at Wandsworth Prison on 3 January 1946.

We entered Nigel's cell and I sat on the bench alongside him as Helena and Willie both stood leaning against the wall and watching over him.

'We only really have two questions Nigel' I said 'Why and who gave you the job?'

'Why?' he asked incredulously. 'You really want to know why? Money, that's why. A hundred grand to be precise. Ten grand up front and another ninety once I'd done the job. Look, I can't get a job in this wretched country for love nor money, despite having had a decent education, and that bunch of layabouts called the royal family just sit on their backsides all day or ride around in the fancy Rolls Royce's and get paid millions a year for doing nothing.'

'And you think that justifies blowing them up?' asked Helena.

'Why should they have everything while the rest of us have nothing?' he replied.

'Don't give me that' I responded 'You live in a nice house in a nice area of the country. You're not exactly sleeping rough on the streets are you?'

'I knew you wouldn't understand' he muttered, utterly depressed and defeated.

'OK' said Helena. 'Do yourself a favour. Tell us who gave you the job and who supplied you with the C4 explosive, and maybe we can put in a good word for you. You can't just buy this stuff in the local hardware shop, so where did it come from?'

'I don't know where it came from. Some foreign bloke delivered it.'

'Does this 'foreign bloke' have a name?' asked Willie.

'Probably, but he didn't tell me what it was. He apparently read one of my rants about the royals on Facebook and then he contacted me and asked me if I was interested in earning some decent money. I said of course I was, and he offered me the job. I said no at first, but then he doubled his offer from £50,000 to £100,000 and I said yes. About two weeks later he met me in King's Lynn and gave me the gear. It was all in that gym bag you found. Thirty blocks of C4, a box of detonators, a mobile phone to use to set it all off with, and a detailed set of instructions for me to follow.'

'Where's the phone and the instructions?' asked Willie.

'They're both still under the floorboards in my bedroom' he muttered.

Willie banged on the cell door and a policeman let him out. He spoke briefly to George and Colin, and the two of them headed back to the house in Hunstanton to collect the mobile phone

and the instructions. Mr and Mrs Collins had left to go home twenty minutes earlier.
Willie re-entered the cell.

'Do you recognize any of these as the man who gave you the explosives?' Helena asked, showing him half a dozen photographs of the terrorists we knew about.

'No. No. No' he said to the first three photographs. Then 'Yes, that's him, he's the one that gave me the C4, and that one there was with him.'

The two people he'd identified were Akram Lajani, the Iranian Kurd, and Khalid Khan, the Afghan planner we'd seen in the Valley of the Kings. We spent a further ten minutes asking questions, but Nigel Collins had told us everything he knew. So we left.

At Helena's suggestion I telephoned Craig Overton at MI6. Fortunately he was at his desk, and I filled him in on what had happened in Norfolk. He knew quite a bit of it, as Rivka had told Moishe and Moishe had informed Craig. But the one bit of news that was a surprise to him was Khalid Khan being in the UK. That he hadn't known.

'How the hell did that bastard manage to get through Immigration Control' he asked without really expecting an answer.

'He probably came ashore having hitched a ride in a Scottish fishing trawler or something similar, and then caught a night train to London.' I said joking.

'The sad thing is Michael' he said through gritted teeth 'you're probably right, or at least something similar. How the hell are we supposed to keep terrorists out of the UK when we've got nearly eight thousand miles of coast line? In reality, anyone can get in if they're clever enough, and these are not only clever, they're the best of the best.'

'Anything more we can do?' I asked

'Yes' Craig responded 'Check out Watton and Thetford as soon as you can. The trouble is we don't know what's being planned, where it's going to happen, or when.'

'I'll let you know if we find out anything' I said, and hung up.

Watton is a small market town in central Norfolk, and all we had was an address of a house in somewhere called Griston Road. We drove the two Range Rovers into Watton and parked in the car park of the Willow House, a nice two storey Tudor style black and white building with a thatched roof. It was basically a pub that had several rooms for rent, plus a decent restaurant. We'd chosen it because the food had received several great ratings, and we all liked decent food. The rooms weren't massive, but they would do us nicely. Having dumped all our luggage in our rooms, we all congregated in the bar and having found Griston Road on a local map we borrowed from the pub, we then set off as luckily enough it wasn't very far away. We walked in groups of twos and threes up the road and then continued on past the house. Martin bent down to do up his shoe lace as we passed the entrance, and he managed to get several crafty photos of the house and garden on his mobile phone. We completed a circuit of the local roads and got back to the pub about forty minutes later. It was a pleasant afternoon, so we all sat outside on the benches and tables with a few lagers and glasses of wine, chatting through a plan of action.

'The trouble is' began Helena 'we have no idea what is being planned. All we have is a few phone numbers and addresses.'

Just then Helena's mobile rang and she stopped speaking as she answered it. She stood up and walked round the car park while speaking quietly into the phone. About five minutes later she returned to her chair and sat down again.

'That was Moishe on the phone' she began. 'It appears that Sergei Polyakov has struck. He hacked into the three banks in San Diego as we expected, but I'm afraid he's also hacked into several banks in London, Frankfurt and Hong Kong. Moishe is busy trying to calm down the various PLO factions that have lost millions, but it's not going to be easy. In total over two hundred and eighty five million dollars has been transferred out of various PLO accounts, and every cent of it has very publically turned up in various Israeli government accounts.'

'Can he keep the PLO from reacting?' asked Sam.

'Moishe thinks so. He said thank goodness he'd warned the head of the Palestine National Council in advance. He's told them every cent that has ended up in the Israeli accounts will be paid into the special bank account he set up for this very purpose within twenty four hours. The PLO can then redistribute it back to where it was taken from.'

'You never know' said Sam 'it might even do some good in that it shows good will on the part of Israel.'

'I have to say Sam' mused Jo 'you really are one of life's eternal optimists aren't you?

Whatever the situation, you somehow always manage to see the good in people.'

'I try my best' said my wife.

Chapter Nineteen

We wandered into the main street of the town, which is Watton High Street, and it basically runs from one end to the other, for the most part lined with shops on both sides. We bought the local paper and browsed through it looking for anything that might inspire the terrorists to take action.

'What about this' asked George? 'According to this article in the 'Watton and Swaffham Times', and I quote 'A special service will take place at St Mary's Anglican Church in Watton on Saturday the 10th to commemorate the 75th anniversary of 2 Group, Bomber Command at RAF Watton. The service will be attended by his royal highness the Prince of Wales representing the royal family, Air Chief Marshall Fitzpatrick on behalf of the RAF, Geraldine Masters, Watton and District's Member of Parliament, and the service will be led by The Right Reverend Peter Mayhew, the Bishop of King's Lynn.'

'If I'm not mistaken, that's tomorrow' said

Jo.

'If I was going to blow up a church' I said 'I'd want to ensure the explosives were all in place and ready to go long before the day. Can we get in there and check it out?'

'Good idea' said Helena.

'Anybody know where the Vicarage is?' asked Jo. 'The Vicar should have keys.'

'I'll ask in the pub' said George as he shot inside the Willow House. He was back a minute later.

'It's more or less opposite, but just along the main road a bit, and the church is at the bottom of a road off to the left of the main road.'

'Let's go' commanded Helena, and we all trooped off to the vicarage. Most of us stayed outside as Helena and George went and knocked on the Vicarage's front door. The door was opened by a lady I estimated to be in her fifties, who I assumed was the Vicar's wife, and after a minute's conversation she invited Helena and George inside. They were back out five minutes later with the Vicar following close behind them.

'Good morning Vicar' said Sam

'Apparently St Mary's doesn't have a Vicar, it has a Rector.' said Helena.

'And that's me' chimed in The Revd. Simon Fordham.

'If you don't mind me asking Rector, what's the difference?' asked Colin.

'A Rector is in total charge of an institution be it a hospital, a school, a church etc, whereas a vicar is the person charged to preach and handle the day to day ministry of a church. Rector's also preach and teach etc, but they have additional legal responsibilities.'

'Well I'm sorry to say it Rector' said George 'but I think this particular legal responsibility of yours, ie the church building, may be well and truly threatened with its very existence, so can we get inside and have a search around?'

'Of course' he replied as we walked down the road leading to the church.'

'Have there been any strangers in the building lately?' I asked.

'We get strangers most Sundays' replied the Rector.

'No' I said 'Sorry Rector, I mean strangers coming into the church, not on Sundays.'

'Oh I see. Not really, well I say that, there was of course the builders who came in to sort out the possible woodworm in the beams etc. Obviously they had full run of the building while they were spraying and we were asked to stay out for 12 hours while they sprayed everywhere. I have to say, the church stank for a 24 hours after they'd gone.'

'When was this Rector?' Helena asked.

'When, oh now let me think. Well they first called at the Rectory offering a free damp and woodworm survey on Thursday of last week. They did the survey on Friday, the following day, and then came back on Tuesday of this week and sprayed everywhere.'

'So you hadn't noticed any woodworm and called the company in. They just called by and offered their services out of the blue?'

'Well yes, now you mention it.'

'The name of the company and their address?' I asked.

'Sorry, I don't know. I don't have any paperwork, they just said they'd post their invoice once the work was completed, but I haven't received anything yet.'

'And I don't suppose you ever will' I thought quietly to myself.

We had by now arrived at the church, and the Rector unlocked the large front door.

'Rector' said Helena 'by all means come in, after all it's your church and your responsibility, but please don't touch anything until we've checked everything out.'

The Rector meekly agreed, and we all spread

out. George found a ladder and climbed up onto the roof areas of a couple of rooms built inside the main body of the church.

'I've got what looks like ten blocks of C4 all taped together with a detonator and a mobile phone.' He shouted down to us. 'I've pulled the detonator out and these blocks are now safe to move.'

George handed the ten blocks down to Rivka who Helena had asked to take charge of anything we found. She, like George, Colin and Jo had received training in handling explosives of most types.

'If there's one lot' said Helena 'there are bound to be lots more. Keep searching and look everywhere.' she commanded.

'There's the same this side' said George who had now moved his ladder and climbed onto the roof of the room the other side of the main entrance.'

'I cannot believe this' said the Rector, holding his head in his hands. Who would want to blow up this beautiful building that stood here since the year 1135?'

'Terrorists don't care about the building or its history Rector' I explained. 'They're only interested in the visitors to tomorrow's anniversary service.'

'Can it still go ahead, or will we have to cancel it?' he asked pleadingly.

Helena walked over and answered the question.

'We'll do everything we can now to ensure the building is totally clear, and I've called in the bomb squad who should be here in about fifteen minutes, and they will take over from us, and hopefully they'll be able to give you the all clear for tomorrow's service.'

A shout came from Willie who was crawling on his hands and knees behind the altar.

'I've got some more of what I assume is C4 here. Can someone who knows what they're doing come and take over please, while I look elsewhere?'

Colin shot straight over, made the explosives safe and handed the lot to Rivka. By the time the Bomb Squad arrived and took over, Rivka had collected nearly one hundred blocks of C4, each set of blocks with a detonator attached to a mobile phone. They had planted blocks of C4 inside the church organ, underneath the floor tiles below the front pews where the dignitaries were due to sit, they'd spread C4 along several of the wooden beams that supported the roof, and as the Bomb Squad leader eventually told us, there was more than enough C4 spread around the church to spray the debris from the explosions over a hundred yards in every direction.

We returned to the Willow House, collected our bags and were about to head off when Helena's phone rang again. This time it was Craig on the line. Again she went 'walkabout' as she talked, and we sat outside the pub on the benches until she returned.

'No need to go to Thetford' she said looking thoroughly depressed. 'A bomb has just gone off in the market square. Five people have been killed and over thirty have been injured. Nobody has claimed responsibility, but Craig said there was a demonstration taking place at the time supporting Palestine's right to exist as a nation in its own right. Inevitably, Israel will get the blame on the TV news and in radio reports as the press know nothing about the Cairo Conspirator's as Craig is now calling them.'

'So what do we do now?' asked Jo.

'I suggest we all head back to the aircraft' said Helena. 'Then sit and carefully chat through our options. We still have other addresses and phone numbers to follow up on, and let's just hope we can get there and stop any more carnage before it happens.'

Chapter Twenty

We sat on the Gulfstream going through the various options. The only other address we had was from the notes section of Ali's iPhone, and this was an address in France. So that's where we decided to head next. During the flight, Rivka and Jo searched the internet looking for anything Palestine related due to occur in France, while Sam and Willie looked for any events in France where there would be gatherings of dignitaries.

The address we'd got from Ali's phone was in the village of Mougins, which is located on the heights above Cannes, and although we didn't know the village it was an area we knew as it is in the district of Grasse. Sam and I had been to Grasse a few years earlier with Helena when we were looking for the Faro Forger. Mougins is a just a 15 minute drive from Cannes, and in modern times, the small village has been frequented and inhabited by many famous artists and celebrities, including Pablo Picasso, Yves Saint Laurent, Christian Dior, Winston Churchill, Catherine Deneuve and Édith Piaf to name but a few. In fact Pablo Picasso spent the last 12 years of his life living in Mougins where he died in 1973. Picasso's former studio was in the old village in a building that is now the tourist office.

We flew to Nice Côte d'Azur airport, which is just a sixteen mile drive to the town. We hired a couple of cars and eventually found a couple of parking spaces. What a fantastic atmosphere this little French village has. I'd spent most of my life telling everyone that I wasn't at all keen on France or the French people. In fact my favourite phrase for years had been 'France is a beautiful country, but unfortunately it's full of French people'. How wrong can you be, and I unreservedly apologise to all I insulted. I think it stemmed from my very first visit to France when I arrived in Calais, and was annoyed that I couldn't get a decent cup of tea, and these wretched people insisted on speaking French. I ask you, how inconsiderate of them all. French people speaking French in France! After numerous visits over the last few years I've now realised that France is indeed a beautiful country, and on the whole most French people are very friendly and will go out of their way to be helpful. Well, at least I'm now admitting that I was wrong for all those years. Anyway, as I was saying; what a fantastic atmosphere the little French village of Mougins has. It's built on a hill with amazing views over the surrounding countryside, and all set amongst pines, olives and Cyprus trees. As soon as you arrive in the village, you can't help but be seduced by the charm of the narrow roads, bordered by colourful flowers and superb ancient houses. Picturesque door ways with each stone carefully restored, beautifully designed window frames, absolutely delightful detail everywhere you look. Then on the outskirts of the village you will find luxurious properties hidden behind magnificent Mediterranean parks and gardens. Without doubt, it's these simple details that make Mougins one of the most attractive villages in the south of France. And yet living somewhere in this village was someone who wanted to destroy it all, and our task was to find them.

We consulted a local map and located the address we'd found in Ali's mobile phone. The house was located in the centre of Mougins and virtually opposite a patisserie. We ordered a selection of cakes and numerous glasses of fresh orange juice. As we sat watching the house opposite, we started chatting with the waitress/owner who was serving us. Apart from us she wasn't very busy, and so she was quite happy to tell us in her broken English about the history of the little town and the people who lived here. We asked about various buildings, and eventually Sam casually asked about the pretty white house opposite with the lovely blue shutters.

'Ah, house belong Madam Favreau' replied our hostess. 'Strange lady. She come to live here less a year ago, but I have no idea why. I speak to her not often, she choose to live in France, but hates France. As I say, very strange lady! She blame our wonderful President De Gaulle for abandoning her beloved Algeria, where she come from. She then move to Gaza with her husband who was two month later killed by soldier during demonstration. After he killed she move here, but why if she hate France. Strange lady Madam Favreau.'

'Thank you' said Sam, bringing the conversation to a close. Our hostess left, and once she'd gone we started chatting amongst ourselves.

'So she hates France because they abandoned Algeria' I said 'and she hates Israel because Israeli soldiers killed her husband. I think we need to keep an eye on her.'

'The trouble is' said Willie 'we have no idea what she looks like.'

'Madam Favreau, she come now' said our host as she walked past us delivering cold beers to the next table. 'That is Madam' she said nodding her head towards an elderly woman I estimated to be in her mid to late sixties. Then I suddenly realised, I'm now in my early forties, and that means I must be approaching middle age. I have to say, the sudden realization came as a shock. Willie brought me out of my thoughts.

'So what do we do about her' he asked Helena.

'Watch the house for the moment, then next time she goes out, Martin can go in through the back and plant a few microphones and cameras so that we can see what she's up to. We need to book into a hotel somewhere. Michael, can you and Sam try and find us some hotel rooms as near to here as possible please.'

In the end we decided to search the internet, and Sam found a large holiday villa designed to sleep ten that was currently vacant and that we could rent for a week. We had no idea how long we would actually need it for, but it was only two minutes' walk from Madam Favreau's house, and that was fine by us. Helena drew up a rota and we took it in pairs to sit and watch the house. Colin had gone for a stroll earlier and had ascertained that the house had a back door, but it only led into the rear garden, and there was no way out from the rear garden without coming through the front.

Two hour shifts were the order of the day, and we varied our watching location between three different coffee shops and bars, all located on the same street as Madam Favreau's. Whoever was on watch was connected to Helena via one of Martin's top of the range two way radio's, and Martin was ready and waiting to break into her house the minute Madam left. That was in fact roughly seven hours later while Colin and Jo were on watch, and the second she left, Colin told Helena who told Martin, who grabbed George, and the two them left straight away carrying Martin's four suitcases between them. They also grabbed Rivka and asked her to replace Colin on watch duty while he joined them in the house to install all the equipment. Jo was already off following Madam and she would use her mobile phone to notify Helena the second Madam started heading back to the house.

It only took 53 minutes to install the cameras and microphones with three of them on the job, and they left after completing a thorough audio and video check on all the equipment with Marika. Everyone apart from Jo and Rivka was back at the villa fifteen minutes later.

'Hi Jo' said Helena answering her mobile which showed her on the screen that it was Jo calling from her mobile.

'I'm currently watching Madam' said Jo 'who is sitting having coffee in a bar with a face we all know very well. Mr Sadiq Rouhani, our Moroccan terrorist. He's got a large sports bag, or holdall type bag on the floor, and I bet she takes it when she leaves.'

'Where exactly are you Jo?' asked Helena. Jo told her.

Helena immediately spoke to Rivka through the two way, told her where to find Jo and asked her to follow Rouhani when he left, and she instructed Jo to follow Madam back to the house, or wherever she went.

'George, can you please go with Rivka, and take a pistol with you. You never know what's going to happen with these dammed terrorists.'

George and Rivka left and walked as fast as they could without drawing attention to themselves, to the bar Jo was still sitting in, and they sat at a separate table, not too far away, but they didn't even acknowledging Jo's presence, as agreed with Helena.

Nothing happened for another twenty minutes, and then Rouhani got up, and leaving the sports holdall behind he walked out of the bar. Rivka and George got up and followed him down the street holding hands and giggling like a loved up couple. Because of the line of business he was in Rouhani was always suspicious of everyone, and he twice looked back to see if anyone was following him. Unfortunately there were no shop doorways to duck into or hide in, and after his second quick look back he became suspicious that he was being followed. So he took several quick turns up narrow roads and alleyways, and pretty quickly established that yes, he was being followed. He decided to call Ahmadi and tell him he was being followed, but before he could dial the number Rivka, who had realized what he was doing suddenly ran, closed the gap between them and pulled a Glock out of her pocket which she pointed straight at Rouhani's forehead.

'Don't be an idiot Rouhani' she commanded in a loud voice, as George joined her, he too pulling out his pistol and pointing it at the terrorist.

'We're from Interpol, and there are more

of us in the town. It's over, put the phone down and come with us.' said George.
Rouhani held up both hands and twisting very slightly as he bent down to place his mobile phone on the floor, his right hand slipped inside his jacket pocket. As he stood, he started to pull a gun out of the pocket, but before anything else could happen, Rivka put a bullet in the centre of his head, literally between his eyes. Rouhani crumpled to the floor, as dead as a dodo, and Rivka and George quickly went over to the body and covered it with a dirty old bit of tarpaulin he'd spotted lying in a nearby builders skip.
George rang Helena and explained what had happened and that they had had no choice, and Helena immediately telephoned the private number Gilles Cazeneuve, the President of France had given her to keep him informed. He said he would contact the local police in Mougin straight away, and inform them that the two Interpol officers on the scene should be free to leave as soon as the local police had taken charge of Rouhani's body. The one other thing George did before the police arrived was to pick up Rouhani's mobile phone and quietly slip it into his own pocket.

Jo meanwhile was still watching Madam

Favreau, who was just about to leave the bar, taking the obviously heavy black and red sports holdall with her. Jo could now see, the holdall was zipped up tight. Madam struggled with its obvious weight, but managed to get to within fifty yards of her house before she stopped for a rest on a bench. Jo was watching from about seventy feet away, and she was giving Helena a detailed running commentary over the two way radio set.

'Sam, can you and Michael take over from Jo please' commanded Helena. 'Jo stay put where you are.'

Sam and I rushed out of the villa and were with Jo in about four minutes. Madam was still sitting on the bench trying to get her breath back for the last bit of her journey. Jo smiled at us, walked straight past us and headed back to our villa. Sam and I sat and watched Madam for a few minutes, and then once again she stood up, picked up the bag and struggled back to the house. She got her key out, opened the door, and both she and the bag disappeared inside. We reported in to Helena who instructed us to return to the villa, as they could now see and hear everything Madam was doing via the video. So we did, just in time to meet up with Rivka and George who had been given a lift back to the villa by the local police, who had taken the body with them.

We all stood watching the big TV screen in the lounge where the video link in Madam's house had now been fed. Madam Favreau took the bag into the kitchen, and straining hard she lifted it up, and onto the pine table that occupied the centre of her kitchen.

'My bet is it's full of C4' said Colin. 'It's obviously bloody heavy.'

'No, I bet it's full of machine guns or something similar.' said Willie.

As it happened they were both wrong. Madam opened the central drawer of the pine table and took out a pair what looked like white latex gloves. She put them on, and carefully unzipped the bag. Holding it open with her left hand she carefully pulled out a glass bottle containing a clear liquid. She held it up to the light, looked through the glass, shook her head as if she hadn't a clue what she was looking at, and then very carefully put the bottle to the back of an empty shelf inside one of her kitchen wall units.

'So what the hell is in that bottle?' asked Willie.

'Whatever it is, she's being very careful not to touch it.' I said.

'Could it be Nitro-glycerine?' asked Colin. 'That's a clear liquid.'

As we were all speculating as to the bottles contents, Madam returned to the open bag and pulled out another glass bottle, which she also put on the same shelf. However, this second glass bottle contained a dark brown, viscose type liquid.

'I think I know what that second bottle is' said Rivka. 'How much do you all know about poisons and nerve agents?' she asked.

We all looked fairly blank, and then Helena said

'We're taught a few basics at Interpol, but in all honesty it's not something we come up against every day.'

'Well I know a bit from my days as a police surgeon' said Sam 'but I'm not sure how much of it I can remember now.'

'Well I had to study the subject in depth' said Rivka taking central stage. 'Every Mossad operative has to as we face the possibility of poison and nerve agent attacks regularly. Helena, do you mind if I give you all a quick bit of education, because I think Madam Favreau now has a selection of real nasty's going into her kitchen cupboard.'

'Please Rivka go ahead. Marika, can you please watch what Madam is up to, and warn us the second she looks like going anywhere.'

'Will do.' Marika replied from her seat in front of the TV monitor.

Chapter Twenty One

'OK' began Rivka once we were all seated. 'Let's deal with poisons first. Some I'm sure you will have heard of. For example Hemlock. It's a highly toxic flowering plant indigenous to Europe and South Africa. It was a popular poison with the ancient Greeks, who used it to kill off their prisoners. For an adult, the ingestion of 100mg of hemlock, or conium as it's more accurately known is fatal. Death comes in the form of paralysis, your mind is wide awake, but your body doesn't respond and eventually your respiratory system shuts down.
Aconite is another plant based poison, this one coming from the plant monkshood. It's also known as wolfsbane, and aconite leaves only one post-mortem sign, that of asphyxia, as it causes arrhythmic heart function which leads to suffocation. Poisoning can occur even after touching the leaves of the plant without wearing gloves as it is very rapidly and easily absorbed. Because of its untraceable nature it has been a

popular one with the “get away with murder” crowd in novels. Reportedly, it has a particularly famous casualty. The emperor Claudius is said to have been poisoned by his wife, Agrippina, using aconite in a plate of mushrooms.’

‘Do these plants still grow wild?’ asked Sam.

‘Oh yes’ replied Rivka. ‘You can easily find them growing all over Europe, but only if you know what you’re looking for.
Then there’s Belladonna. Now this was a firm favorite of the ladies! The name of this plant is derived from Italian and means beautiful woman. That’s because it was used in the middle-ages for cosmetic purposes – diluted eye-drops dilated the pupils, making the women more seductive, or so they thought. Also, if gently rubbed on their checks, it would create a reddish color, what today would be known as blush! This plant seems innocent enough, right? Well, actually, if ingested, a single leaf is lethal and that’s why it was used to make poison-tipped arrows. The berries are the most dangerous part of the plant, and if you put just ten of the attractive-looking berries mixed in with other fruits and berries to make a fruit salad, then the results would be fatal.

‘My God’ said Colin ‘I thought nature

was supposed to be wonderful, but it turns out to be a wonderful killer.'

'Anyone heard of Dimethylmercury?' asked Rivka

She received zero response.

'Well this one is a slow killer – a man-made slow killer! But this is exactly what makes it all the more dangerous. Absorption of doses as low as 0.1ml have proven fatal; however, symptoms of poisoning don't start showing until after months of the initial exposure took place, which is definitely too late for any kind of treatment. In 1996, a chemistry professor at Dartmouth College, New Hampshire, spilled a drop or two of the poison on her gloved hand. Dimethylmercury went through the latex glove, symptoms appeared four months later and ten months later, she died.

Now I'm pretty sure you will know about this one even if you are unfamiliar with its scientific name – Tetrodotoxin. This substance is found in two marine creatures, the blue-ringed octopus and the puffer fish. However, the octopus is the most dangerous, because it purposely injects its venom, killing in minutes. It carries enough venom to kill 26 human adults within minutes and the bites are often painless, so many victims realize they have been bitten only when paralysis sets in. On the other hand, the puffer fish is only lethal if you want to eat it, but if it is well prepared, meaning the venom is taken out, the only thing that's left is the adrenaline of eating something which could kill you.

'I think I'll stick to good old English cod and chips' I said smiling.

'Now I'm sure you've all heard of Polonium' said Rivka. 'It's a radioactive poison, a slow killer with no known cure. Just one gram of vaporised polonium can kill about 1.5 million people in just a couple of months. I suppose the most famous case of individual polonium poisoning was that of the ex-Russian spy Alexander Litvinenko. Polonium was found in his tea cup, a dose 200 times higher than the median lethal dose in case of ingestion. He died in just three weeks.'

'I remember reading about that.' said Jo. 'Is it painful?' she asked.

'Yes, very' replied Rivka. 'They all are. Now in addition to all of those there are three forms of mercury which are extremely dangerous. Elemental mercury is the one you can find in glass thermometers, it's not harmful if touched, but it is lethal if it's inhaled. Inorganic mercury is used to make batteries, and is deadly only when ingested. And finally, organic mercury that is found in fish, such as tuna and swordfish. To be safe keep your tuna consumption down to 170g a week, but it can be potentially deadly over long periods of time. A famous death caused by mercury was that of Wolfgang Amadeus Mozart, who was given mercury pills to treat his syphilis.

'What about cyanide' asked Colin? 'I think Agatha Christie used it a lot in her various novels.'

'Yes, you're right' replied Rivka. 'Cyanide seems to be extremely popular in books, for instance you often read about spies who use cyanide pills to kill themselves when they're caught, or ex-Nazis who did the same when they were caught. There are plenty of reasons for this. Firstly, it is found in a great variety of substances like almonds, apple seeds, apricot kernels, tobacco smoke, insecticides, pesticides and the list goes on. Murder can always be blamed on a household accident, such as ingestion of pesticide - a fatal dose of cyanide for humans is 1.5 mg per kilogram of body weight. Secondly, it's a rapid killer, depending on the dose of course, and death usually occurs within 1 to 15 minutes.

Also, used in its gaseous form – hydrogen cyanide – it is deadly, and as you all know I'm sure, it was the agent used by Nazi Germany for mass murders in gas chambers during the Holocaust.

'Don't remind us' I said thinking back to our visit to Auschwitz during the Salzburg Suicides case.

'The last two poisons I'll mention' continued Rivka 'are Botulinum toxin which causes Botulism, a fatal condition if not treated immediately, involving muscle paralysis, eventually leading to the paralysis of the respiratory system and, consequently, death. Oh, and by the way, the bacteria enter the body through open wounds or by ingesting contaminated food. Also ladies, please bear in mind, botulinum toxin is the same stuff used for Botox injections!'

'Urgh' mouthed Sam 'I never liked the idea of Botox anyway.'

'Lastly there's that good old favourite Arsenic' continued Rivka 'which has often been called the king of poisons, for its discreetness and potency. It used to be virtually undetectable, so it was very often used either as a murder weapon or as a mystery story element. But that's until the Marsh test came and signalled the presence of this poison in water, food and the like. However, this king of poisons has taken many famous lives in its time including Napoleon Bonaparte and your own King George the 3rd of England.'

'OK, so that's a quick run-down of poisons, but they're not nerve agents are they? I asked 'or are they the same.'

'No, nerve agents are totally different, and I'm going to mention a few, but I suspect Madam Favreau now has at least two of them in her kitchen cupboard. One of the nastiest substances around is called Ricin, although it's not technically a nerve agent, even though it has much the same effect, but from what I've seen I don't think she has any of that, but I'll tell you about it anyway.
Ricin is a highly toxic powder which comes from the innocent looking castor bean which in turn comes from the innocent looking castor plant. The plant is commonly used as a decorative plant in many people's homes. Incidentally, it was Ricin that was used when they tried to assassinate former US president Barack Obama back in May 2013.

'You said it was a highly toxic powder' queried George. 'Is it always in powder form and just how lethal is it?'

'Oh, if the powder is inhaled or injected, then just a few grains of it can kill an adult.

A nerve agent is different to poison in that it works by disrupting messages sent by the brain to a person's muscles. It can also affect a person's breathing muscles and if it does that, then it becomes fatal. As for the powder aspect, no, it can also and more often is used as a liquid substance. Also bear in mind, while a nerve agent is usually fast-acting and can kill in minutes, ricin acts much slower, and therefore is a favourite where the killer needs time to make their escape. Ricin will eventually cause multiple organ failure, and death.

'So what exactly is a nerve agent then' asked Jo?

'Nerve agents or nerve gasses are chemical weapons which attack a person's nervous system and prevent their body from functioning properly. Well known examples you'll all have heard of are Sarin Gas, VX and Thallium. They are all nerve agents, but as I said, ricin is not. Sarin is a colourless and odourless agent that was outlawed in April 1997 by the Chemical Weapons Convention, and I may be wrong, but I suspect the first bottle Madam pulled out of that bag was probably Sarin.

'And it's very dangerous' asked Sam'

'In its purest form' replied Rivka 'Sarin is estimated to be 26 times deadlier than cyanide.

Thallium is another one and it is known as the poisoner's poison. Thallium is colourless, odourless and tasteless, and its wide-ranging symptoms are often suggestive of other illnesses. It also has the added bonus of being very hard to trace, meaning that even your Porton Down experts may not know for sure what was administered to someone.'

You mentioned VX' I said. 'I've never heard of it, and what is it?'

'In simple terms' replied Rivka 'VX is without doubt the most deadly chemical weapon ever produced by anyone, anywhere. It's a highly toxic nerve agent, first developed in the UK in the 1950s but under international agreements it was supposed to be all destroyed and outlawed. It causes victims to spasm uncontrollably and involuntarily shut their windpipe, causing them to suffocate.
As little as 10mg of VX, outlawed by the 1997 Chemical Weapons Convention, can kill a human in just a few minutes.

'So just how toxic is VX' asked Helena?

'VX is so toxic that even a microscopic amount can kill. One touch would be enough. According to the experts, VX is primarily a touch hazard, so you would need to be in physical contact with it for its full impact to become clear.

It is usually dark in colour and highly viscose, and I believe that's what Madam pulled out of the bag in the second bottle. Just so you fully understand, if you were to take 1 as an example toxicity figure for Chlorine, then Sarin would be 4,000, and VX would be 20,000.'

'OK' said Helena thinking aloud 'If she's got a supply of nerve agents, what the hell is she going to do with them, and how the hell do we stop her?'

'Are there any prominent Palestinians living in Mougin' I asked?

'No idea' answered Helena. 'Why, what's your thinking Michael?'

'Well if for example there was a prominent Palestinian living here, then if Rivka is right, which I don't doubt for a second, then all Madam has to do is take her bottle of VX and paint some on his front door handle. Next time he touches it, he's dead.'

'OK' said a thoughtful Helena. 'I can see how that could happen, but how and why would the blame fall on Israel?'

'That's easy' said Rivka jumping in. 'A couple of days before Madam used it, an anonymous report would be put on the internet and released to news agencies saying a vial of VX had disappeared from Israel's unlawful supply of the nerve agent. It wouldn't be true, particularly as Israel doesn't have any VX, but the world would believe it.'

'So what do we do?' asked George.

'Easy' said Rivka. 'We walk over to her house, let ourselves in and kill her. It's quick, it's clean, and we secure the stock of nerve agents before they can be used.'

'Is killing the answer you have to everything Rivka' asked Sam?

'What do you want to do then Sam, go over there, sit down and have a nice civilised chat about it with her over a nice cup of tea and a biscuit?'

'I'm sorry Sam' said Helena. 'Rivka is right. It is far too dangerous to run even a one percent chance of Madam using those damn nerve agents. I see no alternative, but I'm open to suggestions if you can think of an alternative?' There was a long drawn out silence for a minute or two, and then Sam spoke quietly.

'I'm sorry Rivka, I mean no offence and I respect you and everything you do, but I'm a doctor and my entire existence is all about saving human life. I do understand, but I find it very difficult that you seem to have no problem in taking human life.'

'I don't wake up in the morning thinking

who can I kill today Sam. But life isn't always cups of tea and roses round the door frame. Sometimes you have to do unpleasant things for the greater good, and sadly that often involves killing I'm afraid. But being Israeli that is what I've been brought up with all my life and trained for, and if it needs doing then I won't hesitate. Plus I can guarantee you that if you don't bite the bullet and kill them, then they'll quite happily kill you.'

'I know' said Sam? 'I understand it, but I don't have to like it.'

'Nobody is ever going to ask you to kill anyone Sam' said Helena reassuringly. 'We all know and understand how you feel about the sanctity of life, but please understand, with deadly nerve agents around, we simply cannot risk even a drop of one of them being used. George, Colin' Helena continued 'can the two of you and Rivka please make your way as inconspicuously as possible to the rear entrance of Madam's house, let yourselves in and if at all possible, take her alive and put handcuffs on her, fastened behind her back of course. Take no chances whatsoever with that muck in her kitchen cupboards, and if you have to, and only if there's no other way, then shoot her. Secure the house and all the nerve agents etc and then if possible we'll see what we can get out of her. She obviously has contact details and we need to find them.'

'Anything you want us to do?' asked Willie.

'Yes there is' replied Helena. 'Can you and Michael go to her front door, knock on it and start asking her about a new census being taken of everyone who lives in Mougin. Tell her you're from the Town Council and that you would appreciate ten minutes of her time. Tell her if it's not convenient you can call back tomorrow. It's simply to distract her while George, Colin and Rivka get in through the back. Wear an earpiece, and I'll let you know as soon as the others are inside the house. Take a clipboard with you and look as efficient as you can. Michael, I know you don't speak French, but just back up Willie who's French is excellent. Mutter the odd word, you know, the occasional 'oui' or 'non.'

'Sam, can you be prepared if necessary to use your doctoring skills should the need arise for shots to be fired and anyone gets injured. Hopefully, it won't be necessary, but just in case.'

'Of course' Sam replied.

Willie and I, both wearing small Bluetooth earpieces, left the villa and walked the two minutes to Madam's house. George, Colin and Rivka waited at the back of her house and as Madam came to the front door, George and co went in through the back.

'Ah, good morning madam' said Willie in excellent French. 'My name is Henri DuPont and I work for the town council here in Mougins. This gentleman is my colleague, Claude Leon.'

'Good morning' she replied looking warily at both of us.

'We are conducting a new census of everyone who lives in Mougin, and we would like to … ah, I see my colleagues have arrived' said Willie looking directly over Madam's shoulder.

Madam spun around to see Rivka standing about ten feet from her, holding a revolver in both hands, the business end of which was pointed straight at her forehead. George and Colin were also in the room, both with guns drawn, and Colin was standing in front of the cupboard containing the nerve agents and poisons. The distraction of her turning round was long enough for me to quickly step forward, grab both her wrists and hold them firmly behind her back while Willie pulled a pair of regulation handcuffs from his pocket and put them on her wrists. The whole thing took just four seconds. It was over before it really began. We pushed madam into the house, shutting the front door behind us, and sat her on one of the kitchen chairs.

'Now' began George who was a highly experienced Interpol interrogator, 'you are going to tell us madam, and by us I mean Interpol, what you were going to do with all those bottles, who else is involved, all their contact names and telephone numbers etc, and you will also cooperate in any and every other way we ask. If you should foolishly choose not to help us, then I will have no choice but to hand you over to my colleague here who is with the Israeli Mossad, and she will take the greatest pleasure in ensuring you receive the maximum amount of pain that it is possible for one human being to inflict on another.'

Rivka had now put her gun away, and was fiddling with a nasty looking knife, with a look in her eyes that said 'just let me at her.'

'My colleague enjoys what most people would I'm sure describe as torture, but she calls it fun. I suppose we are all different, but I assure you madam, I can prevent that and you will not be harmed in any way if you cooperate. Please

understand, for you it is all over, but you can make the rest of your life tolerable by helping us. You have nothing to gain by refusing to do so, and absolutely everything to lose.'
Madam had had enough and she was scared witless.

Chapter Twenty Two

Over the next hour or so she answered every question asked of her, and it was amazing just how much she knew. She was approaching seventy years of age and she was not in the best of health. She resisted for all of five minutes, then realized she would only survive by answering all our questions. Helena and Sam came over and joined us, and the real interrogation began in earnest. She gave us contact details and several plans we had no idea about, and probably wouldn't have done until it was too late, but most importantly, she told us who was behind it all, who was running the show and why.
We had thought ever since we'd been asked by Craig Overton to get involved with this, that it was a terrorist operation, probably sponsored by, or even ran by Palestine or Iran, mainly because of Jahangir Ahmadi and Akram Lajani

being the leaders and both being Iranian, but their involvement was not what we'd thought. Madam had disillusioned us of that idea fairly quickly into her confession.

According to her, this was a purely government sponsored and government run operation involving three different countries, and it wasn't the three I would have suspected, which were Iran, Iraq and the leaders of Palestine. In fact the three countries involved turned out to be Yemen, Algeria and Kuwait. The government in Yemen arranged an initial secret meeting with representatives of both the Algerian and Kuwaiti governments over two years ago, and they chose Cairo as the location for their conspiracy as it was seen as a neutral country for all of them. It is no secret that Yemen hates Jews, and Madam made it clear that Algeria felt much the same. Kuwait had come as a massive surprise to me, but then I don't profess to know much about world politics.

'You may be surprised to know Michael that the governments of Israel and Kuwait do not have any form of diplomatic relations whatsoever' said George, who knew far more about international politics than the rest of us.

'Kuwait refuses entry into the country to anyone with a passport issued by Israel, or for that matter shows through visas and stamps in their passports that they've simply travelled to the State of Israel. Also, during wars between various Arab nations and the State of Israel, Kuwaiti forces were more than happy to participate against the State of Israel.'

'I had no idea' I mused.

'Kuwait allegedly boycotts all Israeli products, and in January 2014 Kuwait even boycotted a renewable energy conference in Abu Dhabi as it was attended by Israel.'

'They really do seem to have a problem with Israel' said Jo.

'Back in 2012' continued George 'A German court ruled that Kuwait's national airline didn't have to transport an Israeli citizen because the carrier would face legal repercussions at home if it did. The Frankfurt state court noted in its decision that Kuwait Airways is not allowed to have contracts with Israelis under Kuwaiti law because of the Middle Eastern country's boycott of Israel. The court said it didn't evaluate whether 'this law make sense,' but that the airline risked repercussions that were 'not reasonable' for violating it, such as fines or prison time for employees. An Israeli citizen, who was later identified in court papers as Adar M., a student living in Germany, sued Kuwait Airways after it cancelled his booking for a flight from Frankfurt to Bangkok that included a stop-over in Kuwait City. The cancellation came a few days before M.'s scheduled departure in August 2016 when he revealed he had an Israeli passport. The airline offered to book him on a nonstop flight to Bangkok with another carrier. The man refused the offer and filed the lawsuit, seeking compensation for alleged discrimination. He also insisted the airline should have to accept him as a passenger. The court rejected his discrimination claim ruling that German law covers discrimination based on race, ethnicity or religion, but not nationality. Germany's Central Council of Jews condemned the ruling, calling it 'unbearable that a foreign company operating based on deeply anti-Semitic national laws is allowed to be active in Germany.' Frankfurt's Mayor at the time, Uwe Becker expressed the same view saying 'An airline that practices discrimination and anti-Semitism by refusing to fly Israeli passengers should not be allowed to take off or land in Frankfurt. Becker said. I assume you know all this Rivka?' asked George.

'Of course' she replied. 'This is the sort of thing the people of Israel have to live with every day. There are numerous countries around the world that would be extremely happy if the state of Israel didn't exist, and several, including the three you've mentioned, frequently sponsor terrorist actions against us, but to be honest, we've just got used to it.'

Having got every scrap of information we could from Madam Favreau, all recorded on both video and audio on tape needless to say, we then handed her over to the French authorities, who under the direction of Gilles Cazeneuve, the President of France, took her away without revealing to any of us what they were going to do with her. We sat and chatted for about an hour or so, trying to decide what to do next and where to go, and narrowed it down to a choice of two options. London and Craig Overton or Israel and Moishe Kravitz. In the end it was Rivka that urged us to forget about Moishe as she kept him up to date with everything that was happening anyway. So after much discussion we decided to head to London and take everything we had to Craig Overton. I still didn't particularly warm to the man, but then I guess anyone doing the sort of job he does might be a bit 'unusual', but at least his team had the technology and expertise to unlock all the information contained in Madam Favreau's mobile phone.

As per usual we headed for Biggin Hill, and having locked the Gulfstream safely away in its hanger, we drove to London and parked under the MI5 building alongside the Thames.

'I've always wanted to see this building' said Rivka 'ever since I first saw it in the James Bond films. It's sought of magical.' she muttered quietly to herself.

'Well magical is not a word I'd use to describe Craig Overton' I said 'but then thinking about it, in a way perhaps you're right. Craig always reminds me of Professor Snape at Hogwarts. A little bit creepy with slightly slimy overtones.'

'Don't be so nasty' said Sam telling me off. 'Craig's all right, he's just single minded about his job and so he takes everything very seriously. Whereas you I'm afraid Michael Turner, you don't take anything seriously.'

'Except you my love.' I replied.

'Oh, thank you dear' replied Sam.

'Ugh' squealed Colin 'Will someone get me a bucket to throw up in, you two are far too much in love. Why can't you be like the rest of us and just ignore your emotions?'

'Oh Colin' sighed Sam 'So sad. There must be someone out there that loves you.'

'Well I've not been scorched by the heat of anyone's affections yet' he laughed.

'Attention everyone' commanded George 'Reichsführer Overton approaching.'

'Good afternoon one and all' began Craig smiling broadly at us all 'and welcome to my humble little abode. You are all most welcome.' Craig shook hands with Helena and Sam and then walked towards Rivka and held out his hand 'And you my dear must be the wonderful Miss Rivka Meyer Moishe has been telling me about over these last few years. Every time we speak he sings your praises, and from what I hear you have excelled yourself during this operation as well.'

'Thank you Mr Overton' she replied

'Craig my dear, please, call me Craig.'

'Does that mean we can now all call you Craig?' I asked him.

'Everyone else, yes. You Michael will

address me as Sir or Mr Overton.'
Craig looked sternly at me, and then laughed. 'Please, all call me Craig, even you Michael. Come on all of you, collect your visitor's badges from reception and come upstairs to my office. I'm dying to see and hear what you've got for me and also to get my hands on that Algerian woman's phone. Well, Simpson's hands, which is more or less the same thing.'
We all managed to cram ourselves into the lift and a minute later we all sat round a large conference table that was off to the side of Craig's office.
Helena took the lead and brought Craig up to date, filling in everything that we'd done since we were last in his office, but she never mentioned what we'd found out from Madam Favreau about the countries behind the conspiracy.

'Michael' said Helena now addressing me 'Can you please fill in Craig on what we learnt from the interrogation of Madam Favreau before we handed her over to the French authorities.'

'Of course' I replied and I then recounted the interrogation that George, Rivka and myself had put her through. It's funny how it had worked out, but Helena firmly believed that I somehow knew how to get people to answer my questions, and I always ended up as part of the interrogation team.

'According to Madam as we simply call her, there is a conspiracy to try and bring down Israel, and the conspirators meet regularly in Cairo.'

'We already know that Michael' said Craig, impatient as usual. 'If you remember, it was me that told you that when I first asked you and Sam to get involved. Probably using terrorists and backed by Iran or Iraq.'

'Not according to Madam' I responded. 'Of course we'll need to check all this out, or you will need to I should say, but Madam told us there are three counties involved in the Cairo Conspiracy, and they are Algeria, Kuwait and Yemen.'

'Not Iran or Iraq?' queried Craig. 'Are you sure?'

'No, neither of them, nor surprisingly the Palestinians. As we all know there is no shortage of countries that would like to see the end of Israel, but according to Madam, it was the leaders of Yemen that called the initial meeting of the three counties and they all agreed to equally finance the operation, but not to get involved directly. They recruited Jahangir Ahmadi, handed it over to him and he put the team together.'

'Bastards' muttered Craig under his breath. 'Yemen is a nightmare for everyone in the area, and nobody really knows what the hell goes on there. Algeria is not much better, but I'm surprised at Kuwait's involvement. It's not like them to show their hand over Israel so openly.'

'Well don't forget Craig' I said 'In fact, none of these three countries have shown their hand openly as you put it. We only know about them from what Madam has told us.'

'Yes true' he muttered. 'Sorry Michael, carry on.'

'As we know, Jahangir Ahmadi, a well-known Iranian terrorist was recruited by the Yemeni government and he was put in charge of the operation. He recruited three other front men to work with, Akram Lajani, Youssef Mahrez and Sadiq Rouhani. Later he recruited Khalid Khan in Egypt when they met in the Valley of the Kings, at least that's the assumption I'm making, but he may have recruited him earlier for all we know. He certainly had Sergei Polyakov on board at an early stage as he has been responsible we're sure for various acts of cyber terrorism.'

'Don't forget Craig' said Helena 'there's also people like Mohamed and Ali Shafer doing his dirty work, as well as Madam Favreau in France and that idiot Nigel Collins who was going to blow try and up the Queen during her visit to the Sandringham Fayre.'

'And he would probably have succeeded' said Craig 'if it hadn't been for all of you.' There was a knock on the door, Craig shouted 'Enter' and Roy Simpson came into the room carrying Rouhani's mobile phone.

'I trust you've got some useful information from that mobile Simpson' said Craig.

Before he got a chance to answer Sam jumped in.

'Why can't you call Mr Simpson Roy?' she asked. 'It just sounds so rude.'

'There are 14 Roy's working in this building and it would just get confusing, and this particular Roy is the only Simpson we have. Besides, the service addresses everyone by their surname and I'm afraid it's not going to change Samantha dear, so you'll just have to live with it.'

'But you call me Samantha and not

Turner' she responded.

'Yes, but there's only one of you named Samantha so it's simple. If I said excuse me Turner, which one of you would answer - you or Michael?'

'Leave it Sam' I said 'You're fighting a losing battle.'

'If it's any interest Mrs Turner' said Simpson 'I really don't mind being called by my surname.' said Simpson smiling 'it's the norm here. Anyway, to answer your question Sir, yes, Rouhani's mobile phone had lots of information on it, and the first thing to note was that his instructions always came from Cairo, never Yemen, Algeria or Kuwait.'

'So' mused Craig 'we must assume the main orchestrator of all this nastiness and bloodshed is holed up somewhere in Cairo dishing out his orders, and so I am still going to refer to it as the Cairo Conspiracy. What else have you gleaned from Rouhani's mobile phone?' he asked Simpson.

'Quite a lot actually Sir.'

Chapter Twenty Three

Roy Simpson began by bringing us all up to

date.

'Firstly, we were able to trace all of Rouhani's received calls back to their source, and every one of them came from Cairo.'

'Mohamed and Ali Shafer's house?' I asked.

'No Mr Turner. Every one of them came from the Kuwaiti Embassy.'

'Did they now?' mused Craig. 'I don't suppose we have any idea who made the calls, or is that too much to ask?' he continued.

'As you know sir, we have all the Middle Eastern countries embassy's in Cairo under 24 hour surveillance ever since this 'conspiracy' started, and we were able to cross reference the dates and times of the calls with who was actually on the premises when the calls were made.'

'Surely they didn't use the embassy's land line phones?' queried Sam, 'even I know they can easily be traced and bugged.'

'No Mrs Turner, the calls were all made from a mobile, but we were able to trace it back to a batch of six pay as you go mobiles bought in Cairo by the Kuwaiti embassy about eight months ago. I suspect whoever was making the calls either went out into the embassy's garden to make the calls, or went out onto the roof. The Kuwaiti embassy is like most buildings in Cairo in that it has a flat roof that has been turned into a roof terrace.'

'What about the cross referencing you started to mention?' queried Helena.

'Oh yes, sorry.' said Roy Simpson. 'We checked everyone's movements where we could and worked our way down in order of seniority. The Ambassador wasn't even in Egypt for over half of the calls, and the same was true of the Consul. However, the Cultural Attaché was in the embassy every time a call was made, including the long call you managed to record on the Nile cruiser Mr Turner. Nobody else we could find was present on every occasion.'

'I assume you've checked out this Cultural Attaché chap?' asked Craig.

'Yes we have sir. His name is Faisal Al-Hasawi, he's thirty two years old, and he has been based in Kuwait's Cairo Embassy for nearly nine months. I'm afraid we can't find any trace of him prior to his arrival in Egypt though.'

'Yes, well that in itself is suspicious.' muttered Craig. 'Is there any way we can trace who he is getting his orders from. I can't believe a thirty two year old has put all this together and managed to recruit the world's top terrorists. He must be a conduit.'

'A what' asked Jo?

'A conduit.' replied Craig. 'Like a cable that links electricity to a lamp for example. The cable is a conduit, it's simply a means of getting the power, ie the electricity, to the active bit, the lamp. In our scenario, Al-Hasawi is the conduit, the means of getting the power, ie the bosses instructions to the active bit, Jahangir Ahmadi and co.'

'Oh, I get it. Thank you' replied Jo.

'Well if we could get our hands on Al-Hasawi's mobile phone sir' said Roy Simpson 'and copy everything that's on it, then we could probably trace it back to see who he's getting his instructions from. But I assume that's not going to be very easy?'

'Nigh on bloody impossible' said Martin, who hadn't uttered a word up until this point. 'Breaking into a foreign embassy, particularly an Arab countries embassy is going to get anyone who's caught shot dead, if not worse.'

'What on earth is worse than getting shot dead' queried Sam.

'Oh I can think of lots of things' answered Rivka. 'Getting dragged into a freezing cold underground cellar, being stripped stark naked by a bunch of sex-starved torturers, having your genitalia attached to electric crocodile clips, and then h…'

'Stop!' yelled Sam 'I really didn't want to know.'

'Then you shouldn't have asked' said Rivka smiling at Sam. 'You really are squeamish aren't you Sam?' she asked. 'Surely you must have seen all sorts of horrors when you were a police surgeon?'

'Yes, I did, but they were all dead and that somehow that made it much easier.'

'Well leaving all that aside' interrupted Craig. 'Martin, could you copy Faisal Al-Hasawi's mobile if you had it, and if so, how long would you need it for?'

'Yes I could, and I'd only need it for about three minutes, but I have to say I'm not that keen on committing suicide by breaking into a Middle Eastern counties embassy and having my bits chopped off as punishment.'

'Then don't break in. Walk through the front door.' said Craig smiling.

'Explain please' said Martin, and so Craig did.

Chapter Twenty Four

The following day we all flew to Cairo in the Gulfstream, having left Madam's mobile phone with Roy Simpson. Hopefully by the time we got back, even more secrets would have been revealed. Having landed and cleared customs we all dropped off our luggage at our pre-booked hotel, the Sheraton Cairo Hotel & Casino, which was just a short walk from the Kuwaiti embassy. After a drink to cool down, we all headed for the embassy get a quick look at the outside of it before putting Craig's plan into operation. The embassy is located at 12 Nabil El Wakkad Street, Dokki, Cairo, Egypt and it is a fairly modern, though in my humble opinion, drab looking building of grey tile and green tinted glass. Craig's plan was in essence very simple: Under the pretext of trying to set up a cultural event with the help of the Kuwaiti Cultural Attaché, Faisal Al-Hasawi, we arrange to meet him in his office and then distract him long enough for Martin to grab his mobile off his desk, link it to a matching phone of his own, and then download everything on it. The basic idea was simple, but succeeding was a different matter entirely. Having done a bit of online research on the aforementioned Mr Al-Hasawi, Roy Simpson told us Faisal Al-Hasawi's main hobby seemed to be dating attractive women, preferably non-Arab and white. Craig's suggestion was that Sam and Rivka should be part of the group that went to see him, and that their task was to mainly to distract him and keep him occupied. Martin obviously needed to go in order to copy Al-Hasawi's phone, and Craig suggested I went and did most of the talking as I possessed 'the gift of the gab' as he put it. Ie, I can talk for hours about nothing, and finally Craig suggested Willie should join us as he was used to working with Helena over a radio link. Craig also suggested Helena, George, Colin and Jo went to the embassy a couple of minutes after us to apply for visas to visit Kuwait, so that they were on hand to cause a second distraction should it be needed. Willie would wear a wire microphone linked to an earpiece that Helena could hide under her hair, and she would then know if the second distraction was needed. It all sounded simple when Craig outlined his idea, but now we were here, we decided to go to the café opposite for a coffee and a final chat before entering the lion's den.

The role of a cultural attaché is usually that of a diplomat with the responsibility of promoting the culture of his or her own homeland. Historically, the post has often been filled by writers and artists, which gives them a steady income, and allows them to develop their own creative work, while promoting their own country's culture abroad. However, many countries have also used the role of their cultural attachés for spying in one form or another as cultural attachés are always granted diplomatic status, and they are therefore protected from prosecution as they have diplomatic protection status. Craig was pretty sure that was the real role of Faisal Al-Hasawi, and it would be interesting to see how much Kuwait's Cultural Attaché actually knew about culture in Kuwait.

'So how are you going to start the conversation' asked Martin?

'My idea' I said 'is to suggest a cultural exchange programme of music and dance between the UK, Egypt and Kuwait. We have some of our musicians and dancers put on performances in Egypt and Kuwait, and Kuwait send some of their musicians and dancers to the UK to perform, as well as here in Egypt. The Egyptians do the same. In other words, a three way cultural exchange programme. If it proves necessary Willie here plays a bit of jazz piano and I'm sure both Sam and Rivka can always gyrate a bit in front of Al-Hasawi, certainly enough to distract him anyway.'

'I actually did a bit of dancing in a Tel Aviv night club during my Mossad training' said Rivka. 'It helped pay for keeping a roof over my head, plus one or two little luxuries.'

'Well I can't dance to save my life' said Sam 'although I suppose I can waltz a bit if it becomes really necessary.'

'We don't need you to actually dance' I said 'simply use your feminine charms to distract him while Martin grabs his phone and copies it.'

'In other words' said Rivka 'you want Sam and I to flirt outrageously with him?'

'Exactly' I replied. 'In an ideal world his mobile phone will be sitting on his desk, and one of you could sit on the desk ensuring you are between him and his phone.'

'I've got various phones in my jacket pockets' said Martin. 'To be frank, it's bound to be an iPhone or a Samsung Galaxy, as I can't imagine Kuwait supplying their people with cheap and cheerful phones, but either way, I'll be able to copy whatever's on it. I can whip it off his desk and copy it to one of the matching models in my pocket providing you can two can distract him for at least three minutes.'

'I can distract him for at least three hours if necessary' smiled Rivka.

'I don't doubt it for a second' said George, 'but what do we do if his phone's not sitting on his desk, and it's in his pocket?'

'That's where Helena comes in.' I replied. 'Willie, you need to let Helena know via your wire that his phone is not available to us. Simply say into the mic very quietly one word, something like 'Call' or 'Ring'. On hearing that, Helena will ring his mobile number, he will obviously fish his phone out of his pocket and answer it, Helena apologises for ringing a wrong number, and Rivka then moves in and uses her undoubted charms to ensure his phone is put on the desk, and not back in his pocket. Martin then does his bit, and then once that's done we all leave. Any more questions?'

'What if he's got two phones? One for the legal work stuff as cultural attaché, and one for the terrorism stuff?' asked Jo.

'Dammed good question Jo' answered Martin 'and if that is the case then I think we may have to resort to a break in of his home during the early hours, but let's hope this works and a break in is not necessary.'

'OK' I said. 'If there are no more questions, let's go'.

Sam, Rivka, Martin, Willie and I left the coffee bar, walked across the road and into the reception area of the Kuwaiti Embassy. I had already telephoned a couple of hours earlier and made an appointment to see Mr Faisal Al-Hasawi, so we were expected. Helena and everybody else waited in the coffee bar until we were shown into Al-Hasawi's office, and then they crossed the road and entered the embassy themselves. Al-Hasawi was a well-built young man, quite good looking according to Sam, he had a healthy tan and a dark, neatly trimmed moustache to go with his almost black neat hair.

'Good morning Mr Al-Hasawi' I said, walking forward and offering my hand, which he shook with a reasonably firm grip. 'I'm Peter Savage, we spoke on the telephone earlier, and these are my colleagues William Shulberg, David Franklin, Christine Cooper and the delectable Miss Shona Divine, our principal dancer. These were the names we'd agreed upon

in the coffee bar, and Shona, who we all knew as Rivka stepped forward and kissed Al-Hasawi on both cheeks in the traditional European style. I could tell straight away that Al-Hasawi was pretty besotted with Rivka from the moment he laid eyes on her, and she obviously realized it to and played up to it. We were in luck and Al-Hasawi's mobile phone was laying on his desk, and we spread out around his office sitting in various chairs, apart from Rivka who perched on the corner of his desk, with her legs pointing straight at Al-Hasawi, as she carefully pushed his mobile phone behind her.
Martin picked it up and slid it in his pocket.

'I'm sorry to ask Mr Al-Hasawi, but may I use your toilet please?' asked Martin.

'Of course Mr Franklin, outside, turn left and it's the second door on your right.'

'Thank you' said Martin and he left the room.
Rivka immediately jumped in and took over the conversation.

'Tell me Mr Al-Hasawi' she began

'Oh please, call me Faisal' he said, almost whimpering.

'Why thank you Faisal' she replied leaning in towards him. 'In that case you must call me Shona. Now tell me Faisal, do you get to see a lot of my type of dancing in Kuwait, or is it not popular?'

'Well I don't know exactly what sort of dancing you do Shona.' he answered. 'Can you give me some sort of idea?'

'Of course Faisal.' she replied, and with that she slid off the desk towards him, and spent the next few minutes humming a quite sultry tune while performing what I can only describe as the most erotic and personal lap dance I've ever seen. Faisal Al-Hasawi was totally hooked and the rest of us were totally ignored. After three or four minutes there was a knock on the door and Martin walked back into the room.

'Thank you so much Mr Al-Hasawi, I feel much better now' he said.

Rivka had stopped her dance routine the minute Martin entered the room, and as she perched herself back on the edge of the desk again, Martin took the opportunity to put Al-Hasawi's mobile phone back on the desk behind her.

'Well Mr Al-Hasawi' I said 'Do you think what Shona and the rest of our group has to offer would go down well in Kuwait?'

'I'm sure every man in Kuwait would love to see what you all do, and particularly what Miss Shona has to offer, but I'm afraid every man in the audience watching would probably be arrested. I fear Kuwait is not ready for your particular cultural offerings Mr Savage, but I would of course be more than happy to arrange private viewings if Miss Shona was agreeable?'

'I'm afraid' I responded 'Miss Shona is contracted exclusively to our company Mr Al-Hasawi, and as such she is not allowed to perform her own unique dance style outside of bookings we arrange within the company. So I am afraid we have unwittingly wasted your time.'

'Oh no Mr Savage. That was not a waste of time. In fact, I think I can honestly say I have never had a more enjoyable five minutes in my life, and for that I thank you all.'

We all thanked Al-Hasawi for his time, shook hands and left. Martin had managed to copy everything from Al-Hasawi's phone onto his own duplicate iPhone, but we would not know if we'd got the information we needed until we got back to Roy Simpson's office at MI6 in London, which was our next port of call.

Chapter Twenty Five

Back in London we all went to see Craig Overton at MI6. We did discuss only two or three of us going, but then we'd only have to waste more time telling the others what had happened, and even then we were bound to forget something. So in the end we all went, and Craig didn't seem to mind. The minute we arrived Martin handed Faisal Al-Hasawi's mobile over to Roy Simpson and he scuttled office to his department to see what secrets he could get out of it. He was back within twenty minutes.

'This is a goldmine ladies and gentlemen, an absolute treasure trove of information. We have lots of highly confidential telephone numbers, numerous text conversations that have not been deleted, and what I believe to be absolute proof that this is without doubt State Sponsored Terrorism.'

'Don't beat around the bush Roy, is it any use or not' I asked, laughing.

'I cannot believe' he replied 'that someone would be so stupid as to not delete text conversations relating to international terrorism, or that they would have the personal mobile phone numbers of the terrorism's sponsors on speed dial would you believe?'

'So who is behind all this' asked Helena.

'It's as everyone here thought, an international conspiracy between protagonists from three different countries, but not ordinary terrorists, but between three governments. Algeria, Yemen and Kuwait, and it's Kuwait that appears to be the real driving force behind all this. Would you believe Faisal Al-Hasawi gets his instructions direct from the mobile phone of his own Prime Minister, Sheikh Ahmed Al-Asaad Hashim?'

'You're joking' said Craig in astonishment.

'Well we know it's the Prime Minister's mobile as we've had his phone number on file for the last eight months' said Roy 'but we don't know for sure that it's the Prime Minister using it.'

'Perhaps not' said Craig 'but you only have to look at the Kuwaiti's hatred of all things Israeli to believe it could well be true. And you say it's definitely the leadership of both Algeria and Yemen as well?' queried Craig.

'Looks like it sir' replied Roy. 'As you know, we have had a department downstairs for the last ten months whose sole task is to discover the personal mobile phone numbers of anyone and everyone we think may have something against the UK. We know we're not the favourite country of Yemen, and Algeria doesn't seem to approve of anyone. So we made a point of obtaining the personal mobile numbers of all world leaders wherever possible, and we have had the personal mobile numbers of all three now for eight months. We obviously passed the information onto GCHQ, and they listen in 24/7 for anything suspicious. Reading the received texts from Al-Hasawi's mobile, it would appear that he receives his instructions from Prime Minister Hashim's personal mobile. The messages are all in code of course, but knowing when and where these various terrorist incidents have happened, we can fairly accurately trace them all back to the Kuwaiti Prime Minister's mobile.'

'Anything else of major importance Simpson' asked Craig?

'There are also confirmation texts received by Al-Hasawi after every instruction from Kuwait. These confirmation texts we traced back to Yemen and Algeria.'

'But what do these three counties hope to gain by all this?' asked a bemused Sam.

'I can answer that' said Rivka. 'The total

destruction of the State of Israel, followed by the legal recognition of Palestine which would occupy the same land. Israel would cease to exist. These three countries, and others have all tried over the years to destroy Israel through numerous United Nations proposals, which always fail to get anywhere due to the permanent members having the right of veto, they've tried other peaceful routes, they don't have the armed forces to declare war on Israel, so it looks like this is the latest and most horrendous ploy in order to achieve their end. Palestine would be much easier to deal with than Israel for all three counties.'

'And I assume' said George 'by using terrorists, the counties themselves that actually instigated and pay for all this don't get blamed.'

'Exactly.' said Craig.

'By the way sir' said Roy Simpson. 'We have a lot of similar information from the mobile phone of Madam Favreau. Every phone we have examined seems to tell the same story, but for what is such a well-organized plot in so many ways, they are all so careless about what they keep on their mobiles'.

'Well I don't suppose any of them were expecting you to be examining their mobiles

Roy' said a smiling Helena.

'No Ma'am, I guess not' he replied.

'Moishe needs to be told about all this' said Rivka 'but if you don't mind I would prefer to brief him face to face, and see what he wishes to do about it.'

'I concur' said Helena 'I think we all need to fly to Israel again, meet with Moishe and help in whatever way he wishes. After all, it is his country that is in the most danger.'

'Agreed' said Craig. 'Is Interpol happy to continue and see this through?'

'Of course' replied Helena. 'We gave our word, and Interpol never goes back on a promise to anyone.'

The following morning we all boarded the Gulfstream, and with George at the controls and Colin seated alongside him, we all headed back to Israel and a meeting with Moishe in Herod's Palace on top of Masada. Every time I saw Masada I couldn't help but marvel at this amazing location, a perfect combination of the wonder of nature or God's perfect creation, depending on your personal beliefs, and man's ingenuity in King Herod building a fortress and a three tier palace at the top.

Helena, Sam, Rivka and I all took the cable car to the top of Masada, where like on previous occasions we were met by Israeli armed guards. They escorted the four of us through the no entry signs keeping the public out, and into the top level of the palace, and then we walked down a level to the central section. On seeing Rivka, Moishe walked forward to greet us all, but he started with Rivka giving her a massive bear hug. He then shook hands with all four of us, and then we all sat down round a large wooden table that had been especially brought up to the palace for the meeting.

'It's so good to see you all' he began 'and can I start by thanking you for all for everything you have done. Israel owes you all a massive debt of gratitude. Rivka has been keeping me up to date with regular calls from her cell phone, or mobile as you British prefer to call them, which is totally secure as it's highly encrypted at both ends, and so I know what's been happening. However, what you don't know is what we've been up to while you and your team have all been busy in Europe and Cairo.'

'Tell me Moishe' asked Helena 'Sorry to interrupt your train of thought, but are relations with the Palestinians still OK, or are they back to hostilities?'

'I have to say' replied Moishe 'things between us have never been better. I talk regularly with my Palestinian opposite number, and because we immediately informed them of everything that the terrorists were doing, and what's more refunded every penny that they tried to dump on us, trust between us has grown. I won't say it is great, but it is certainly a vast improvement over a few months ago.'

'Thank you, that's great news. I'm sorry, you were about to tell us something.'

'Yes indeed' began Moshe. 'About two weeks ago, and just by chance during a general sweep of cell phone chatter, we picked up what we believe was a telephone conversation between Jahangir Ahmadi and Sergei Polyakov. If you remember, Ahmadi is the principal organizer on the ground, and he uses Polyakov for any cyber terrorism they have in mind. No names were mentioned in the phone call, but we put both of their voices through VRS, and … '

'Sorry to interrupt Moishe, but what is VRS?' asked Sam.

'Sorry my dear, I get so used to talking in initials, I forget not everyone knows what they stand for. VRS is our Voice Recognition System. Whenever we manage to record a voice we can positively identify, we immediately load it and store it in our VRS system. VRS then analyses that specific recording and picks out all the little things that make a voice unique. That information is then stored for future reference. Anytime we get a recording where the voices are unknown to us, we load the recording into VRS and it searches its memory to see if it has heard the voices before. On this occasion it came back positively identifying Jahangir Ahmadi and Sergei Polyakov.'

'Anything useful come out of it?' I asked.

'Yes Michael, two things. One, they are planning a cyber-attack of some sort to take place in Vatican City, no doubt blaming Israel again and trying to turn all Catholics around the world against us, and …'

'Again, sorry to interrupt, but do we know when and how?' I asked

'No, but from what they were saying, it's not imminent. However, the other thing we picked up on is that they have a base HQ, and a training camp located in the Hoggar Mountains in the central Sahara region of southern Algeria. The mountains cover an area of roughly 212,000 square miles).

'I presume this camp is nowhere near civilization?' asked Helena.

'No, far from it. This particular mountainous region is located about 1,000 miles south of the capital, Algiers, and it's a largely rocky desert about 3,000 feet above sea level.

'So they're unlikely to be disturbed.' Said Sam.

'Exactly' replied Moishe 'or at least, that's what they think. If you are still happy to be involved ….'

'We are.' said Helena jumping in and replying on behalf of us all.

'Then I would like you all to come to Mossad headquarters this evening. Not just the three of you here and Rivka, but your whole team. We intend to fly helicopters to within 50 miles of their camp, and then send up a couple of high altitude drones with cameras. We need to know how many people are in the camp, who they are, what they are doing etc, etc. I have had enough of these relentless attacks and acts of terrorism from this group and I intend to end it once and for all. Once the drones have counted and identified the personnel so we know if anyone is missing, I will be sending in three jets to blow their HQ and their camp of the face of the earth. I would then like your team, along with myself and a team of Israel's elite troops to go in, remove any terrorists that somehow managed to survive, identify the bodies, and you folk will know and recognize them better and quicker than any of us, and then go through everything that's left. Are you OK with all of that. Being present at the end is I feel the least you all deserve.'

'I think the only person that may have a problem is my wife' I said. 'Being a doctor her aim is to protect and preserve life, not extinguish it.'

'Michael's right' said Sam. 'I don't find it easy seeing people killed, but after everything these terrorists have done and are planning on doing, I can understand what you are doing and why, but I would prefer not to watch it, if that's OK.'

'Of course my dear' said Moishe 'Come with everyone this evening, and when the aircraft go in to bomb the place, you can go for a coffee or something until it's all over.'

'Thank you Moishe' said Sam. 'It's not that I am particularly squeamish, it's just that I took a solemn oath to protect life, and I take that oath very seriously.'

'No problem, I completely understand. Now' continued Moishe 'can I suggest you all return to your Gulfstream and fly to Tel Aviv. I have already booked you all into our best hotel there' Moishe leant forward and handed me the booking confirmation for all our rooms, 'and Rivka will come and collect you all around 7.00 pm this evening. Please make sure you all have warm clothes to wear. The desert can be very cold at night.'

We did as Moishe suggested, all shook hands and descended back down in the cable car and were driven back to our aircraft, where Helena brought everyone else up to date, and we then took off for the short flight to Tel Aviv.

Chapter Twenty Six

The single word 'Mossad' has become a very evocative word in the world, and it means many things to many people. In fact the literal translation of Mossad is 'The Institute' which is short for 'HaMossad leModiʿin uleTafkidim Meyuḥadim' which in English means 'The Institute for Intelligence and Special Operations'.

It is one of the three principle units in the Israeli Intelligence Community, along with the Aman, or military intelligence, and Shin Bet, which is responsible for internal security. Mossad is responsible for intelligence collection, covert operations, and counterterrorism. However, in contrast to all other government departments and the military, the goals, structure and powers of Mossad are all exempt from the basic laws of Israel. Its activity is subject to highly secret procedures that have never been published, and its director answers only to the Prime Minister.

The largest department of Mossad is called 'Collections', and it is tasked with many aspects of conducting espionage overseas. Employees in the Collections Department all operate under a variety of covers, including both diplomatic and unofficial roles. The 'Political Action and Liaison Department' is responsible for working with allied foreign intelligence services, as well as those nations that have no normal diplomatic relations with Israel. Mossad also has a 'Research Department', tasked with intelligence production, and a highly specialized 'Technology Department' concerned with the development of tools for Mossad activities.

Mossad was originally formed on December 13, 1949, as the 'Central Institute for Coordination' at the recommendation of Prime Minister David Ben-Gurion to Reuven Shiloah. Ben Gurion wanted a central body to coordinate and improve cooperation between the three existing security services; the army's intelligence department known as 'AMAN', the Internal Security Service known as 'Shin Bet', and the foreign office's 'Political Department'. In March 1951, Mossad was reorganized and made a part of the prime minister's office, reporting directly to, and only to the prime minister. Mossad's former motto was 'be-tachbūlōt ta`aseh lekhā milchāmāh', a quote from the Bible (Proverbs 24:6): 'For by wise guidance you can wage your war', but the motto was later changed to another Proverbs passage: 'be-'éyn tachbūlōt yippol `ām; ū-teshū`āh be-rov yō'éts' (Proverbs 11:14). This is translated by the New Revised Standard Version of the Bible as: 'Where there is no guidance a nation falls, but in an abundance of counsellors there is safety.'

Mossad has two different sized 'units' that do what has described as 'the dirty work' or 'wet work'. These are 'Metsada', a small and highly efficient unit which is responsible for attacking the enemy. 'Metsada' runs small units of combatants whose missions include both assassinations and sabotage. 'Kidon' is a unit belonging to the Caesarea department, which is one of Mossad's eight departments. It has been described as 'an elite group of expert assassins, who operate under Mossad's Caesarea branch of the espionage organization. Not a great deal is known about this mysterious unit, the details of which are some of the most closely guarded secrets in the Israeli intelligence community. What is known is that it recruits from former soldiers from the elite IDF special force units. The 'Kidon' has been a large part of the country's policy of assassinations where it deems it necessary, a policy that Israel has used more than any other nation in the West. Israel has made no secret of its assassination policy, and one named source recently stated that Mossad has carried out at least 2,700 assassination missions on behalf of Israel.

So this was the organization we were about to work with. I must say, having read up on what little is known about Mossad, they scared me a bit in the ruthless way they went about protecting their country, but then no other nation is under the same level of attack that Israel seems to face on a daily basis. Moishe had told us the first thing he was going to do was send in surveillance drones, but to be honest I knew very little about them, so I sat down with Richard, our own resident expert and asked him to give me a guided tour of the world of drones.

'Well for a start, drones is slang' began Richard 'they're officially referred to as UAV's, which stands for Unmanned Aerial Vehicle. They are basically aircraft without a human pilot aboard. UAVs, or drones if you prefer are one of the three basic components of a UAS, or Unmanned Aircraft System which includes a UAV itself, a ground-based human controller, and a system of communications between the two. If you remember you used a similar set up yourself in Mijas when you wanted to get a look at the Simpson's villa.'

'Oh I remember all right' I replied 'but to be honest it was all pretty new to me and I didn't really know what I was doing or how it worked.'

'Well the military use two types of control, either under remote control by a human operator or autonomously by on-board computers. We use them in the police, but the military put them to far greater use than we do, and they use them in all sorts of ways we don't.'

'For example?' I asked.

'UAVs were originally used for missions too considered either too dull, too dirty or too dangerous for humans' said Richard. 'While they originated mostly in various military applications, their use is rapidly expanding to commercial, scientific, recreational, agricultural, and all sorts of other applications, such as policing, peacekeeping, and surveillance, product deliveries, aerial photography, agriculture, smuggling, and now even drone racing. It is now a well-known fact that civilian UAVs now vastly outnumber military UAVs, with estimates of over a million units having being sold annually.'

'So how else are they used by the military?' I queried

'I'll try and keep it simple' he replied. 'UAVs typically fall into one of six categories: Target and decoy operations, which provide ground and aerial gunnery a target that they can simulate as an enemy aircraft or a missile. Reconnaissance, which is basically a means of providing battlefield intelligence, which is what Moishe will be doing tonight. Then there's actual combat, where drones can provide safe attack capability for particularly high-risk missions, logistics, ie; delivering cargo and of course research and development.'

'So who makes these things?' I asked

'Mostly the US, although lots of other countries produce various units, but in my opinion the best all come from the States.'

'How are they powered?' I asked Richard.

'Small UAVs mostly use lithium-polymer batteries, while the much larger vehicles rely on conventional aircraft engines.'

'Is it possible to communicate with them while they're flying' I asked? 'I mean, I know you can control a UAV's movements, but can you change things once you start to get information fed back from the UAV?'

'Oh yes, very easily nowadays. Most UAVs use a radio for remote control and exchange of video and other data. For very long range flights, military UAVs also use satellite receivers as part of satellite navigation systems.'

'Do human beings still play a part' I queried?

'Oh God, yes' replied Richard. 'Ground control is still basically a human being operating a radio transmitter and receiver, along with a smartphone, a tablet or a computer, or any combination.'

'So basically, you have to get this gear from the US or not at all?'

'No, not quite. The global military UAV market is dominated by companies based in the United States and here in Israel. Four of the top five military UAV manufactures are American, and they are General Atomics, Lockheed Martin, Northrop Grumman and Boeing, the other being Chinese. Israeli companies mainly focus on small surveillance UAV systems, however if you calculate market share by the quantity of drones sold, Israel is way out in front with 60.7% of all UAV's sold in the market.'

'Do all countries use the same drones?' I asked.

'No' answered Richard 'for example the German military favours the German-made LUNA drone for their reconnaissance operations. These are small and are usually launched from a box kept on a soldier's utility belt, from which he can control the tiny helicopter from a handheld terminal, which also shows images from its three cameras.

'I never realized these things could be so small and yet do so much.' I said. 'Well all I can

say Richard is a big thank you for my drone education studies.'
As I spoke I glanced at my watch and realized we'd soon need to meet up with Rivka, and head off to Mossad's HQ here in Tel Aviv. Somewhere not many people get to visit.

Chapter Twenty Seven

The exact location of Mossad's HQ is a closely guarded secret, although many people over the years have put forward various suggested locations, all here in Tel Aviv. I had no idea where we were going, and just to make it really easy for us, Moishe had sent a 20 seater coach to pick us all up. We all boarded and took our seats, and just as we were about to leave, what looked like thin metal sheets slowly descended between the two panes of glass on all the coaches double glazed windows. As this was happening, Rivka walked forward and pulled a concertina style door across the front of the coach so that we were now all cocooned inside a large box.

'Just a security precaution' she said 'I hope you understand.'

We all said fine and we headed off. The journey took about fifteen minutes, and then we slowed to a halt and the coach's engine was switched off. With that, the plates inside the windows all ascended and we could see that we were parked in an underground car park.
Moishe was there to meet us and after a few hellos and handshakes, we all followed him up two flights of stairs. We then walked along a passage to a large lift, which we just about all managed to squeeze into. I expected the lift to go up, but instead it descended, quite a long way. The doors opened and we all emerged into a large open hallway.

'Welcome, and I apologise for all the cloak and dagger with the windows on the coach, but we are incredibly strict about our security, and it's not that we don't trust you, it's simply that if you don't know where you are, you can't tell anybody else, even under torture. An awful lot of our operatives don't even know where this place is as even they have to arrive in special security coaches and vans as well.

We are about to enter the operations room' he continued 'and I will explain what is happening on the screens in front of you. Please don't ask questions of my staff as they all have very strict and extremely delicate jobs to do, and they won't appreciate being put off. We will watch the surveillance footage live as it comes in, and then decide the next step. Is everyone OK and happy?' he asked, and we all either nodded or muttered something positive.

Walking into the operations room reminded me a bit of when I visited Mission Control at NASA's Cape Canaveral in Florida. There were about thirty people in the room, what seemed an equal mix of men and women, and every one of them sat in front of a PC type computer. There was a massive cinema type screen stretching across the wall in front of us, with ten really large TV monitors stretched out across the front underneath the screen.

The cinema screen was showing a map of Algeria with a red spot of light pinpointing the exact location of the terrorist camp. In the top right hand corner of the screen was a flashing green light, which Moishe informed us was the location of the surveillance drone. It was slowly heading towards the red light.

'The drone is travelling at a speed of 280 miles per hour at a height of 35,000 feet. There are no commercial flights in this area of Algeria, so the risk of running into something else at this height is incredibly remote. The drone is quite large, but it is what I guess in layman's terms you'd call a 'stealth drone'. In other words, it does not give off a signal to any radar that might be watching. Once the drone gets closer it will descend to 5,000 feet where we will receive crystal clear images. The on board computers will track every individual it sees and count them. Once it spots someone, it continues to track them to ensure the same person is not counted twice. The screen in front of you will then split into three parts. One will show the normal image, but bear in mind it is now early evening in Algeria and the natural light will fade in about an hour. The second section of the screen will show the same image but in infra-red, and the third section of the screen will show heat imaging.

Once we have a count, the cameras will start to zoom in, and the images they will see and show us will be fed into our facial imaging computers, and the software will hopefully be able to identify some of the terrorists, although we have no idea if any of the big names Michael and Sam met in Egypt are in the camp this evening. Any questions so far?'

'I have one' said Sam 'How does the

drone know where to go and what to do?'

'Ah, OK, good question Mrs Turner' replied Moishe. 'You see that gentleman in the maroon shirt over there, well he programmed the satnav location of the terrorist's camp into the drone before it took off from here about three hours ago. When it gets to about one hundred miles from the camp, the drone will send a message to him which will beep and appear on his computer monitor, and he will then switch off the automatic flight mode on the drone and take over manual control. He has two monitors in front of him, the left one shows him where on the map the drone is, and that's the image you can all see on the large cinema type screen in front of you, and the second monitor is showing him the view from the drone's forward facing camera. Ie, the pilot's eye view.'

'I see, thank you Moishe, this is fascinating and so clever.'

'Yes it is, and please don't ask me how it all works. I know how to use the technology, but I have no idea what makes it all function. We have specialist technicians for all that.'

'Will we really be able to see people's faces from a TV camera 5,000 feet away and travelling at 280 miles an hour?' asked Jo.

'We can even zoom in on someone's chin and tell whether he shaved this morning' laughed Moishe answering Jo's question. 'Satellite technology started all this with the United States 'Corona' program back in 1959. The Corona program was a series of American strategic reconnaissance satellites produced and operated by the Central Intelligence Agency Directorate of Science & Technology with substantial assistance from the U.S. Air Force. The Corona satellites were used for photographic surveillance of the Soviet Union, the People's Republic of China, and other areas beginning in June 1959 and ending in May 1972, but the US, the UK, Germany, France, Russia, China etc have all come so much further over the years. To be honest, I think most people would be horrified to know just how much we can watch people if we so wish. I'm afraid there are no great secrets left in the world, and very few places people can hide. We now have the technology to watch and listen, and Mossad is not afraid to use it to protect our people.'
At that point there was a loud beep from the computer monitor in front of the maroon shirted man, and Moishe said.

'The drone is now only a hundred

miles away and is rapidly dropping to 5,000 feet as it was programmed to do. The automatic tracking and routing will remain in place and operational until we actually arrive over the camp. At that point, my colleague over there will take full control and put the drone into an orbit mode. The cameras will all adjust themselves automatically and start the count. Once the count is complete the software in the drone's on board computer will tell it to zoom in on different faces, capture the image and then feed it back to us for input into the FRS.'

'Sorry Moishe' said George 'I've forgotten, what's FRS?'

'Facial Recognition System' he replied. 'With any luck it should tell us if any of the big five are in the camp. The FRS has the photographs of Jahangir Ahmadi, Akram Lajani, Youssef Mahrez, Khalid Khan and Sergei Polyakov all loaded, and its first programmed task is to find them if they are there. We've also loaded the faces of every other known terrorist as there may be people there we have no idea about.'

'How long now roughly?' I asked

'Another ten minutes' answered Moishe 'and then we should start getting the

count through. It will appear in the bottom right hand corner of the wall screen.'
The next ten minutes seemed to drag by, but sure enough after eleven minutes the edge of the camp came into view. The picture we were watching slowly rotated anticlockwise as the drone orbited around the edge of the camp, and then numbers started appearing in the bottom right hand corner just as Moishe had predicted.

'God, there's a dam sight more people there than I anticipated' commented Moishe. 'I expected about 50 or 60 at most, but we're already up to 128 and still rising.'
The counter eventually stopped at 187 and it was interesting to look down on the activity in the camp.

'How come they can't hear the drone or see it?' asked Willie.

'Well for a start' replied Moishe 'they are making one hell of a lot of noise themselves. Look, there's about 15 or 16 of them down there in the bottom left hand corner' he said pointing at the screen. They're all busy firing machine guns at targets, and with that noise they wouldn't hear tanks arriving. But even if they were all quiet, they still wouldn't hear us. When we dropped to 5,000 feet we turned off the more powerful jet engines we used to get the drone to the location, and switched over to the silent on-board electric motors. You can barely hear them when you're standing next to them, never mind being 5,000 feet away.'

'And the visibility?' queried Colin.

'Matt paint and non-reflective surfaces' replied Moishe 'No, they have no idea we're watching them. OK team, let's see who is who. Activate zoom search please.'

As we stood there watching, the camera view suddenly zoomed in until two faces, side by side, were big enough to fill the giant wall screen. It was just like being at the cinema. The faces swept across the screen as the drone took still pictures of each face, fed them into the FRS and then moved on photographing more. This went on for several minutes, and then a woman's voice in front of us turned round in her chair and said to Moishe.

'Got one sir, Sergei Polyakov is sitting outside what I assume is the canteen drinking a cold beer.'

'Oh excellent news. Keep searching.'

'Sorry' I asked 'but how do you know it's a cold beer and not a warm beer?'

'Show him Rachel.' laughed Moishe.

'This is the picture I have on my other screen' she said, and as she spoke, the massive picture on the wall screen changed to that of a man's hand holding a bottle of Heineken beer with very obvious cold condensation running down the outside of the bottle. 'Does that look cold to you sir?' she queried looking at me.

'I bow to your superior knowledge and wisdom' I replied bowing to her.

Moishe just laughed and the screen changed back to the search of faces.

Rachel called out again.

'Got two more sir. The Shafer brothers from Cairo, Mohamed and Ali.'

'Wonderful' said Moishe 'This day just gets better and better. Now if only the ring leaders were here.' he said to himself.

The search went on for another ten minutes and then a shout from Rachel again.

'They're all here sir, Ahmadi, Lajani, Mahrez and Khalid Khan have all just emerged from that big hut with the green metal roof. They're all walking over towards the machine gun target practice area.'

'Excellent. Captain Kravitz, get Colonel Jakub on the phone for me please.'

Ten seconds late the red phone next to Moishe rang. He picked it up.

'Colonel Jakub, please leave now. The coordinates you were given earlier. Please, wipe the camp, and everyone in it off the face of the earth.'

He listened for a moment, and then said 'Thank you Colonel' and then Moishe replaced the receiver.

'Colonel Jakub is leading a flight of three fast bombers, who will be over the terrorist's camp in approximately forty minutes. They will then proceed to drop twelve small, but incredibly effective bombs on the camp. It should neutralize everyone there, and enable us to go in and examine what and who, if anyone, is left. Sam, if you don't want to watch what's about to happen at the camp, can I suggest that in about thirty minutes you and one of my colleagues head off to the canteen for half an hour. We will then join you when it is all over, and then we'll all fly down to the camp together to pick over the bones and see if we can find anything useful.'

'Thank you Moishe, I'll do that if you don't mind.' Said Sam

'Problem sir' yelled Rachel. 'Our four terrorist leaders have just got in a Toyota Land Cruiser, and if you follow the track it's on, I'm afraid it leads to a helicopter pad we hadn't noticed earlier. It looks like a Sikorsky S-76 is waiting for them sir.'

'Damn them. OK, Sam, forget about the canteen, you're coming with us and we're all leaving, right now. Rachel, contact Colonel Jakub and inform him I am going after the terrorists leaders with the Interpol people, and then get the drone to follow the Sikorsky. Keep me informed as to its movements. Helena, can we please use your Gulfstream to get to the area?'

'Of course Moishe, but it's basically a civilian jet, we have no weapons.'

'Oh I know that, I just need an aircraft to get me to the area as fast as possible, and yours is the nearest, plus it's faster than my personal transport. Once we're in the air I can liaise with a military flight I'm about to organize.'

Moishe turned back to the rows of computers.

'Rachel, get Colonel Jakub on the phone again and get him to order a couple of F15E fighters to go after that Sikorsky, and also ask him to get a fully armed Apache down there as well. I want that Sikorsky back on the ground, and preferably in one piece. The F15's can force him down and if they won't cooperate and it proves necessary they can shoot him down. Tell him to get all three to head for wherever the

Sikorsky is headed. Come on' he commanded to the rest of us. 'Let's go chase some terrorists.'

Chapter Twenty Eight

Once we were in the air, Moishe used the Gulfstream's sophisticated communications set up to talk with Rachel again. Back in Tel Aviv, she'd already spoken to Colonel Jakub who had two F15E's already en route towards the Sikorsky. Colonel Jakub had tasked two F15E's that were on joint exercises with the Italian Air Force taking place just outside Naples in southern Italy, and these were the nearest aircraft to Algeria. He ordered them to leave the exercises immediately and relocate to wherever Rachel directed them to go. With a top speed of well over 1,600 miles per hour and a distance of only 650 miles to Algiers, it wouldn't take them long to get to the intercept area, providing of course the team back in Tel Aviv were able to track the terrorist's helicopter wherever it went.

'The Gulfstream is very fast for a civilian plane Moishe' said Helena 'but I'm afraid it's no match for your F15 fighter jets. It will all probably be over long before we get anywhere near the scene.'

'I doubt it' he replied 'I want those

bastards alive, and the pilots have been given strict instructions to tail the Sikorsky wherever it's going and if possible try to force him down, but that's not easy with fighter aircraft. If our Apache helicopter arrives on the scene then that's a whole different ball game, but it travels at a quarter of the speed of the F15's, and I doubt if it will arrive in time to be of much use, but I have to try.'

'Do you really think the terrorist's will come quietly and surrender if they're forced down?' I asked. 'Surely they'll realise that the F15's aren't prepared to shoot them down, in which case they can just head for the nearest town, land the helicopter and disappear in the crowds.'

'Thank God you're on my side Michael and not there's' said Moishe. 'Let's hope that in their panic they don't come to the same conclusions as you, because if they do we could easily lose them. But anyway, it will take them quite a while to get to civilization. Their camp was located in one of the most remote areas on the planet, and at the speed the Sikorsky travels our F15's should reach them long before they reach any towns.'

'Do we know where they're headed?' asked Jo as she was handing out mugs of hot coffee to everyone.

'No, but Rachel may have an idea by now.' answered Moishe. He called her up on the Gulfstream's radio, and their conversation came through loud and clear on the aircraft's speakers.

'Do we have any idea where they're headed for yet Rachel' Moishe asked.

'Not really sir. They're heading North East, in the general direction of Greece, but goodness knows why or where exactly. They are flying at about 5,000 feet and at that altitude and current speed the F15's should locate them visually in about 20 minutes.'

'Do they have them on radar yet?' asked Moishe.

'Oh yes sir. They locked on about 15 minutes ago. There's no way they will lose them, but the pilots are not sure what they can do to force them to land if they can't actually shoot them down.'

'Get them to fire a couple of warning shots across the Sikorsky's bows, so to speak. That might make them think twice and force them down. How's the Apache doing?'

'Making good progress sir. Fortunately, because the Sikorsky is heading in the general direction of North East and therefore towards our helicopter, the Apache is heading at top speed straight across the Mediterranean, and should link up with the Sikorsky a lot quicker than we originally thought.'

'OK Rachel, thanks. Please keep me informed of any developments.'

'Yes sir' she replied, and the connection was broken.

'So where are we heading for sir?' asked Rivka.

'Wherever that damned Sikorsky goes.' he replied, lost in thought.

Very little happened aboard the Gulfstream for the next fifteen minutes. George and Colin were in the cockpit, with Colin doing the flying at George's request. He'd decided Colin was better at any quick flight manoeuvres should they prove necessary, so he'd happily taken the co-pilot's seat. Helena and Richard were sitting together in a pair of seats facing Willie and Jo who were sitting in the pair opposite them. Sam and I sat behind them with Martin and Rivka facing us. Moishe was on his own in the office area in the rear of the Gulfstream. The radio came to life and Rachel was on the other end of the call.

'The F15's have just got visibility on the Sikorsky sir and are asking for updated instructions. They are currently flying at 20,000 feet and have dropped speed drastically to match that of the Sikorsky. What should I tell them to do or should I patch the lead pilot, Captain Berman through to you sir?'

'Good idea Rachel, patch him through, but stay on the link and listen in.'

'Patching through now sir. You are connected.'

'Good evening Captain Berman, I am Moishe Kravitz, Mossad's Director of Operations and I need that Sikorsky on the ground as soon as possible, preferably with everyone on board in one piece.'

'Understood sir. We can fly alongside the Sikorsky, one either side and flag him down, and if that doesn't work we can fire warning shots, but if he just ignores us sir and continues flying, there's very little we can do other than shoot him down.'

'I wish to avoid that if at all possible. Are they aware of your presence yet Captain?'

'It very much depends on what electronic equipment they've got on board sir. Their radar may well have picked us up, particularly now we have slowed to match their speed, but we are still 15,000 feet above them, and roughly 500 feet behind them, so there is no way they can visually see us.'

'Captain, there is an Apache heading your way and I think at this stage it might be best simply to continue doing what you are doing and tail them from above and behind. I too am on my way and once we have everyone in place we will re-evaluate the situation.'

'Understood sir, we'll continue to match whatever they do. Thank you sir'

'Thank you Captain.'

Moishe broke the connection with Captain Berman, and spoke to Rachel.

'Rachel, now the F15's are tailing the Sikorsky, send the drone back to the terrorist's campsite and patch the pictures through to the Gulfstream so that I can see for myself what's happening down there. Major Deichman is heading to the camp with a Sayeret company of 120 specialist troops to mop up anyone left, but I'd like to see the latest pictures as soon as the drone is back in position.'

'Yes Sir, will do.'

Moishe could see the confusion on our faces and he knew we had lots of questions, such as what are Sayeret's, who is Major Deichman, how did they get there so quickly etc.

'As soon as we became aware of the terrorist's camp in the Hoggar Mountains' he began 'I ordered a Sayeret unit to head out there on a Hercules transport, from which they free fall parachuted into the surrounding hills. They then headed off on foot to the camp. Sayeret's are our Special Forces units in the Israeli Defense Force, and there is a very broad range of specialist units within the Sayeret's. Most of the units are usually a company or battalion size in strength. Sayeret units originally started as reconnaissance units in the Israeli Defense Forces, and as far as the general public are concerned that's what they still are. However, in reality they specialize in various other tasks including a lot of intelligence gathering and surveillance. Most of these units also specialize in commando and various other Special Forces roles, in addition to their reconnaissance duties. They are the ideal force to clean up what's left of the camp, and they should be arriving there within the next 20 minutes.'

'So if I've got this right' I tried to summarize 'there are 120 special forces troops about to arrive at the terrorist's camp, which you have already blasted out of existence, and the four leaders of the terrorists are being shadowed by two F15's and are about to run into a fully armed Apache attack helicopter.'

'That's about right Michael'. Moishe

responded 'I want to get these bastards alive if possible and get them to confirm that they are doing all this at the behest of three separate governments. Terrorism against anyone is bad enough, but state sponsored terrorism against an entire nation is beyond the pale as far as I'm concerned, and I want the rest of the world to know what Kuwait, Algeria and Yemen are up to, and how the terrorists they've employed are quite prepared to use the innocent people of God knows how many different countries to fulfil their desire to destroy Israel.'

'Every Israeli in the world is tasked with defending their country' said Rivka 'and we are all extremely proud to do so. We know a lot of countries around the world can't stand Israel and disapprove of what we stand for, but we all fervently believe we have the right not only to exist, but to defend ourselves through whatever means is necessary. I'm sorry, I try not to get political, but on this subject I can't help it.'

'Aren't you glad she's on your side Moishe?' I asked jokingly.

'You laugh Michael, but Rivka is the personification of everything Israel stands for. Personally I have nothing against the Palestinians, the Arabs, the North Africans, any other nation, and I would be quite happy to live in peace with all other nations, but I'm afraid that is not the view of so many other counties who are trying to destroy Israel and everything we stand for. I can't let that happen, so we do what we have to do.'

'I completely understand' I meekly replied, not knowing what else to say.

Chapter Twenty Nine

Forty five minutes later we were approaching the same deserted area of the Sahara that the Sikorsky was currently flying over, when Captain Berman, the lead F15 pilot suddenly came over the radio.

'Sorry Sir, but the Sikorsky has just spotted us. We are approaching the outskirts of the city of Ghardaïa, and it looks like the Sikorsky is going to land.'

'Damn' said Moishe 'I wouldn't mind betting the terrorists are going to ditch the helicopter and lose us as they hide themselves in the city. What do we know about Ghardaïa?' Moishe asked nobody in particular.

'I've just Google it Sir' replied Rivka. 'It says Ghardaïa is located in northern-central Algeria in the Sahara Desert and it lies along the left bank of the Wadi Mzab valley. Ghardaïa is part of a something called a pentapolis, which is a posh word for a hilltop city amongst four others, all of which were built almost a thousand years ago. It was founded by the Mozabites, a Muslim Ibadi sect of non-Arabic Muslims, including the Berbers. Apparently it is a major centre of date production and they also manufacture rugs and cloths. The city is divided into three walled sectors, and it is a fortified town. It has a population of just under 100,000. That's it I'm afraid Sir.'

'Um' muttered Moishe. 'Not a massive city, but being fortified it's certainly going to have walls and tunnels and it is certainly big enough to hide from us. Can you shoot them down captain without killing them all?' Moishe asked.'

'The problem now sir is that they're very close to the edge of the city, and if I try and shoot and shoot them down now we'll probably end up killing innocent civilians as well. However sir, the apache has just arrived on the scene and he can do a much better job of surveillance on them than me. As you know sir, F15's are not known for their hovering skills.'

'Quite so Captain.' said Moishe 'Well thank you for shadowing them, and keeping me up to date. Are you still on the line Rachel?'

'Yes Sir' she replied.

'Can you patch me through to the Apache, and what's the pilot's name?' he asked.

'It's Captain Keppler sir. Patching you through now.'

'Good afternoon Captain Keppler. I do believe we've met before. I am Moishe Kravitz, Mossad's Director of Operations.'

'Yes sir, I recognize your voice. We met about six months ago at a military conference in Tel Aviv.'

'Yes, I remember now' mused Moishe. 'You were demonstrating the new advances on the Apache helicopters we'd just acquired. Tell me Captain, how are those new bits of technology working? Can you see what is happening with the Sikorsky, and more importantly what is happening with its passengers?'

'I've only just this moment arrived sir, but it seems the Sikorsky has just landed and its passengers, six of them as far as I could tell, have run through the main gate and into the city where they appear to have split up. I am hovering above the city, but once they'd dived into various buildings I had no way of tracking them. I tried heat imaging, but there are thousands of people in Ghardaïa and the terrorists could be anywhere now. I'm afraid we just got here too late sir.'

'Well thank you Captain. There's no point in us or you hanging around here. We'll never find them now. Please head back to base Captain and thank you. Time I'm afraid was just not on our side.'

Moishe turned to Helena.

'The same applies to us I'm afraid. Once they made it through the city gates we'd lost them. Can we please head back to Tel Aviv, and on the way we can think about what the hell we do next? Damn and blast' he exclaimed 'We were so close.'

Chapter Twenty Nine

Nothing much happened for the next few days. We booked into a hotel in Tel Aviv, but everything had gone very quiet, there was no sign of any of the terrorists, and to put it bluntly, we were stuck with no ideas. It was eventually decided we should all head back to London and talk to MI5, meaning a meeting with Craig.

We flew back and left the Gulfstream in its usual hanger at Biggin Hill and drove to London. Rivka was still with us as Moishe had decided she could best be of use staying with us than staying in Israel with him. The day after arriving back in the UK we were about to head to the MI5 building alongside the Thames when Helena received a phone call on her mobile. She listened intently to the caller and then simply said.

'Of course. We're on our way.'

She turned to face us all and said

'Forget MI5, that was the Prime Minister's office and we've been summoned to Ten Downing Street. Something has happened, I don't know what, but Charles Fisher wants to see us all straight away.'

'Does that include me?' asked Rivka.

'Yes, all of us.' replied Helena. Craig is also on his way and will meet us there.'

We arrived in Downing Street ten minutes later and were all shown into the Terracotta Room, which now had about fifteen or sixteen armchairs formed into a rough circle with half a dozen small coffee tables located in the centre of the room. Apart from ourselves, there was nobody else present. We were asked to sit and make ourselves comfortable and in response to a question from Jo, the lady who showed us in replied that the Prime Minister would sit on the sofa nearest the fireplace, and that he would join us soon. About three minutes after we had all sat down, the door opened again and Craig Overton entered the room.

'Ah, hello Craig' said Sam 'Have you got any idea what's going on and why we've all been asked to come here?'

'Hi everyone' muttered Craig looking around at us all and nodding to people as he did so. 'Sorry Sam, but I have no more information than any you.'

Just as he finished speaking, the other door at the far end of the room opened and three people entered; Charles Fisher; the Prime Minister, James Conway ; the Foreign Secretary and Mary Connelly ; the Home Secretary. All three of them sat in their chairs and joined us in the circle.

'Firstly' began Charles Fisher 'Thank you all for coming so quickly, and thank you for what you have already done for this country, and for our friends in other countries.'

He cleared his throat and continued. 'About ninety minutes ago, all electrical power in all government buildings in Whitehall including both the Foreign Office and the Home Office was shut down for a period of exactly twenty minutes. At the same time as this was happening a message came through to the security people in this building claiming that it was the work of 'The Cairo Conspiracy.'

'They actually used those exact words

Prime Minister; The Cairo Conspiracy?' asked Helena in shocked tones.

'Yes they did, and apart from anything else what worries me the most is that using those precise words can only mean one thing; they have a mole somewhere.'

'Have any of you used the term 'The Cairo Conspiracy' to anyone outside of the group of people in this room?' asked Mary Connelly.

We all looked blankly at each other as everyone shook their heads.

'Carrying on' said Charles Fisher 'along with the message claiming responsibility for cutting of the power came a threat. They have given the British government seventy two hours to hand over the people involved in tracking them down, in other words all of you, or they say they will shut down all of London's electrical power for a week.

'Two things' said James Conway. 'Firstly, we protect our people, which obviously includes all of you and we would never hand you over to anyone, whatever the threat. Secondly, the UK does not submit to or give in to any form of blackmail, and thirdly, we do not believe they are actually capable of doing what they claim.'

'What about the twenty minute power cut

they have already done' asked Helena?

'Firstly' continued the Foreign Secretary 'we were totally unprepared for that as it came out of the blue so to speak, and secondly, now we know about their threat we can guard against it.'

'Can I ask Prime Minister?' I began 'Have they named the people they want handed over, and have they said when and where this should take place?'

'Yes, that's another very worrying aspect of this. They have listed by name every one of you here now, including you Rivka, which is why we requested your presence. As I say, they have named all of you, and stated that you will all be killed for interfering in what they claim is their legitimate fight against as they put it 'the scourge that is Israel.'
Your 'executions' as they refer to them are apparently due to take place in Egypt at an exact location and time to be notified to me in twenty four hours' time.'

'How did you receive this threat Prime Minister?' asked Craig.

'A pre-recorded taped message via a phone call direct to the phone on my desk here in number ten.' He answered.

'They have totally infiltrated the workings

of the government' said Mary Connelly.

'The first thing we need to do is find the mole' stated Craig. 'We need to work on that first, and fast.'

'Any ideas Craig?' asked Helena.

'Yes, replied Craig, 'but let me check out a few things before I say anything. I suggest we all move to a secure government safe house immediately, and stay there until this is all over, or we feel it is safe to leave. Prime Minister, is Unit Seven being used at the moment?'

'No it's not Craig. An excellent idea. You should all go there immediately and work from there as your base. I'll notify them that you are on the way.'

'Please don't Prime Minister. No telephone line is completely safe, particularly at the moment. I will arrange everything and keep you informed. I'm very sorry to ask this, but can you three politicians please only discuss this in the basement secure room here in number ten, and please put nothing in writing.'

'Of course Craig' replied Charles Fisher. 'I promise you all, you could not wish for anyone better to protect your lives. We will be in touch should anything happen or there are any new developments.'

'Can I please have a copy of the pre-

recorded message to take with me? asked Craig 'and can all communication from this moment on be under protocol 3B.'
Mary Connelly leaned forward and handed Craig a memory stick.

'Of course' she said smiling. 'I'd already assumed you would want this'.

'Good luck to you all' said Charles Fisher turning his back on us as he headed for the door.
We all stood as the three politicians left the room, with Craig escorting them to the door. He started speaking to us all as he returned to his seat, while at Craig's bidding we all retook our seats.

Chapter Thirty

'OK' Craig began 'Like it not, from now on I'm afraid you all have to do exactly as I say, and I'm sorry my dear, but that includes you Rivka.'

'No problem' she smiled 'I love to be dominated by a man.'
Craig went bright red with embarrassment and didn't know quite what to say in reply. He eventually managed:

'Excellent. Well this is the plan.'
Craig flopped down into his armchair, pulled out and filled his pipe with tobacco, lit it and

then filled us in on his thoughts.

'As you know, I asked the Prime Minister if Unit Seven was available. For obvious reasons it is not common knowledge, but in fact the government, MI5 and MI6 all share a total of twenty three 'safe houses' located in different parts of the UK. They are all simply known as 'Units', and their locations are kept as secret as possible. They are numbered one to twelve and fourteen to twenty four. It was decided back in the 1970's not to have a Unit Thirteen as too many people felt it was not wise to use what is regarded an unlucky number for a safe house. Unit Seven is in fact the most secure of all the 'Units' and it is located in Kent, giving easy access to London and the coastal ports. To all appearances it is simply a large twelve bedroom eighteenth century manor house, but underneath the main building is a secure two level basement filled with the latest technology, and in the event of war, it is where the Prime Minister of the day would run the country from if it proved necessary.'

'So we are all going to be living in an underground basement until this is all over?' asked Sam. 'I hate being underground, which is why I prefer London buses to the tube.'

'My dear' replied Craig 'Fret ye not! You

and your beloved here' he said pointing at me 'will be staying in the manor house itself, as will you all. The grounds are safer than the SAS base in Hereford, and the security at the house is in fact supplied by the SAS. The basement is used for safe communications with the outside world and discussions we may need to have regarding the task we are currently engaged in. By the way, Rivka my dear, you can communicate with Moishe anytime in complete electronic safety from the secure rooms, as I have done on many occasions in the past.'

'Will we need to be flying the Gulfstream to wherever this 'Unit Seven' is located' asked George?

'No' answered Craig. 'The jet stays where it is until it's needed. It is a bit of a giveaway and not the easiest form or transport to try and hide. I've already sent a unit of protection officers to Biggin Hill to keep an eye on it. We'll all be travelling in closed armoured vans straight from here, although to the outside world they'll simple look like simple tradesmen's vehicles.'

'When do we leave, and do we need to pack anything?' asked Helena.

'I'll arrange for my people to clear your hotel rooms' replied Craig 'collect your bags, including those on the Gulfstream and then

bring everything to Unit Seven. As for when do we leave? Well that would be right now.'
Craig stood up, and like good little sheep - we all did the same.

We descended back down two flights of stairs in Number Ten, and then Craig guided us through several perfectly ordinary looking wooden doors and we suddenly found ourselves in an extremely long tunnel. The light tan colored brick lined tunnel was easily wide enough for three people to walk side by side, and it was very well lit by lights running down the centre of the tunnel's roof

'I had no idea there were any tunnels under Number Ten'. I said to Craig.

'Most people have no idea they exist' he replied. 'Even most of the staff working here don't know about them, and if you were to ask anyone it would simply be denied. They were built during the Second World War on the orders of Churchill who wanted simple and direct 24 hour access to the Cabinet War Rooms and bunkers. The tunnels are all bomb proof, and they also provide a secret exit from Downing Street if the Prime Minister wants to leave the building without anyone knowing. Located at the end of this particular tunnel, of which there are seven in total, is a large underground car park where the vehicles for our journey have already been brought.'

'Where exactly are we going' I asked?

'Er, sorry Michael, but if I told you I'd have to kill you.' he laughed. 'No, seriously, as I said earlier, Unit Seven is in fact a rather nice Manor House, which is located in North Kent, the nearest town being Dartford. It sits in several hundred acres of very secure grounds, all patrolled by the army 24 hours a day, and the entire security operation at the property is supervised by the SAS. There isn't a safer property in the UK.'

Helena had by this time speeded up and joined us, She asked Craig

'Do you think we will be in Unit Seven for long. I'm usually the hunter, and I have to say, I'm not used to being the hunted.'

'Oh, er, well I shouldn't think we'll be there more than two or three days. We have literally thousands of people tracing the terrorists as we speak, and the minute we know exactly where they are we will all become the hunters again.'

We suddenly arrived at a door in the tunnel wall, and Craig pulled it open for us all to walk inside. There were five different closed vans parked inside, each with a driver. One was a bright green colored florist's van, one was a grey coloured builders van, one belonged to British Telecom, the UK's main telephone provider, one was a tatty looking white van proclaiming on the side it belonged to a heating and ventilation company, and the last van into which Craig, Helena and I climbed apparently belonged to the Post Office.

'So who owns all the vans' I asked Craig?

'I do' he answered. 'Well er not me personally you understand, but they are all owned by MI5. As you can see they are very all built to the same standard and are extremely comfortable and very well equipped inside. The roof, all the side panels and the floor of each vehicle is Kevlar lined, and the windscreens are all triple glazed and bullet proof. The tyres are all self-inflating and to be honest I don't think there are safer vehicles in the country. A bazooka shell might scratch the paintwork, but that's about it. By the way, all the drivers are SAS.'

'Are we travelling down in convoy' asked Helena?

'No' replied Craig. 'Five different routes, all vehicles leaving the car park at different times and from two different exits.'

'You said earlier Craig' Helena continued 'that you had an idea who you thought or suspected the mole might be. Tell me honestly, do you suspect one of us?'

'Good heavens no.' he replied, then paused. 'I've always thought Michael here was a bit suspicious, he's always far too happy for my liking, but I've got used to him now.'

'Gee, Thanks Craig' I responded as both he and Helena laughed.

'No' he continued smiling 'I'm afraid I suspect one of my own people. In fact it's someone you've all met - Roy Simpson. He's been very down the last couple of weeks and from what I've discovered it wouldn't surprise me if the terrorists have threatened his family and Simpson is feeding them information under extreme duress. I sent one of my female operatives to have a word with his wife, but a neighbour said she and the two children left home with two men she'd never seen before last Tuesday.'

'So what are you going to do about it' Helena asked?'

'I've had Simpson brought down to Unit Seven and I'll talk to him there. I don't want to be right, but I suspect I am. Something similar happened to an operative just over three years ago, when the partner of a Russian spy we were investigating kidnapped our interrogators wife and threatened to kill her unless he said the Russian was innocent.'

'What happened' I asked?'

'All my people are warned about such possibilities when they first join MI5 and long before they sign the Official Secrets Act. We train everyone in how to respond should they be threatened, and fortunately our interrogator came straight to me and told me what had happened. We soon traced our Russian friend's partner to a rented house in Hemel Hempstead, and an hour later the SAS went in and put a bullet through his head. Our interrogator was safely reunited with his family and he's carried on working for us. I don't take kindly to having any of my people threatened.'

'So which of our lovely prisons did the Russian spy end up in' I asked?

'Oh, him. Well actually he's, er, back in Moscow, secretly working for me. I get regular monthly reports on what the Kremlin is up to. Mostly fairly low level stuff of course, but there is the occasional gem and so far he has proved to be extremely useful.' Craig leaned forward and looked through the windscreen. 'OK' he exclaimed 'it looks like we've arrived. Welcome to Unit Seven.'

Chapter Thirty One

Sam, George, Colin, Jo, Willie, Richard and Rivka all arrived within ten minutes of each other, and we all congregated in the Manor House's main lounge. Five minutes later Roy Simpson arrived with two other technicians from his department. Helena and I were the only two people who knew Roy was our suspect mole, and at Craig's request we both said nothing and treated him exactly as we had done previously. The Housekeeper at Unit Seven, a middle aged lady named Dolores, showed us all to our various rooms where we had a shower, put on some clean clothes and then as requested congregated back in the lounge. Once everyone was back Craig asked us all to follow him and we headed down two flights of stairs to the 'Secure Room.' To be honest the secure room didn't look any different to any of the other rooms we'd seen, but Craig assured us we could talk freely about anything within its four walls.

'I will start' began Craig. 'I'm afraid my colleague Roy Simpson has left us. His wife Mary and his two young children had been kidnapped by two of Ahmadi's men about three weeks ago, and they had threatened to kill both of his children first, and then his wife if he didn't cooperate with them. I'm afraid that for the last two weeks Simpson has been feeding Ahmadi bits and pieces of information, including during this last week your whereabouts.'

'God, I can understand why he did it' said Sam 'I would have done exactly the same if Michael's life had been threatened.'

'That's all very well Sam, and I too understand the impossible situation he found himself in, but every MI5 operative is warned about the possibilities and extensively trained in how to deal with it. The first thing everyone is taught to do is that they must report the threat to me immediately and I will deal with it, but Simpson never said a word. I understand why, and I sympathise, and that is why Simpson will not be prosecuted. He is an MI5 technician, and not an undercover operative. So with immediate effect Simpson and his family will be reunited, and then he will be assigned a new post at one of our units in Scotland.'

'That's a bit rough on him and his family' said Sam.

'I know that may seem harsh' replied. Craig 'but I cannot possibly have someone who has been blackmailed on the staff at MI5's

London HQ handling highly sensitive information. Now, let's move on. In fact it looks like we may not be here very long at all as I've received information that GCHQ in Cheltenham have picked up two of the terrorist's mobile phones and they are now listening in to all their communications.'

'Brilliant' muttered Jo.

'Yes, it's good news' said Craig 'but I won't rest until they're all behind bars or dead.'

'Dead would be my preference' said Rivka.

'Mine to' said Craig. 'Now from what GCHQ are telling me it sounds like all six of the terrorists have relocated to the Spanish holiday island of Tenerife. Airport checks are fairly minimal there, and a group of six men on a golfing break doesn't look at all suspicious, and it sounds like that's their cover story. At the moment we don't know where they have booked to stay, but we should have that information soon. I suggest Helena, Michael and Sam come with me to GCHQ where we can track what they are up to, check exactly where every one of them is located, whether they are still all together, and then while we are away the rest of you can hopefully get some very well earned rest.'

Nobody was in the mood to argue with Craig as everyone was feeling shattered and in need of rest, so apart from Helena, Sam and myself, everyone else decided to have a much needed rest. We met Craig back in the main entrance hall, and the four of us descended to the underground garage again, and on Craig's instructions we all climbed inside the British Telecom van. It was by bigger and certainly the most comfortable of the five vehicles we had all travelled to Unit Seven in, and the journey to Cheltenham was completed in silence as both Helena and Sam had fallen asleep. Craig was still wide awake, but as I was dozing Craig thankfully left me in peace.

We were all woken up as we arrived at the entrance to GCHQ, and our vehicle was admitted through the front main gate, but then halted before the second gate. Craig showed the guards his credentials and then vouched for the three of us. The guards obviously knew who Craig was, and showing him due deference they admitted us all.

'Obviously I've heard of GCHQ' said Sam 'but to be perfectly honest Craig, I don't really know what happens here'

'No problem my dear' said Craig 'I will

explain. The initials GCHQ stand for the Government Communications Headquarters, and it is an intelligence and security organisation responsible for providing signals intelligence, what we in the trade refer to as SIGINT in our jargon, and any other information which may be of use or interest to the government and armed forces of the United Kingdom. GCHQ is now based here in Cheltenham in this newish building which has become affectionately known as 'the doughnut' due to its circular shape and hollow centre. GCHQ is the responsibility of the Foreign Secretary, although it is not a part of the Foreign Office.

'So is GCHQ fairly new then' asked Sam?

'Good heavens no' exclaimed Craig. 'GCHQ was first established just after the First World War as the Government Code and Cypher School and it was known under that name until 1946. You all know that during the Second World War we had a department located at Bletchley Park which was responsible for breaking various German codes, including the famous Enigma codes, well that was at the time part of the Government Code and Cypher School. In 1946 it changed its name and became GCHQ. You may remember that in 2013, GCHQ received a considerable amount of media attention when the former National Security Agency contractor Edward Snowden revealed that the agency was in the process of collecting all online and telephone data in the UK via something called the Tempora programme.'

'Yes, I vaguely remember it' I said 'but you still haven't explained in simple layman's terms exactly what GCHQ does and why we are here.'

'OK' responded Craig 'I take your point. At the end of 2003, GCHQ moved to this current building which was specially created for the purpose, and at the time it was the second-largest public-sector building project in Europe, costing £337 million.

So to try and answer your question. GCHQ gains its intelligence by monitoring a wide variety of communications and other electronic signals. For this, a relatively large number of what we call listening stations have been established, both here in the UK and many overseas. The listening stations are here at Cheltenham itself, Bude, Scarborough, Ascension Island, and we share a facility with the United States at Menwith Hill. There is also

Ayios Nikolaos Station in Cyprus which is run by the British Army for GCHQ.

The aforementioned Edward Snowden unhelpfully revealed in his article in The Guardian newspaper that GCHQ had even spied on foreign politicians visiting the 2009 G-20 London Summit by eavesdropping on their phone calls, reading their emails and monitoring their computers. It was true, but we'd have rather kept that bit of information to ourselves. GCHQ also has had access to the United States internet monitoring programme called 'PRISM' which is said to give the National Security Agency and FBI easy access to the systems of nine of the world's top internet companies, including Google, Facebook, Microsoft, Apple, Yahoo, and Skype. Whether this is true or not I cannot confirm as my technical knowledge is limited, but knowing GCHQ it wouldn't surprise me. What you may be interested to know is that in 2017, US Press Secretary at the time, a man named Sean Spicer, alleged that GCHQ had conducted surveillance on US President Donald Trump, basing the allegation on statements made by a media commentator during a Fox News segment. The US government formally apologised for the allegations and promised they would not be repeated.'

'So' I said 'I repeat Sam's original question, not that all you've told us hasn't been really interesting, but why are we here?'

'Yes, sorry' smiled Craig. 'I do get carried away sometimes. We are here to directly listen in to Ahmadi's mobile calls, and try and decide between the four of us what to do next.'

We left the van and were escorted into the building by a smartly dressed young lady who guided us to a private secure listening room, complete with a nice teak coloured conference table and eight comfortable leather chairs. We were all greeted by Sir Duncan Greenhall, GCHQ's Director of Overseas Communications, a smartly dressed man I estimated to be in his mid-forties with hair already greying at the temples.

'Good morning all of you' he began 'and nice to see you too Craig'.

We all muttered thank you and took it in turns to shake his hand. He invited us to sit round the table as he introduced himself, and briefly explained what he did. Then he got down to business.

'Now, to bring you up to date. We now

have access to three of their mobile telephones, those belonging to Ahmadi, Lajani, and Mahrez. We know that Khalid Khan was with them on the helicopter, and we know he is still with them, although his mobile seems to be turned off at the moment. Also, they have now been joined in Tenerife by Sergei Polyakov.'

I sort of put my hand up like a schoolboy and said :

'Sorry to ask this Sir Duncan and please excuse my ignorance, but if they are all together, what use are their mobile phones as they are hardly likely to telephone each other are they?'

'Yes, I see where you're coming from Michael, but stop and think about it for a moment. Every mobile phone, or cell phone as our American friends call them, needs and contains a microphone. They have to or they wouldn't work. They're needed for talking on the phone, recording voice mails etc. What is not generally known outside of these walls however is that once we have tracked a mobile phone, we can remotely switch its microphone on or off at will, therefore turning their mobile phone into a transmitter we can listen to. The user will be totally unaware of what has happened and therefore we can hear everything they say, and of course record it for posterity.'

'Good God' exclaimed Sam 'Does that mean you could switch on my mobile phone and listen to what Michael and I are saying in private?'

'Technically speaking? Yes it does Sam, but in reality no we can't. We have very strict guidelines and in every case there has to be written permission granted from two senior GCHQ personnel, one of which is always the Director, and also you have to be doing something very suspicious, or be on a wanted list supplied by the police or the security services for example. We do of course get requests occasionally from other external colleagues, but again, we always require a very good reason and written permission. So don't worry Sam, your intimate moments and whispered sweet nothings are perfectly secure from our prying ears.'

Craig laughed, as did Helena, and then Sam and I both started laughing.

'Tell me Sir Duncan' I asked thinking aloud as I spoke. 'If you can remotely turn on the microphone, can you also turn on the phone's camera?'

'Yes we can Michael, but it is rarely of any use to us. Mobile phones are usually carried in the users pocket or stuffed in a ladies handbag.

Otherwise they are invariably laid on a table, either face up or face down, but either way, we get to see nothing except a black pocket, a table surface or the ceiling.'

'Mmm' I muttered 'I see your point.'

'To continue' said Sir Duncan 'We now know exactly where our five terrorists are located. They have booked themselves into a resort named 'The Royal Tenerife Country Club' in an area of the island known as 'Golf Del Sur'. They are all sharing a large apartment and have provisionally booked to stay for a week. As far as we know they only have normal luggage with them and five sets of golf clubs which they picked up from a hire shop when they landed at the island's southern airport. They also collected two hire cars, a dark blue Range Rover and a large black Mercedes.

'How did they all get to Tenerife Sir Duncan' asked Helena?

'Ahmadi, Lajani, Mahrez and Khalid Khan all flew in to South Tenerife Airport on a commercial flight from Morocco' he answered 'but how the hell Sergei Polyakov got there we have no idea. If he came in by boat, which is what we suspect, then he could have brought all sorts of weapons and technology nasties with him.'

'So Craig' I asked 'Do we get the team back together and go down to Tenerife and arrest them all?'

'No Michael, at this stage we gather more information. If you remember the Prime Minister informed us that the UK was under threat from Polyakov that unless the government handed over the people involved in tracking them down, ie, you and the rest of the team, they say they will shut down all of London's electrical power for a week.'

'We're hardly likely to have forgotten' mused Sam.

'Fear not my dear' said Craig in his best comforting voice. 'Nothing is going to happen to any of you and we will stop their threat to London.'

'But surely Craig' I argued 'if we go to Tenerife and arrest them, or better still as far as Rivka is concerned simply kill them, the threats to us and to London die with them. End of story!'

Craig looked at Sir Duncan, and they both gave a very long, knowing and pitying smile.

It was Sir Duncan that replied:

'OK Michael. How does your idea help if the item of technology they are using to blackout London is still in London, and all it needs is a phone link to set it off remotely? How does it help if they are determined to destroy London, and as a revenge tactic they have also left a small nuclear device hidden somewhere between Downing Street and Buckingham Palace. How does it help if they've left canisters of Sarin gas next to the Israeli embassies in London, Paris, Berlin and Washington, all timed to go off at a certain time in the event of their not getting what they want from the British government. How does it help if .....

'OK, OK Sir Duncan, I get your point. Sorry I just hadn't thought it through.'

'Oh please don't apologise Michael, I really admire your get up and go, but until we know exactly what they are up to and what they have left in different places, I'm afraid it's not a case of get up and go, but rather sit down and listen. Talking of which, this room is now yours for as long as you need it Craig. Over here is a computer on which you can switch into any of their phones and listen to what's being said. Don't worry, you can say what you like, they won't hear anything their end. We are listening all the time to all the phones, but you folk know these people better than we do, particularly Michael and Sam who have spent time with them. Listen in and see if anything they say

means anything.
The good thing is they are all speaking English as neither Polyakov nor Khalid Khan speak Farsi or Arabic. The only common language they have is English, but just in case we have Farsi, Arabic, and Russian speakers listening in. You know where to find me Craig, and good luck. We've only got 42 hours before their deadline is up.'
Sir Duncan left the room, closing the door behind him.

'Well I guess we better start listening' muttered Craig and he headed over to the computer and pressed the relevant keys. The computer, an all singing, all dancing, top of the range laptop, was linked to a pair of extremely high quality speakers buried in the walls of the room, and we could all remain at the conference table while listening. There was a TV monitor on the wall at the end of the conference table, and every time one of them spoke, the speakers name appeared like subtitles at the bottom of the screen.

'The TV monitor is also linked to the computer' said Craig explaining 'and GCHQ have fed the relevant voice recognition software into the system so that we know who is saying what.'
We sat there listening to them for over two

hours, but nothing of any great interest was said. Mahrez complained about the limited range food on offer at the pool bar as they didn't cater for Moroccan tastes, even though Morocco was in his opinion very close to the Canary Islands. None of them said anything of any relevance to the situation as far as we were concerned, and then out of the blue Khalid Khan said:

'So what do we think? Are the bloody British going to hand over their spies or does Sergei make the phone call and blackout London?'

'Are you sure it will work Sergei? asked Lajani. 'There's a lot of distance between here and that deserted warehouse rooftop in Woolwich, and why the hell Woolwich and not the centre of London?'

'Has it not occurred to you my dear Akram that the British will have been searching for the device from the minute they received our threat, and that search will have started in central London. We spent a long time finding the right spot with the right line of sight. Don't worry, it will work.'

'But what if children are playing there and discover it?' argued Lajani 'after all the building has been deserted for many years and we've seen children playing there.'

'Yes, but they were playing in the grounds of the warehouse, but not on the roof. Besides, nobody would dream of looking inside an old oil drum.'

'And you are sure it will work. I'm sorry Sergei, but I always worry about things I don't understand.'

'Look Akram, and all of you' said Polyakov 'It's very simple. At the allotted time, which is now roughly thirty six hours from now, I simply dial the mobile phone attached to the oil drum. On the third ring, the drum's lid opens, the satellite dish rises up out of the drum, and automatically turns the signal on. That signal is strong enough to take out all of London's electricity. Please, I guarantee you it will work.'

'Come on Akram' said Ahmadi. 'Stop worrying. We got Sergei involved because he's the technical expert. Let's leave it to him to know what he's doing. He screwed with Downing Street didn't he? Just stop worrying.'

They then changed subject and all started talking about football.

'So, we now know the device is located in an old oil drum which is on the roof of an unknown deserted warehouse in Woolwich.' I said. 'Is that enough information to find it Craig?'

'Mmm, er, yes, I would think so. I suggest we give all the information to Stephen in Greenwich. I know that strictly speaking Woolwich does not come under his jurisdiction, but Stephen knows all about this situation and what's at stake whereas the Superintendent in Woolwich doesn't. I'm sure Stephen can work with his opposite number and get a search of every deserted warehouse in the area underway.'

'There can't be that many deserted warehouses in Woolwich can there?' asked Sam.

'I wouldn't have thought so' said Craig 'but I must emphasize to Stephen that if they do manage to find the oil drum, it's not to be touched until the bomb squad have got there and thoroughly checked it for booby traps and explosives. Leave it with me, I'll go and ring him now.'

Chapter Thirty Two

Craig returned to the room about fifteen minutes later.

'Well that's all underway' he said. 'Stephen spoke to the Superintendent in Woolwich, and I had a quick word with him as well. The search has already started. The Superintendent in Woolwich said there are less than ten buildings that have been deserted for years in the area, and he thinks they'll find it pretty soon. They'll let me know as soon as it's been disarmed, or neutralized or whatever it is you do to these sort of devices.'

'So what do we do now Craig' I asked?

'We do what you suggested a few hours ago Michael. We get up and go.'

In fact we left GCHQ five minutes later having thanked Sir Duncan for his hospitality. The drive back to Unit Seven was uneventful and we arrived back in time for a wonderful roast dinner Dolores had prepared while we were away. Craig had telephoned her say we were on our way back, and he'd requested his favourite evening meal of roast beef and Yorkshire pudding, roast potatoes etc. I have to say it was an excellent meal all washed down with a couple of bottles of red wine, a rather good Cabernet Sauvignon.

After the meal we all gathered in the lounge to discuss what we should do next. Craig was adamant that the threat wasn't over and we needed to know what else they'd got planned. The only people the terrorists didn't know were Rivka, George, Colin, Jo and Willie. The rest of us they'd either seen personally or knew what we looked like at least. In fairness Jo pointed out, Sadiq Rouhani had seen both Rivka and George, but as Rivka quickly said, having had a bullet put through his head in a back street of Mougin stopped him from identifying either of them.

'I suggest we all fly to Tenerife in the morning' said Craig. 'That way Rivka, George, Colin, Jo and Willie can keep an eye on them without raising suspicion. Richard, can you bug their apartment at the Country Club so that we can see what they're up to??

'Not really Craig' he replied. 'I don't have either the equipment or the expertise. You really need Martin and Marika for that.'

'Mmm, that's no good, Kurt has them both on an operation in Hong Kong, and even if he'd let us, there's not time to pull them out and get them here. OK, option two. Ladies,' Craig said addressing Rivka and Jo 'do you think you could use your undoubted charms to get close to our terrorists and then get yourselves invited back to their apartment for a drink. You may find something of use there. If not we will just have to arrest them and hope there are no nasties spread around Europe waiting for a signal to set them off.'

'God, that's a bit risky isn't it' asked Sam.

'It's no different to what you did on the

Nile cruiser Sam my dear, when you literally threw yourself into the arms of Jahangir Ahmadi.' replied Craig.

'Yes, but I had back up in the form of my husband.' countered Sam.

'So will Rivka and Jo' replied Craig. 'George, Colin and Willie will be listening in outside the terrorist's apartment, and they will all be ready to jump in and rescue the girls should the need arise.'

'So are we going to book into the same resort' asked Helena?

'No, I think not' answered Craig. 'The company that runs the 'Royal Tenerife Country Club' also owns a couple of other resorts in the area, and I think it will be safer to be located at one of those. I have booked us three, two bedroom apartments at the 'Santa Barbara Golf and Country Club' which is a short four or five minute drive from the 'Royal Tenerife Country Club'. We can't risk one of the terrorists going for a stroll and bumping into one of you.'

'When do we leave' asked Helena?

'I suggest we all go and pack right now, grab a bit of shut eye and then get up and meet back here at 7.45 am and leave for Biggin around 8.00 am. That way we'll have a reasonably full day in Tenerife to execute our plan, and time ladies and gentlemen is something we don't have a lot of.'

Chapter Thirty Three

Our drive from Unit Seven to Biggin Hill was fairly short and quite quick as both places are located in the southern UK county of Kent. Upon arrival at the airport we stowed all our bags on the Gulfstream and Colin flew us to Tenerife South airport. Tenerife is the largest of what are known as the Canary Islands. There are four main islands; Tenerife, Gran Canaria, Lanzarote and Fuerteventura. Because of their location off the west coast of Africa, roughly 60 miles from the coast of Morocco, they enjoy a fantastic all year round climate, warm and sunny, but being in the Atlantic Ocean they can sometimes they can get a bit windy. The islands are all Spanish, and there are several other smaller islands in the group, the main three being La Palma, La Gomera and El Hierro, but these are not so well frequented by tourists as the big four. I guess the Canaries are to Europeans what the Caribbean is to Americans. Guaranteed sunshine fairly close and at a reasonable price.

The Gulfstream was parked in a pre-booked private hanger, and we piled into three good sized hire cars Craig had also pre-booked. We then drove to the 'Santa Barbara Golf and Country Club', unloaded our luggage and the ladies checked us all in while three of us men tried to find somewhere close to park the hire cars. Unfortunately, the resort didn't have its own car park, and so all three vehicles ended up several streets away. We walked back to the resort, showed the reception desk our passports, and headed to the top floor where Sam and I were sharing an apartment with Helena and Richard, George and Colin were sharing with Rivka and Jo, and Craig was sharing with Willie. Our rooms at the resort were all self-catering and all three had fantastic views out to sea, plus every facility you could think of. However we had all had a long, tiring day, and so we decided to go to the resorts main restaurant for a meal before the girls drove to the Royal Tenerife Country Club's pool bar for a drink where they could hopefully try and get 'up close and personal' as the saying goes to the terrorists. The meal was excellent, and then rather than any of us known to the terrorists risking being seen, Rivka, George, Colin, Jo and Willie decided to get two taxi's to take them the short distance to the Royal Tenerife Country Club. They were just about to leave when Craig held his hand up and brought everything to a halt. He was finishing a call he had received on his mobile, and we all waited for what we assumed would be an update.

'Great news' he said, 'but let's all go to my room where we can talk in private.'

As soon as we got there Craig filled us in on his call.

'The telephone call was from Stephen. He said the police found the oil drum on a roof near the Woolwich Ferry terminal. It was indeed an old warehouse that had been empty for about three years. Once the army's Bomb Squad had checked the area and the oil drum for booby traps etc, they disarmed the device Sergei Polyakov had rigged up inside it. The other good news is that GCHQ, having been listening to the terrorists various conversations for several hours are now one hundred percent convinced there are no other devices in any other locations ready to go off.'

'Does that mean we can now safely take them out?' asked Rivka.

'Yes it does, but hold your horses. While we've been here having a nice meal, our terrorists have been talking amongst themselves, and apparently they are expecting a boat delivery of weapons and other unspecified equipment to be landed on Tenerife by boat around 1.00 am when I guess they expect everyone to be asleep.'

'Do we know where' asked Helena.

'A beach called San Blas, which GCHQ tell me isn't far from here. There's one big hotel at San Blas, but the rendezvous point is about half a mile further along the coast and out of sight of the hotel.'

'Do we know anything else about the delivery, what's on the list etc' asked Willie?'

'Er, no, afraid not, but they did say a larger ship was bringing it all to Tenerife from Morocco, and then a small 'silent running' dinghy as they described it was going to bring everything ashore, unload and then return to the main ship. I'm going to speak to the Royal Navy and get them to intercept the main ship. GCHQ tell me they've got a nice big cruiser in the area and they tell me the Captain will take great delight in having something for his crew to do.'

'So what do you suggest we do now then Craig' I asked.

'I suggest ladies and gentlemen that we all arm ourselves, and head for the area of San Blas and await our terrorists. I've asked for back up and there are a couple of dozen marines on the way here, but it's already 11.00 pm and the marines may not get here in time.'

'Do we try and arrest them' asked Helena.

'I'm afraid not' answered Craig. 'These people's automatic reaction is to shoot first and ask questions later. I suggest everyone takes a weapon with them, and that includes you Sam. I will not have your death on my conscience, and I need you to be there in case of any gunshot wounds.'

'Can't you just hand this over to the Spanish police to deal with' asked Sam 'You know how I feel about guns.'

'Yes I do, and I'm sorry Sam but I must insist. If we tried to get the Spanish police involved at this stage it would take hours just to get to talk to the right man, by which time the terrorists will have collected whatever it is they are collecting, and have been long gone and for all we know completely disappeared. No, I'm afraid it has to be us, and everyone has to be armed.'

Chapter Thirty Four

We piled into the three cars, and drove fairly sedately to the area known as San Blas. The last thing we needed was to be stopped by the police for speeding and then have to try and explain why every one of us was carrying a gun. San Blas from what we could see was a small resort area, with several shops, bars and restaurants, but by the time we all arrived it was just gone midnight and everything was closed and very quiet. We urgently needed to find somewhere to hide where we could all see what was happening without being seen ourselves. With everything now being closed, and the place had a slightly eerie feel to it, but I guess most places feel like a bit weird at that time in the morning.

'How about that terrace area up there' said Jo 'pointing at a raised area with several bars and shops along the front facing the sea. 'The nearest one, that tea shop called 'Hattie's' will give us a good view along the beach.'

'Yes it would' agreed Craig 'but I'm afraid it's too far away, and there's no real cover or protection for us. Let's get down onto the beach itself. There are several small boats, piles of sun loungers and pedalo type things over there, and I would think we can make enough cover for ourselves out of that lot.'

'How will we know when they're here' asked Helena?

'GCHQ have me on speed dial and they will let me know the second the terrorists leave.'

'Do we know if they're all coming to the beach' I asked.

'Good point Michael' answered Craig 'but I'm afraid we've no idea. We'll just have to wait and see who turns up.'

We reached the spot that Craig had referred to, and there were indeed I estimated about sixty to seventy white plastic sun loungers piled up in four separate piles, each pile about six foot high. There were also six pedalo's pulled up on the beach and six small two man sailing boats, each with their sails lowered, roughly rolled up and lying full length in the hull of each boat.

'This will do fine' said Craig. 'Find yourself a hiding place that will hide you from the terrorists when they arrive, but be prepared to move round when they go down to the dinghy. I want those weapons, so keep quiet and be patient.'

We did as Craig asked, and spread ourselves out amongst the boats and sun loungers. The four girls each climbed inside one of the sailing boats and then laid full length underneath the sails, but with a small gap so they could see what was going on. George and Colin both laid on the beach in a full length position, guns drawn, alongside a couple of the pedalo's which actually hid them quite well. Craig, Willie,

Richard and I all took cover behind the four piles of sun loungers.

'From now on' said Craig 'nobody speaks except me.'

'No change there then' muttered Colin, but Craig never heard him.

Nothing happened for nearly thirty minutes, then Craig announced that GCHQ had just informed him that Akram Lajani, Youssef Mahrez and Sergei Polyakov were on their way to the beach. Apparently Jahangir Ahmadi and Khalid Khan had stayed behind in the apartment.

'Total silence please everyone' said Craig 'and have your guns ready. Remember, these people don't talk, they just kill.'

We waited in silence and then roughly four minutes later, the three terrorists arrived in a large, silver coloured Toyota Land Cruiser which they parked at the top of the beach, about fifty feet from where we were hiding. They sat in the car not talking, and after a further two minutes, exactly at the stroke of 1.00 am, Lajani started flashing a torch out to sea. Three on/offs, a gap and then three more. Fifteen seconds later there was a light from the sea, three on/offs, a gap and then three more.

'Bloody hell' whispered Richard 'I didn't see the boat coming at all.'

'Me neither' I whispered back.

'Shut up the pair of you' commanded Craig in a very quiet but firm whisper. 'Are you two bloody idiots deliberately trying to get us all killed?'

We both looked suitably sheepish, but said nothing. Fortunately the terrorists were still in their car and couldn't have heard us anyway, but Craig had made his point. A minute or so later the three terrorists got out of the car, quietly closed the doors and slowly started to walk down the beach towards the sea, the shoreline of which was only about thirty feet away. The route they were following would take them to within about forty feet from our hiding place, and as they walked past us muttering in Arabic amongst themselves, we slowly moved round to keep the piles of sun loungers between us and them. Thank God it was a sandy beach and not pebbles, or they would definitely have heard us. We still couldn't hear the dinghy, although we could now just about see it. It was all black, as was the clothing of the single man driving it. I looked way out to sea in the direction the dinghy had come from, and I could just about make out a larger ship just this side of the horizon. I looked at Craig, and then pointed at the ship. He followed my finger and then acknowledged he'd seen the larger vessel. The dinghy had new reached the shore and the three terrorists were now unloading everything onto the beach. We had no idea what was in any of the boxes, but there were about ten black, what I assumed were plastic cases. They were all roughly the same size, about three feet by two feet and roughly a foot deep.

We waited until they were all ashore and then Craig shouted

'Stop what you are doing. We are all heavily armed and prepared to shoot.'

Every one of us held an extremely powerful torch in our left hand, which we all turned on at the same time as had been previously arranged. The terrorists all looked at each other and then everything happened at once. The man who'd arrived in the dinghy suddenly gunned its outboard engine as he turned the dinghy towards the open sea. As he did so, Rivka fired her silenced weapon, and a hollow point bullet from her Glock exploded in his back, just below his neck. He fell forward and the dinghy started to go round in circles as he lay across the arm of the outboard. The other three terrorists had decided to make a fight for it as we'd expected, and they had all pulled out guns and started firing at the torches, which in the dark was all they could see. However, Craig had foreseen this, and all the torches had either been placed on top of the sun loungers, on the edge of the sailing boats or on the beach as we turned them on. We had immediately all moved well away from the lights that were shining in their eyes by the time the shooting from the terrorists had started. George I saw shot at Lajani who was hit and immediately fell to the floor dropping his gun, and at the same moment Colin shot Mahrez who fell backwards into the still circling dinghy. Sergei Polyakov was smarter than the other two, and he'd started to run to his left along the shoreline immediately the first torch had come on, but it didn't stop him firing back at us as he ran. I noticed Rivka to my right who was now quietly kneeling down on the sand, gun held in both hands and pointing it at the retreating Polyakov. She gently pulled the trigger, and the Glock gently cracked as the bullet exploded from its barrel. The second noise I heard came as Polyakov's head also exploded a fraction of a second later, or maybe I just imagined the noise.

'Everyone OK' yelled Craig as we all walked towards the still circling dinghy. George and I held the small black boat still as Richard reached in and turned off its engine. We had by now all congregated by the boat and the three dead terrorist's bodies. George and Colin headed down towards the dead body of Polyakov, which they picked up and began carrying back to the rest of us. Sam had by now joined me and I put my arm around her and Richard was doing exactly the same to Helena. Jo started looking round and then suddenly said

'Where's Willie got to?'

We all looked around, but we were all a bit blinded by the torches which were still on. Craig then asked us go over and turn them all off, and then collect the torches and bring them back with us. As we walked towards them Helena suddenly said

'Oh my God, I think Willie's been shot.'

Willie was lying face down on the beach in front of a pile of sun loungers. We all ran forward and Sam immediately knelt down beside him. She turned Willie over and felt at the side of his neck for a pulse. She gently lowered him back down and said.

'He's gone I'm afraid. Willie's dead.'
Jo started crying and Helena held back a tear.

'I'm so sorry everyone' said Craig 'and I know you don't want to hear this, but in our line of work I'm afraid this will occasionally happen. Willie knew that, but he still wanted to help and do his bit. Willie was the unlucky one, but it could have been any one of us. Let's get Willie into the back of the car and take him to the nearest hospital.'

'No' said a very determined Helena. 'Willie worked directly for me and he was my responsibility. I want him taken straight to the Gulfstream and flown immediately to the hospital in Salzburg where he will be treated with the utmost respect. George, Colin, please see to it, and before you say anything Craig, I will not allow you to interfere in this matter. My decision is final. The rest of us will stay here with you and finish the job.'

'I bow to your decision Helena, but shouldn't George and Colin stay here first and help finish the job as you put it. After all, apart from Rivka, Jo and myself, George and Colin are the only two people with firearms training?'

'No I'm sorry Craig, Willie needs to be taken to the morgue in Salzburg as soon as possible. From what I've seen of Rivka over the last few weeks, she could probably finish the job on her own.'

'It would be my pleasure' she said.

'Never the less' responded Helena 'we still have seven of us here. I'm quite sure that will be sufficient to take out two men who are totally unaware of what has just happened.'

'OK' said Craig 'I reluctantly accept your decision, but in that case George can I please request that with Helena's permission, you take all the weapons they unloaded here back with you on the Gulfstream, along with I'm afraid the four dead bodies of the terrorists. I hate to ask, but there is not time to go into long, complicated explanations with the Spanish authorities, and I don't think they would take too kindly to MI6 and Interpol running an operation on their soil without their knowledge anyway. Can you please keep the weapons safe and untouched until you can fly them to London for me?' George looked at Helena who gave him a nod.

'Thank you Helena, and thank you George and Colin. As for the rest of us, I suggest we head for the Royal Tenerife Country Club.' We all helped load the four dead terrorists and their weapons into the Land Cruiser, and then

George drove it to the Gulfstream's private hanger at Tenerife South airport, while Colin drove Willie's body, now covered in one of the small sails we had taken from one of the sailing boats, to the same private hanger in one of the rental cars. The great advantage of having the Gulfstream in a private hanger was that because it was an official Interpol registered plane, the aircraft or anything put on it was never examined by local customs officials. The rest of us then spread ourselves among the remaining two rental cars and with Richard and myself driving we headed for the Royal Tenerife Country Club.

Chapter Thirty Five

The Royal Tenerife Country Club, unlike the Santa Barbara Golf and Ocean Club, is mostly a collection of low level white painted buildings. There are several two story buildings, but our remaining two terrorists were we knew in a ground floor apartment with its own private tiled terrace behind it, which then overlooked the local golf course at Golf del Sur.
We decided to split our forces so to speak, and so Craig, Richard, Helena and Sam would go to

their front door, while Rivka, Jo and me covered the rear exit from the grounds of the golf club. If you are familiar with golf clubs you will realize that they provide very little cover, particularly this one which had very few trees to hide behind, so the three of us crept along the outside wall that separated the apartments from the golf club until we got to their apartment. All three of us were armed with hand guns, and Rivka suggested that Jo and I took position against the wall to the left of the apartment while she took position against the wall to the right. That way, if they tried to come over the wall we could see them and if necessary shoot them from both sides.
Craig, Richard, Helena and Sam had walked down to the front door of the apartment and at a set time would ring the doorbell. We assumed the two remaining terrorists, Jahangir Ahmadi and Khalid Khan, would think it was their three colleagues returning with the weapons they'd been to collect.

Craig drew his gun and taking a deep breath rang their doorbell. I guess there should have been a signal of some sort, like three knocks on the door or something, but obviously ringing the bell was not the right thing to do. Both terrorists immediately ran out of the open patio doors at the rear of their apartment, but instead of jumping over the wall onto the golf course and into our waiting guns, they both vaulted over the walls into the adjoining apartments. They then did the same again and before we realized what had happened they were three apartments away.

There was no way we could fire at them as the other apartments had innocent guests in them enjoying their holidays with a restful night's sleep, and besides, the apartments all had windows and large glass patio doors. The chances of them being bullet proof were pretty remote. So the three of us ran along the wall, but by the time we got to the end we saw them both running up towards the resort's reception area.

'Damn' I yelled 'They're heading for their other car.'

We gave chase, and saw them split up. Khalid Khan ran off to the right down a short passageway between apartments, and Ahmadi did the same, but going left instead of right. I didn't know it at the time, but Craig and Sam had headed right in the same direction as Khan having realized the terrorists were on the move.

Helena and Richard had decided to head straight for the car park and with guns drawn they were both waiting for the terrorists there. I assume Ahmadi had spotted Helena or Richard, and either recognized one of them or realized they were heading into a trap, and he'd immediately told Khalid Khan to head off to the right while he raced off to the left. Khan had made a big mistake in heading right as he ran straight into Craig and Sam. Craig already had his gun drawn as did Khan. Upon seeing each other they both shot at virtually the same time. Both guns had silencers attached and so there was very little noise, apart from a small scream from Sam as she realized Craig had been shot. Luckily it was only a flesh wound in his right arm, but it was enough to make him drop his gun to the floor. Sam immediately bent down and picked it up, and she then looked up ready to point it at Khan. Fortunately she didn't have to as Craig's shot had been more accurate than Khan's. Khan was dead, and she and Craig slowly walked over to his body keeping an eye open for Ahmadi as they did so, but there was no sign of him.

Jahangir Ahmadi had disappeared, and none of us had a clue where he'd gone. We all congregated in the car park, and then Craig suggested we split into pairs and search for him, and then meet back in the car park in fifteen minutes. Sam and I went together. Sam had given Craig his gun back and he was now holding it in his left hand, but he assured us he had been trained to shoot with both hands, as had all Interpol officers.

'Where would you go if you were Ahmadi' asked Sam.

I thought about it for a moment or two, and then said

'I think I'd try and get back to the apartment, collect my passport and other possessions, and then make my escape across the golf course.'

'That makes sense' said Sam. 'Let's head back that way. If he's not there at least we can collect anything he's left behind.'

The Royal Tenerife Country Club is built on a hill and follows the natural contours of the golf course surrounding it on all sides, and the apartment the terrorists had occupied was right at the bottom of the resort. There were two main approaches, down maroon painted concrete paths. Rather than split up we decided to stick together and take the right hand path leading to the lower apartments. We saw nobody on route and obviously neither the two shots nor Sam's little scream had woken any of the guests. The apartment's front door was still open ajar after Craig and Richard had put their shoulders to it in order to get in once they'd heard the terrorists making a run for it. I gingerly opened the door and looked into the lounge. I could see nobody and so very tentatively I walked inside with Sam close behind me. We looked in both bedrooms and the kitchen and ascertained that the apartment was empty.

'You search in here Michael, and I'll have a look in the bedrooms' said Sam, as she left the lounge and started rummaging through the mess of clothes and papers strewn around the main bedroom floor. I started going through the drawers in the cabinet under the main TV set in the lounge, which meant I had my back to the front door. I heard nothing until

'Well, well, Mr Michael Turner' said a quiet but menacing voice.

I slowly turned round to see Ahmadi standing in the lounge, just inside the front door, pointing a silenced gun at my head.

'You and your colleagues have been a real annoyance to my mission and you have all totally screwed with our plans. As much as it would make sense for me to simply walk away from this mess and make my escape, I can't do that without killing you first.'

I saw the smile on his face as he started to draw his finger tight on the trigger. I couldn't help it, but I shut my eyes, screwed up my face in a grimace and turned he head away from him. I heard him shoot me with three quick shots, but I felt nothing other than a numbness. My mind then said to me that if I was dead, I would only have heard the first shot and not the other two. Why did nothing hurt? Why hadn't I fallen to the floor? Why could I still ask myself these stupid questions? I decided to open my still closed eyes. I turned my head back and looked at Ahmadi who was now a crumpled mess on the floor.

I immediately looked left and saw Sam standing there, still pointing her gun at where Ahmadi had been standing. She'd shot him in the head just as he was about to shoot me.

'My God Sam' I said as I ran over to her. 'Are you OK?'

I put my arms around her and held her as close

as I could.

'No, I'm not OK' she replied shaking 'and I don't think I'll ever be OK again. I've just shot and killed a man which is against all I stand for as a doctor.'

'But Sam' I responded 'you wonderful woman, you saved my life.'

At that moment Richard and Helena came bursting through the front door with Craig close behind them.

'Fantastic' said Craig. 'You got him, you killed the bastard. Well done Michael.'

'It wasn't me' I said 'Ahmadi was pointing his gun at me, and was about to kill me when Sam shot him in the head.'

'Are you alright Sam?' asked Helena, moving towards Sam and giving her a hug.

'I'll be alright I suppose, but I never thought I could ever kill someone, but when I thought Michael was about to be killed I…, I had no choice.'

Craig moved into boss mode and told us we needed to get the two bodies away from the resort and onto the Gulfstream.

'Richard, there's a golf cart with a big flat platform on the back they use for moving suitcases around the resort up near the reception area. Can you go and bring it down here please?'

'Where do I get the key?'

'For goodness sake Richard, you're a technical whiz aren't you? Just hot wire the damn thing.'

Richard left and headed off towards the reception area. Meanwhile Rivka and Jo wrapped Ahmadi's body in bedclothes as best they could, while Helena and Craig packed up everything they could find in the apartment into the terrorists own bags and suitcases. I sat on the lounge sofa with my arm around Sam. She was still shaking. Five minutes later Richard returned driving the golf cart which he backed up to the apartments front door. We loaded Ahmadi's wrapped body onto the back section of the golf cart along with a couple of suitcases, and Craig and Richard headed up to the car park and our own vehicles. The rest of us picked up the remaining bags suitcases, and after a quick check to make sure nothing had been left behind, we all walked up the hill to join Richard and Craig at the cars. We loaded everything, including the bodies of Ahmadi and Khalid Khan, which Craig had already put in the boot of one of the cars, and we all headed back to Tenerife South airport, where we drove into our own private hanger which we'd rented, and we then waited for the return of the Gulfstream.

Everything, including the bodies of Ahmadi and Khalid Khan, the weapons, paperwork, personal possessions of the terrorists etc were all taken to MI6's London HQ, and that was the last I ever saw of any of it. Sam recovered and a week or so later she was more or less back to her usual self. The Gulfstream picked us up one more time, and we all flew to Salzburg for Willie's funeral. We met his mother and father and his younger brother, and if you can say such a thing, it was a good funeral. Sam and I flew back to the Algarve, and
eleven days later we received a request for us to return to London for a special meeting.

Epilogue

At 10.00 am on the 23rd of October, the UK based Ambassadors of Kuwait, Algeria and Yemen were summoned to a meeting at 10 Downing Street. At exactly the same moment, in three other counties, the three resident Ambassadors of those the same three countries were also summoned to meetings at The White House in Washington, the Élysée Palace in Paris, and the Federal Chancellery in Berlin, Germany. It would also have been ideal if their could have been the same unequivocal summons issued from Israel, but Kuwait, Algeria and Yemen do not have any diplomatic relations with, or for that matter even recognise the state of Israel.

The four meetings were all identical in that the format had been very carefully agreed in advance by all four countries, in that the three Ambassadors were required to stand and listen as a formal letter, which in diplomatic circles is referred to as a communique, was read to each and every one of them. The ambassadors were shown none of the usual diplomatic courtesies whatsoever, nor were they invited to sit down. In each of the four simultaneous meetings, the same identical communique was read to the three ambassadors who were required to stand in a row facing the relevant countries Prime Minister, President or in Germany's case Chancellor. Other members of each host countries government and armed forces, stood alongside their respective leaders in order to show their government's full support of the communique and its contents. All of us who had been involved in the destruction of the Cairo Conspiracy, including Rivka, were present at the Downing Street meeting and we all together sat at the side watching. The communique read as follows:

It has come to our attention that your three governments, that is Kuwait, Algeria and Yemen, have conspired together in an attempt to bring down and destroy the state of Israel, by means of a highly illegal international conspiracy using numerous terrorists employed by your three respective governments for that sole purpose. To that end, the terrorists you employed planned and carried out numerous obscene acts of terrorism in all of our countries. We, that is the governments, intelligence services and armed forces of the United Kingdom, the United States of America, France, Germany and Israel have unequivocal proof of these matters, and any attempt by any of you or your countries to deny such involvement will not be tolerated.

State sponsored terrorism is an anathema to anyone and everyone who considers themselves to be civilised, and as such it is seen as an international crime. It is abhorrent to all members of the civilised world, and any and all such action will not be tolerated.

We the undersigned require that within the next twenty four hours, the current leaders and all members of the existing governments of your three nations resign from office with immediate effect, and in the course of doing so offer your citizens free and fair elections which four of our five nations will supervise. We are well aware that your governments will not agree to this action willingly or wish to do so, but please understand, this is not a request. It is an instruction. Failure to comply with any of the required actions outlined in this communique will result in an immediate range of international reprisals.

Signed :

Charles Fisher - Prime Minister of the United Kingdom
George Wagner - President of the United States of America
Gilles Cazeneuve - President of France
Helmut Groening - Chancellor of Germany

Charles Fisher then addressed the three men standing in front of him.

'The reprisals in question are not outlined in this communique, and they have not been, and never will be put in writing anywhere, but please understand and please ensure that your leaders and your governments fully understand that these instructions have been issued to you by the governments, intelligence services and armed forces of five nuclear powers, and the instructions you have been issued with are not open to any debate or comment. Please do not speak, just leave and make sure our instructions are implemented in full.'

At that moment, armed troops stepped forward and escorted the three ambassadors out of the building to their waiting vehicles. Identical words and scenes had taken place at the same time in Washington, Paris and Berlin.

'What do you think James' asked Charles Fisher of his Foreign Secretary who was standing alongside him? 'Will they do what we've said, and do you think they believe we will nuke their countries?'

'I don't know Charles, and to be honest I'm not sure I believe we'll nuke anyone' replied

James Conway 'but sure as hell I believe George Wagner will quite happily nuke and take out all three of their countries, and if Congress and the Senate knew everything that has happened over the last few months they'd help him push the damn button.'

'What do you think Mary' asked the Prime Minister?

'I think I'm glad I'm only responsible for the Home Office' she replied smiling.

The following day, after having been tipped off by a selection of various anonymous telephone calls, international TV coverage including that of CNN, Sky News, the BBC, Al Jazeera etc, were all on air and broadcasting from Kuwait, Algeria and Yemen, where all three nations had announced that the existing regimes had all resigned and that during the next four months, free and fair elections would be held in each of the three countries, with independent oversight ensuring there was complete freedom and fairness from the USA, the UK, Germany and France.

Kuwait was in theory what is called a constitutional emirate, with a semi-democratic political system. That is a kind of hybrid political system which is divided between an elected parliament and an appointed government. It was members of the appointed government section that had authorised the 'Cairo Conspiracy', and it was the appointed government that resigned en mass, once the members of the elected parliament had been informed of what they had been up to.

Algeria is what's known as a constitutional presidential republic, whereby the President is the head of state, while the Prime Minister is the head of government. The country has a multi-party state with over 40 legal, political parties, but commentators around the world are unanimous in their agreement that the real power in Algeria does not rest with its legal constitutional agencies, but with other informal powers including military men and others from the ruling party. It was these men that resigned on the 24th of October.

Yemen's politics and hence its government had been in an uncertain state since the coup d'état of 2014. An armed group known as the Houthis or Ansar Allah had seized control of the Yemeni government and announced it would dissolve parliament, as well as install a presidential council, a transitional national council and a supreme revolutionary council. These three councils were to govern the country for an interim period, although the deposed president, Abdrabbuh Mansur Hadi declared he was still in office and was working to establish a rival government in Aden. At that time Yemen's government had been completely dominated by just one party, the General People's Congress, and that had been the case since unification. Various government ministers and three army Generals all resigned on October the 24th, and it was hoped by all onlookers that peace might at last come to the region.

As for us?
Well after the meeting Sam and I bid our farewells and then headed back to the Algarve where we vowed to steer well clear of the Police, Interpol, MI5, MI6 and GCHQ. We knew our vow wouldn't last, but we could dream.

THE END

Printed in Poland
by Amazon Fulfillment
Poland Sp. z o.o., Wrocław

57277075R00195